SMASHED

LAS VEGAS MYSTERY

SMASHED

LAS VEGAS MYSTERY

Rex Kusler

THOMAS & MERCER

Text copyright © 2014 Rex Kusler
All rights reserved.

Published by Thomas & Mercer, Seattle

www.apub.com

Amazon, the Amazon logo, and Thomas & Mercer are trademarks of Amazon.com, Inc., or its affiliates.

ISBN-13: 9781477819852
ISBN-10: 1477819851

Cover design by Brian Zimmerman

Library of Congress Control Number: 2013920362

Printed in the United States of America

For Geraldine Cowden

CHAPTER I

It was 3:36 a.m. on a Thursday in late March when they came upon the body.

Manny Nisperos and his wife, Carmen, were eastbound on Greenawalt Road, returning home from a winning night of slot play at Shillington's Casino just west of the Strip on Flamingo Avenue. They were in high spirits—until the periphery of their headlights played across the motionless form crumpled on the westbound side of the road.

It was a small figure—not a child, probably, but if an adult, a slight one. Whoever it was lay in the middle of the intersection of Greenawalt Road and Wampler Street in Henderson, Nevada, arms and legs stretched across the pavement in the image of a dancer in mid-leap.

Manny eased the car to a stop just before they reached the victim, so the edge of their headlights illuminated her. For now they could see that she was a girl—a black-haired, teenage girl wearing black pants, a black jacket, and black sneakers.

The two of them stared with wide eyes at the body. It was obvious she wasn't breathing.

"Oh, my God, Manny!" Carmen gasped. "She's..." She couldn't bring herself to utter the word "dead," which was okay with Manny. He wasn't ready to hear the word yet, himself. "What happened?... What is she doing there?"

"I don't know," Manny said. He shifted into park, set the brake, and turned on his flashers. "I'd better take a look. You call 911."

"Oh, my God, it's a young girl!" Carmen said, as though she were trying to convince herself of the horror lying in front of her. "She's not moving. Is she dead?"

"How would I know?" Manny said. "I haven't looked at her yet." Her babbling annoyed him. She was pretending the obviously dead girl might not be. She was forcing him to be the one to make the call. He threw his door open and got out.

Carmen dug her cell phone out of her oversized purse and punched buttons.

Manny approached the body tentatively, as though it might suddenly jump up and attack him. He walked in a wide arc around to the girl's head, telling himself he was maintaining a safe distance so as not to step on any evidence. From ten feet away he leaned forward and peered at the girl's face. Her mouth and eyes were open—like those of a doll.

"She's definitely not breathing," Manny said. "She's dead all right!"

"*Oh, my God!*" he heard his wife exclaim from the car. "There's a dead girl in the middle of the road! She's not breathing! Can you send an ambulance right away?"

As though there was any need to hurry.

CHAPTER 2

"My house is bigger than yours," Alice James said. "So we'd have a little more room. Also, I have more furniture than you, and it's in better condition and more elegant. If I move in with *you,* I imagine you'd want to put your furniture in storage or give it to Goodwill. Moving all of my stuff would require a lot more time and effort."

"That's true," Jim Snow agreed. "Your home looks like it was staged to be photographed for *House Beautiful.* My house looks like somebody lives there."

"Someone who never bothers to clean up," Alice said.

She was seated behind her desk in one of the two offices of the James & James Detective Agency. Her posture was erect, and she sat with her hands folded in her lap. Alice looked stunning this morning, attired in a black skirt suit with her teal blouse open at the collar, her prominent cheekbones and full lips accentuated by a subtle application of eyeliner, blush, and lipstick. Her straight black hair nearly covered her ears, revealing a pair of elegant gold earrings. She was forty-two, but she looked much younger than that. When a white woman in a bar had commented on her youthful appearance, Alice had just smiled and shrugged. "It's my heritage.

Black don't crack," she said, laughing a little at the woman's shocked reaction. "That's what my mother told me, anyway."

Jim Snow pretty much looked his age. Slouching in his swivel chair to the right of Alice's desk, his thinning brown hair was cut short and parted along the side. He wore dark blue slacks and a plaid shirt. At forty-seven and a couple inches over six feet, Snow's muscular frame overshadowed his body fat, but only when he made an effort to suck in his gut. Usually he didn't bother.

"Where would I put my weight-lifting equipment, Alice?" Snow wondered. "It takes up an entire room."

"We'll both need to make concessions, Jim." She was using her patient voice with him. "With both of us living in a three-bedroom home together, I'm afraid there won't be room for that. Have you considered joining a fitness center?"

"I've tried that," Snow said. "It's no fun standing around waiting to use a piece of equipment occupied by two chubby women wearing pancake makeup and flirting with every guy in the gym. What if I move my weight-lifting equipment into my office here? I hardly ever use that space. I'm always in your office. I could get rid of my desk and share yours."

Alice looked down at her desk and shook her head.

"What?"

She looked up at him. "Jim, we've been together a year and a half, but you still have every rough edge you had the day I agreed to help investigate your brother-in-law's murder. Maybe I should have stayed in Homicide."

"This detective agency was your idea," Snow reminded her.

"Times like this I'm not so sure it was a good one. There's a reason people say it's not so smart mixing personal relationships with business."

"Well, I do a lot of things that aren't too smart. But I don't want this next step to be one of them. I don't understand why we need three bedrooms. There are only the two of us, and we'll be sharing the same bed."

Alice leaned back in her chair and folded her arms. "For guests, Jim."

"Okay," Snow said. "One bedroom for us, one for guests, and one to work out in."

"When my relatives come to visit, if they all come at the same time, one guest room isn't even enough. My mother needs a bedroom, and my two brothers share the other. One sleeps on the bed and the other sleeps on a cot. So even three bedrooms is stretching the accommodations."

"How often does that happen?"

"A couple times a year. Sometimes more often," Alice said. "It depends…"

"On how bad they've been bitten by the gambling bug that year?"

"It depends on how much they miss me."

"You have an extraordinary family, Alice. You know, part of the thrill of coming to Vegas is the experience of staying in a luxurious room at a resort—not camped out on an old cot in a guest room. You should invite them to stay at a nice hotel when they decide to visit."

Alice frowned at him. "That would be rude. Jim, those rooms are expensive; they don't have money for that."

"Then tell them to stay at Motel 6. Those places are inexpensive and they can bring a dog."

"I know you're joking," Alice said, "but that's not very funny."

"This whole idea is pretty serious," Snow said. "What do I do with my house after I move in with you? And after I'm living with you, your relatives, when they come to visit, will need to approve of me. And there are bound to be lopsided cultural differences that produce friction. I'll be outnumbered."

Alice raised her eyebrows while she considered this. "You mean like Custer at the Little Big Horn?" she said evenly.

"Maybe I worded that improperly," Snow said. "I just wonder where I'll sleep if the house is full of guests and your 'little friend' comes to visit."

Alice stared at him in silence for a moment before asking, "Are you claiming that my menstrual cycles drive you away?"

He shrugged. "If we were to track our disagreements on a calendar, I'm pretty sure we'd find clusters of them around the same three- to four-day period every month."

"Jim," Alice said, then stopped herself and took a breath before continuing. "It was your idea for us to move in together."

"No, it wasn't," Snow countered. "The question may have come out of my mouth, but you planted the concept in my head."

Alice tipped her head at an angle, unfolded her arms, and returned her hands to her lap. "And how did I manage to do that?"

"How would I know how you did it? I don't think those geniuses at that think tank at Stanford could figure that out."

The sound of the front door opening and closing could be heard, followed a moment later by two chimes from a bell in the reception area.

Snow got up. "Looks like our client is here," he said, glad for the interruption. This wasn't going particularly well. "I'll go bring her in."

The woman was standing at the counter in the lobby, studying a life-size cardboard cutout of Betty Boop wearing a red dress. On the counter in front of Betty Boop were a desk bell and a black tabletop sign that read "Ring Bell For Service."

The woman, in her late twenties, had long brown hair, plain features, and small, puffy, red eyes. She was of medium height and buxom. She wore jeans fitting tightly against her wide rear and a black, scoop-neck blouse calling attention to her ample breasts.

"I was admiring your receptionist," she said.

Snow smiled. "We're quite happy with her. She works below minimum wage, never complains, and, if she doesn't work out—we can recycle her."

"That's pretty clever." The woman smiled and offered her hand. She spoke softly. "I'm Cassie Lane."

Snow shook her hand. "Why don't you come on back to my associate's office and we can talk there."

She followed him down the short corridor to the office on the right. Alice stood and walked around to the front of her desk and took Cassie Lane's hand. She offered her a seat and went back behind her desk.

Snow lowered himself into his swivel chair in his usual spot to the right of Alice's desk.

"May I ask how you heard of our agency?" Alice inquired.

Cassie crossed her legs, rested her elbows on the arms of her chair, and interlaced her fingers before answering. "I got your name from a friend of a friend who worked with someone whose murder you investigated. I was told you have a lot of experience with those types of cases."

"Yes, we do, Cassie," Alice said. "Jim and I are both former homicide detectives with Metro. We received a lot of training and spent quite a few years on the job. What is it we can do for you?"

"To begin with, I'm wondering how this whole thing works," Cassie said. "Do you work together as a team, or will it be just one of you who handles my case?"

7

"That's up to you," Snow said. "We can go either way. If we work as a team, which we usually prefer for more complex investigations, we charge expenses and one hundred per hour total for both of us. If one of us works alone, it's sixty per hour. The advantage of hiring both of us is that we can cover more ground and interpret what we find, coming from two different perspectives. That's why homicide detectives work in pairs. For simple investigations, naturally, you would only need one of us."

"Okay," Cassie agreed. "So, I guess I'd like to hire both of you. I doubt you'll find anything simple about this investigation. But can I set a limit? I don't think I want to spend more than four thousand. I don't have a lot of money."

"That's up to you," Alice said. "We do require payment in advance for an agreed-upon minimum. When time runs out, we suspend our investigation until we receive further payment."

"You can pay as much as you're comfortable with," Snow said. "One day at a time if you want, but it's more convenient if you pay at least a couple days ahead to prevent the investigation from being interrupted. If we manage to complete our investigation while there is still time remaining on your retainer, we'll refund the overpayment within thirty days."

"Alright," Cassie said. "That sounds acceptable. How do we get started?"

Alice opened a desk drawer and brought out a form. She slid it across the desk in front of Cassie. "This is our standard contract. You need to read it, sign it, and provide us with a personal check or a money order for the retainer."

Cassie reached into her purse for her checkbook and a pen as she glanced over the text on the contract. When she was finished reading it, she signed and dated it. Then wrote out a check and handed both to Alice.

With this done, Cassie straightened in her chair and folded her hands in her lap. "Where do I begin?"

"Wherever you like," Alice said. She opened her desk drawer and took out a large spiral notebook and a pen.

Snow pulled a smaller notebook out of his rear pocket.

Cassie took in a breath and let it out. "I had been having an affair with a man I met at work before he went back with his wife. I'm a slot technician at the Boulder Nugget Casino on Boulder Highway. He was a steady customer there. He was a professional horseplayer, and he placed the majority of his bets at the Boulder Nugget sports book."

"We're quite familiar with that casino," Snow said. "They have an excellent buffet. And I can see why your friend chose the sports book there. It's impressive, the largest I've seen in Las Vegas."

"Jim," Alice cut in.

"What?"

"Let's let Cassie tell her story." She inclined her head toward Cassie, whose eyes, Snow saw, had begun to brim with tears.

"Sure," he said. "Sorry. I didn't realize I'd gone off on a tangent." He sighed and rolled his eyes.

"That's not a problem," Cassie said, sniffling.

Alice opened a side desk drawer, pulled out a box of tissues, and slid it across the desk toward her.

Cassie leaned forward and tugged one free from the box. Sinking back into her chair, she dabbed at her eyes with it.

"His name was Billy Ryan, and he was murdered exactly one week ago outside of his home in Henderson at three thirty in the morning. He'd been playing craps at the Boulder Nugget. The person who shot him supposedly robbed him, stole his SUV, and hit a teenage girl with it minutes later on Greenawalt Road. She was left for dead in the middle of the intersection.

9

"The police couldn't find any witnesses of the shooting or the hit-and-run, and the SUV was found abandoned near the scene of the hit-and-run a couple hours later. Police noticed the damage to the front end. They said the DNA on the front of the car matched the victim of the hit-and-run. But they haven't found the person who did it. And I don't think they ever will."

"Why do you believe that?" Snow asked.

Cassie dabbed at her eyes with the tissue once more. "Because I think the police are on the wrong track. They interrogated Billy's wife, Gina, and her two brothers at their home. But they aren't even considering them as suspects, because there was no life insurance policy, and Billy and Gina had just gotten back together.

"They said there's no motive and no evidence pointing to Gina or her brothers. They told me they checked all three of them for gunpowder residue and didn't find any, but it seems to me they could have used gloves. Though it's true that Gina and her brothers did let the police into the house to search it, and they didn't find anything.

"Both brothers legally own handguns. But they're 9mm and hadn't been fired. Billy was killed with .38 caliber bullets." Cassie shook her head slowly, pressing the tissue to her nose as she did. "Anybody can get a gun like that without it being traced to them. Everybody knows that. But the police are just focusing on the robbery and carjacking angle. They think someone saw Billy flashing a wad of cash and followed him home from the casino."

"Was Billy at the casino alone?" Snow asked.

"He'd been playing craps at the Boulder Nugget with a friend of his, Dean Kale. He's also a professional horseplayer. He's a really nice guy. They hung out together in the sports book and sometimes gambled together in the casino after they finished their business with the horses."

"Did you ever notice any tension between them?"

"No," Cassie replied. "Billy and Dean were really good friends. I don't remember ever seeing them argue—other than playful banter. You know how guys are."

"Who do you think the shooter might have been?"

"I can't be sure," Cassie said. "My guess would be Gina. She's domineering and vindictive. She acts like she's royalty, and she treated Billy like he was her servant. Nothing he did for her was good enough. She was verbally abusive toward him. After he finally left her, she doted on him and seduced him back into her web. But I don't think she really wanted him back after he rejected her. I think in her mind the relationship was ruined."

"Why did she want to reconcile with him?" Alice said.

"She may have wanted him back so she could punish him," Cassie said. "I believe Gina has a very sick mind."

"Does she have a job or any other source of income?"

"No. Billy has been supporting her ever since they got married six years ago."

"What will Gina do for money now, with no life insurance?"

"Billy has a lot of money socked away," Cassie said. "She'll get that."

"What about her two brothers?" Snow said. "How do they fit into this?"

"They were living in Detroit—the family comes from Michigan. The brothers worked in an auto assembly plant. When they got laid off, they went to live with their parents in Muskegon. After a year and a half, their parents had enough of them and threw them out, and Gina took them in. They're boorish, mean, and sadistic. Billy tried to get along with them, but it was impossible. He was intelligent and successful; they're both losers.

11

They threatened to kill him a number of times, describing how they would do it. Once they threatened to smother him while he was sleeping by wrapping his head with duct tape."

Snow sat up. "Did you tell the police about these threats?"

She nodded, scowling. "They insisted they were just joking, and Gina backed them up."

"And they're both still unemployed and living with Gina?"

"They got jobs finally. One of them works at a quickie oil change place. The other one moves furniture. But Gina insists they don't make enough money to move out on their own. It was a horrible situation for Billy," Cassie said. "You can just imagine."

"Yes," Snow agreed. "It sounds pretty bad." He studied her face. "You say Billy and his wife supposedly worked out their differences. How long ago did Billy move back in with her?"

"Three weeks ago. Two weeks prior to his death."

"How long did your affair with him go on?"

"Six months," she said. "He started flirting innocently with me at the casino. I liked him; he made me laugh. We got together for a friendly drink initially. Nothing serious to begin with. The relationship grew slowly from there. Two months later Billy moved in with me."

"So, you were living together for four months," Alice said. "And three weeks ago he moved back in with his wife." She scribbled in her notebook. "Was that the end of your involvement with him?"

"Yes."

"Has there been anyone else you've been involved with recently?"

Cassie hesitated. "Yes. Dean Kale."

"How did that get started?" Snow asked.

"He's always been a good friend to me," Cassie said. "After Billy left me and moved back in with Gina, Dean was there for me. We grew closer and our relationship blossomed."

"Is it still in full bloom?" Snow asked.

"Yes," Cassie replied. "Dean's a very nice person."

Snow nodded. "Any ex-husbands in your past?"

"I've never been married," Cassie replied. "Billy was the first man I've ever lived with. I had high hopes for our future together. But that turned out to be wishful thinking, unfortunately."

Alice looked up from her notes. "What is it you hope to gain from our investigation, Cassie?"

"Just peace of mind, I guess," Cassie said. "We never spoke to each other again after Billy moved out of my house. But I still cared for him a great deal. It bothered me that he would end our relationship so suddenly just to move back in with *her* after the way she treated him. After I found out about his murder, I haven't slept well since. All I can think about is Gina. I can't move forward with my life until she's arrested for Billy's murder and the hit-and-run killing of that poor young girl."

"What if we find that Gina had nothing to do with it?" Snow asked. "I have to tell you, from the surface of it, it does look like robbery most likely was the motive."

"All I want is justice," Cassie Lane said. "I want to know who did this, and I want her locked up where she won't be able to harm anyone else."

"We'll do our best, Cassie," Alice said. "We can promise you that."

CHAPTER 3

Gina Ryan was in her early thirties, and one of the most strikingly beautiful women Jim Snow had ever met. She stood an inch under six feet tall, with trim legs beneath her white cotton shorts and pert breasts pressing against the sheer fabric of her sleeveless pink blouse. If she was wearing a bra, it was even thinner than her blouse.

She had large, unsettling green eyes and high cheekbones, and wore her blonde hair cut straight in a line below her ears, curled inward toward her pouting lips.

"I'm Jim Snow," he said. "And this is my associate, Alice James."

"Come in," Gina said, with no change to her disinterested expression. She led them into her living room, where she seated herself primly on the sofa. With her knees together, her legs angled to the side and her hands at her sides, she looked as though she were being interviewed for television.

Alice and Snow sank into the matching chairs across from each other at the ends of the couch.

"I'm curious who hired you," Gina said.

"As a rule we don't like to give out that information," Alice said.

"If I were to speculate, I would have to say it was Billy's former mistress, Cassie Lane. Did I guess right?"

Alice said nothing.

"I had a feeling it was her," Gina said. "Doesn't it seem strange to you?"

"In what way?" Alice said.

"I would think Cassie Lane would be the most likely murder suspect. She didn't handle her breakup with my late husband very gracefully. She was angry and bitter. She called him incessantly, in a state of frenzy. She even showed up at the door a couple of times, demanding to talk to him. He finally did, just to try and calm her down, but both times she slammed the door, sobbing hysterically on the way out.

"And then, like a storm cloud breaking up, her wrath ended— two days before Billy's death. That was the last he heard from her that I know of."

"Did you let the police know about that?" Snow asked.

"Of course. As soon as they showed up to investigate. They said they would check into it. But they like the robbery/carjacking premise much better—I suspect because it requires less effort. And I have to admit, it does sound feasible."

"It sounds most likely to me," Snow agreed. "And like you said, if Cassie Lane murdered your husband—why would she hire us to find the killer? It makes no sense."

"Exactly," Gina agreed. "That's what I find most troubling. I wonder if she killed Billy; it may be her intent to falsely incriminate me somehow with your help." She raised her hands off the couch and turned them palms up. "Who knows? But I think it's certainly possible she hatched a frantic, half-baked plan to obtain the ultimate revenge by killing Billy, expecting I would immediately become the focus of the police investigation.

She probably assumed there was a large life insurance policy I'd be in line for. But there wasn't, so the second part of her scheme hasn't worked out for her. The police seem to have excluded me as a suspect, since I had nothing to gain and everything to lose by Billy's death."

"If your suspicion is correct," Snow argued, "why would Cassie steal Billy's car after she shot him?"

"That's what is so poorly conceived about it," Gina replied. "I think Cassie stole his car to make it look like *I* was trying to make it look like a robbery/carjacking. But the police aren't that convoluted in their thinking. After they searched my house and found no evidence, no life insurance policy, and no reports from anyone of recent conflict between Billy and me, they just focused on the robbery/carjacking theory and ran with it."

"Gina," Alice said, "how well do you know Cassie Lane?"

Gina crossed her legs and interlaced her fingers. "Not very well," she replied. "We hardly spoke at all to each other before Billy's death. I used to see her with Billy occasionally while they were together out in the open. She only lives a little over a mile from here, and we apparently shop at the same stores.

"Cassie and I did run into each other in Albertson's one morning a few days after Billy's murder, and she seemed subdued and genuine in her grief. She was actually friendly and kind toward me, for a change, and I invited her over for coffee."

"I'm sorry," Alice said, "but are you saying you asked her into your home? The woman you think killed your husband? That seems odd to me."

"I know, it sounds crazy. But yes, that's right: I did ask her over, and we had a good talk. She came across as warm and sensitive. To my surprise it seems we may be forming a friendship of one sort or another. I'm a little suspicious of it, but I think she's just overly passionate. And apparently she's one of those people with extreme emotional swings who doesn't deal well with rejection. But none of us is perfect."

"That's true," Alice said. "But I have to go back to my question: If you suspect Cassie of murdering your husband and attempting to incriminate you, how could you consider her a friend?"

"My first suspicion after the shooting was that Cassie did it. I've had more time to think about it since, but I still objectively consider her a likely suspect," Gina said. "That doesn't mean I'm convinced she did it. I just wonder about the possibility of it. Now that I've had a chance to see another side of her, I find myself enjoying her occasional company. What can I say? This whole business is crazy. And no one is ever completely trustworthy, no matter how close we get to them. Look at what happened with Billy. I opened myself up to him, and he cheated on me."

"That's true." Frowning, Snow nodded as he scribbled in his tiny notebook.

"How did you feel when Billy left you to move in with Cassie?" Alice asked.

Gina shrugged. "It was frustrating for me, but not a major setback. I understand men very well. Most of them seek classy, beautiful women for marriage, while indulging their adventurous side with any woman willing to copulate with them. I suspect a likely reason many executives put in late hours at work is to give them the chance to roll around on the floor of their offices with the cleaning lady before heading home to their wives."

Snow raised an eyebrow. "So you were confident Billy would end the relationship with Cassie quickly and move back in with you."

"Absolutely," Gina confirmed. "Cassie Lane is a slot technician, for heaven's sake. She does have some redeeming traits, but what could she have to offer someone like Billy long term? Convincing him to move in with her was the final act in her desperate play on my husband. And it was a short one."

"May I ask," Alice said, "what is your background, Gina?"

Gina tipped her head back slightly and smiled. "I was born and raised in Muskegon, Michigan, with my two younger brothers. Not long after high school graduation, I moved to Chicago, where I got into modeling. I worked, quite successfully, in that field for nine years until I married Billy. At that point I decided to give up my career to become a full-time, nurturing wife and mother… I only accomplished half of that goal."

"You've never had any children?" Snow asked.

Gina frowned. "We did. We had a girl a year after we were married. But she was stillborn. Neither of us had the heart to try again after that experience. Billy got a vasectomy right away."

"That's terrible," Snow said. "I'm sorry to hear that."

"What was Billy's profession?" Alice asked.

"He was a marketing executive for a large corporation in Chicago. And he was quite successful at it. But somewhere along the way, he became obsessed with horse racing. He found he had a talent for that. He studied the race tracks around Chicago for years and made quite a bit of money betting on the horses."

"Did he actually go to the tracks?" Snow asked. "Or did he place his bets off-track?"

"Both. Whichever was more convenient to him."

Snow leaned forward, his face suddenly aglow. "Did he have some sort of a system? How did he pick his horses?"

"Jim," Alice warned.

"What? It's salient."

She cocked an eyebrow at him, but didn't press the point.

"I don't know for sure how he did it," Gina said. "But it wasn't simple. He spent hours studying the *Daily Racing Form*. I know that he considered a lot of factors and that he only bet two or three races at each track each day. I never was interested in it, so I didn't understand what he was looking for to make a good bet. But he did it full-time for three years, and he made good money at it.

"And now that he's gone—that income is gone too. Now I'm not sure what I'll do to survive financially. I may have to go back to work, and I'm afraid I'm getting too old to get back into modeling, except maybe on a smaller scale and for less money. That's the only professional experience I have."

"You and Billy didn't have much money saved?" Alice said.

"Half a million dollars is all," Gina said. "That won't last forever."

"Probably not," Snow muttered, thinking about his own dwindling net worth of seventy-five hundred dollars in his online brokerage account. "Gina, what can you tell us about the night of Billy's shooting?"

"Not much, unfortunately," Gina said. "We were in bed, sound asleep. All any of us heard were the two gunshots, and then the sound of a car speeding away."

"A single car?" Snow asked.

"Yes, just one car. I assume it was Billy's Nissan. Of course there may have been another car driven by the killer's accomplice— if there was an accomplice—that drove off before the gunshots. None of us were awake until after the shots were fired."

"Who else was in the house with you at the time?" Alice asked.

"My two brothers, Lance and Damon. They've been living here with me for the last year or so while they get back on their feet. Up until two and a half years ago, they both had good jobs in the auto industry in Detroit—and that turned out to be the wrong place to try and make a living long term. But they both have jobs now—they're doing fine."

"What did you do after you heard the shots?" Alice said.

"I got out of bed and looked out my bedroom window, but couldn't see anything because it faces the backyard. So I came downstairs and peeked out of that window." She pointed at the picture window next to the front door. Staring at it, she pressed her lips tightly together and began to sob, her words catching in her throat. Struggling to regain her composure, she swallowed, took in a breath, and continued: "And that was when I saw Billy lying facedown at the foot of the driveway. There was a lot of blood. He wasn't moving, and there was no one else around. Lance and Damon were both down here by then. Lance went to the kitchen to call 911. Damon and I went outside together to look at the body." She sobbed again.

"Take your time," Alice said. "I know this is difficult for you."

Gina brushed the tears from her cheeks with the fingers of both hands, then folded her arms and turned her eyes to Snow, and then Alice. "Shortly after that, the police and an ambulance came. But it was too late for the paramedics to do anything. The detectives later told me both bullets went right through his heart. He was shot in the back as he was walking up the driveway toward the front door.

"A half hour after the police got here, three detectives showed up along with some crime scene people. They all started looking around for evidence. They checked all three of us for traces of blood and gunpowder. Of course they didn't find any. They wanted to come in and look through the house and wanted to know if that was okay. I told them that was fine with me—we don't have anything to hide."

"Did they find any evidence near the scene?" Snow asked.

She shook her head. "I asked them about that. They said they didn't. No shell casings or anything like that. They checked Billy's pockets, and he still had his billfold and cash. So they said the thief must have panicked after he shot him, and just drove off in Billy's car without taking the time to look for money."

"If it was a robbery, it sounds like an amateur. How much cash did they find on him?"

"A little over thirteen thousand," Gina said. "That was typical for him, because he bet hundreds of dollars a race, sometimes as many as twenty races in a day. He usually left for the casino with about ten thousand, so he must have had a good day."

"How much was he making?" Snow asked.

"He averaged over a thousand dollars a day," Gina said. "That's what he told me."

"Wow. That's pretty decent money."

"Yes," Gina said. "He was good at it. But he gave a lot of it back at the crap table. That was his weakness."

"He had been playing craps the night he was shot?"

"Yes. He and a friend of his, Dean Kale. Dean is a fellow horseplayer. They hang out together in the sports book at the casino. Dean is a professional also, but he hasn't been at it as long as Billy. Less than a year."

"Dean Kale also makes money betting horses?" Snow asked with raised brows.

"Yes, he's very good."

"So, when they left the casino—I understand it was around three in the morning," Alice said. "They drove home in separate cars?"

"No," Gina said. "Billy had picked Dean up on the way to the casino that morning. Sometimes they commuted together because Dean's home is on the way to the Boulder Nugget. Dean said that Billy seemed to be too drunk to drive, so he suggested he drive Billy home and keep his car overnight. Billy didn't want him to do that, but he let Dean drive the car to his house. Dean said Billy seemed to be okay at that point to drive the rest of the way home, because it's only a few miles and there wasn't much traffic at that time of the morning."

"Where did the hit-and-run occur?" Alice said.

"That was at the intersection of Greenawalt Road and Wampler Street."

"Would Billy have driven through that intersection on his way home?"

"Yes," Gina said. "Greenawalt Road is the shortest route to get here from Boulder Highway. He always takes that road when he's coming from that direction."

"He was intoxicated. I wonder if there's any chance that it was Billy who hit that girl."

"Absolutely not," Gina said. "For one thing, you had to know Billy to know how impossible that was. He was a wonderful man. If he were to hit someone by accident, he would have stayed right there and called for an ambulance. For another, the accident occurred after the shooting. The police told me our 911 call was recorded at 3:32 a.m., and the call for the hit-and-run was placed at 3:36. Also, I was told that the evidence showed that the girl's body had been hit in the crosswalk in the middle of the westbound lanes and dragged westward. That's the direction heading away from our house. Billy would have been eastbound on Greenawalt coming home."

"This Dean Kale," Snow said. "What sort of person is he?"

"He's a wonderful man," Gina said. "He's always been a good friend to both Billy and me. He's been very kind and supportive through all of this. But it also hit him pretty hard. He and Billy were very close. He's as devastated over this as I am."

"I wonder if you'd mind giving us his phone number," Snow said. "We'd like to talk to him. He may be able to throw some light on this for us."

"I doubt he'll be able to help you much," Gina said. "He doesn't know much about that night. But if you give me your business card, I can call him and ask him to get in touch with you. I'm sure he'll call you right away."

———

Behind the wheel of his Hyundai Sonata, Jim Snow cranked the engine to life. He turned his head to Alice. "What do you think?"

"That woman is a convoluted mass of contradictions. I found it hard to believe that she would give up a modeling career during her prime years to become a housewife. I modeled for a short time in my early twenties while I could get the work, which was a minor miracle. I wouldn't have given it up for anything. And I never met any other models who felt any differently about it than I did."

Snow shifted into gear and pulled away from the curb that fronted the Ryan residence. "I don't know," he said. "She seems like a very bright, sophisticated woman. She's sensible and doesn't allow her emotions to rule her actions. I think it only seems like she's waffling, because she's trying to be fair and objective, considering all of the angles."

"She does project that image," Alice said. "I think I'd like to do a background check on Gina and Billy and her two brothers. See what turns up."

Snow nodded. "While you're at it, maybe you could call one of your contacts at Metro and get some information from the hit-and-run report on that girl. We might get a lead out of that."

"Alright," Alice said. "It probably won't be helpful, but you never know."

"While you're doing that, I think I'll head over to the Boulder Nugget before the ten a.m. shift change and see if I can get any information out of the crew that was working that night." He glanced at his watch. "Maybe you could meet me over there for lunch."

Alice smiled. "I'm guessing you've got another coupon for the buffet."

Snow chuckled. "You're correct. Two for one. You've just won a free lunch, Alice."

"Oh, that's wonderful," Alice said, feigning delight. "We haven't eaten at the Boulder Nugget buffet since yesterday."

CHAPTER 4

Snow set his food tray on the table and lowered himself into the chair across from Alice. "Okay, so what did you find out?"

"A lot," Alice said. She took a sip of ice tea, straightened her silverware, and dropped her hands into her lap. "I don't know if this is of any use to us, but Gina Ryan never worked for a modeling agency in Chicago or anywhere else. She worked for a number of escort agencies in Chicago from the age of eighteen to twenty-seven before she married Billy Ryan. She has three convictions for prostitution and served ninety days in jail for the third offense. Not a bad record, I imagine, for a career spanning nine years."

"A hooker? I wonder if Billy knew about that before he married her."

"Probably not," Alice said. "I doubt many men do background checks on their fiancées, and it doesn't do any good to search her maiden name on the Internet; Gina Brown is a fairly common name."

Snow picked up his knife and fork and began slicing off a section of roast beef on his plate. "What about the rest of her family?"

Alice shook her head. "Her parents are both teachers in Muskegon. Her two brothers have clean records. So did Billy Ryan. Although Gina did exaggerate Billy's job title. He wasn't a marketing executive. He worked as a sales rep for a pump manufacturer."

"That's not bad," Snow said. "Those guys can make pretty good money. Though probably not as much as he was raking in playing the horses."

"Unless Gina was lying about that too. I don't see how we can believe anything she tells us."

Snow chewed his roast beef and swallowed. "She's pretty convincing. She had me going."

"I think she gets most guys going," Alice said with a knowing look.

"What about the hit-and-run?" Snow said.

"We might have a possible connection there. The girl's name was Brittany Wile. She was sixteen years old and three months pregnant. She was walking home from a friend's house. She was wearing earphones when she was struck by Billy Ryan's car, listening to music on her MP3 player. So she apparently didn't hear the approaching car."

"You think she might have been the primary target?"

"It's not likely," Alice said. "Though it did cross my mind that the father of her baby might not have wanted the complication in his life, especially if he's not a minor. He could have been in big trouble and potentially facing prosecution for statutory rape."

"So he hijacked a car to use as an untraceable murder weapon, killing the owner in the process to prevent being identified."

"Right. A bit much. And besides, the timing is too precise. Brittany Wile was run over only a few minutes after the car was stolen. If the perpetrator were planning something like that, he'd have given himself more time to lie in wait for her."

"Not necessarily," Snow said. "He may have seen a small window of opportunity and jumped at it. Young guys can be pretty impetuous."

Alice shrugged. "If he knew she was walking home at three thirty in the morning."

"And what is a teenage girl doing out by herself on the street at that hour on a school night? What sort of parents would allow that?"

"They probably didn't," Alice said. "They just neglected to lock her in her room that night."

"Alright," Snow said. "Well, I guess we need to dig into that mess when we get the chance."

Alice stabbed at some sliced beets with her fork. "What did you find out here?"

"I talked to the floor supervisor, the pit boss, and a couple of the crew who were working the crap table Billy Ryan and Dean Kale played at that night. I know all these guys fairly well, and they were all helpful. They all remember seeing the two of them; they're both regulars so they all knew them. They remember they were both fairly drunk by the time they colored in their chips, and there was a lot of amiable, competitive banter exchanged between them. They said it's always that way with them. The pit boss checked the database and told me they played craps at that one table for five hours. They'd both been in the sports book all day until around six thirty in the evening. Then they had dinner at Cheng Wong's and played blackjack for four hours before moving to one of the crap tables. All told, Billy Ryan won a few thousand that night. But Dean Kale lost over eight grand. They told me they remember Billy Ryan was playing the pass and come lines—he made over ten straight passes on one streak while he had the dice. And Dean Kale was betting against him on the don'ts. I met with the head of security and he told me he had checked the video footage at that crap table and the casino exit Billy and Dean Kale used. The homicide investigators asked him about it last week. He said Billy and Dean left the casino together and they didn't see anyone who appeared to be following them out of the casino. After I talked to security I had a little time to kill waiting for you to show up for lunch, so I lost a few hundred at blackjack. Too bad I can't write that off as a business expense."

"Well, that solves one mystery," Alice said.

"Which one?"

"Why you keep getting so many of those two-for-one buffet coupons in the mail."

CHAPTER 5

At 2:00 p.m. on a Thursday, when Dean Kale would normally be sitting in front of a monitor with three racing forms covering the entire country and a stack of printouts listing the day's entries at racetracks from coast to coast, he was at home.

He owned a single-story, three-bedroom home near Rodeo Park in Henderson, with a two-car garage and a yard covered with gravel and an assortment of desert flora.

In his mid-thirties, Dean Kale was of medium height and weight, with a square jaw and a head of thick blonde hair cut short. He came to the door wearing jeans, a pair of scuffed brown loafers, and a rumpled chambray shirt. There were bags under his eyes, and his complexion was pallid.

After Snow introduced Alice and himself, Kale nodded solemnly, stepped back behind the door, and waved them inside.

"I'd offer you something to drink," Kale said, "but all I have is tap water. I don't even own a coffee maker; I either get my coffee at the casino when the horses are running or at 7-Eleven when they're dark."

"That's okay," Snow said. "We're fine."

Kale slouched into a stuffed chair with worn edging, and Alice and Snow sat next to each other on the matching couch. It sagged so badly that Snow's knees were nearly even with his chest. He felt like he was sitting on the floor.

Kale saw him struggling to get comfortable and said, "I have to apologize. I've been putting off getting new furniture. I don't usually have company over, and I seldom use it myself. I'm usually at the casino. In fact, I should be there now, but I can't seem to get up the energy to drive there. And I can't concentrate. I keep thinking about what happened to Billy. It's been a week and I'm still having trouble coming to terms with it. Have you two got any leads?"

Snow shook his head. "No," he said. "We're just getting started." Wondering where to put his hands, he finally rested them on his knees. He felt like a downhill skier preparing to schuss off a mountain peak.

Frowning, Kale nodded. "The cops don't have anything either. They hauled ass over here to interrogate me after they finished with Gina and her brothers. I guess that's standard procedure, since I was the last known person to see Billy alive. But I couldn't be of much help to them."

"Did you happen to notice anyone follow you out of the casino that night?" Snow asked.

"No. But neither one of us was paying much attention. Billy was three sheets to the wind, and I was feeling pretty good myself. We should have taken a taxi, I guess, but it probably wouldn't have altered the outcome. I've been thinking: if I had insisted on driving him all the way home, they wouldn't have tried to rob both of us together. But that's nonsense. If I had driven him home, we'd probably both be dead."

Alice sat with her knees together, her fingers interlaced around her shins. She looked as though she were in mid-air doing a cannonball off a diving board. "You were driving Billy's car," she said, "when the two of you left the casino?"

Kale nodded. "He couldn't even walk straight. So I talked him into letting me drive him as far as my house. I wanted to drive him all the way home and then come back for him in the morning to head to the casino, but I couldn't talk him into it. He only had a couple miles to go, and there's never any traffic at that time of the night—or morning."

"Did you notice any cars following you from the casino parking lot?" Alice said.

"To be honest," Kale said, "I wasn't paying attention to the traffic behind me. I never do."

"Gina said that Billy had a lot of cash on him," Snow said. "I assume you did too. Were you two always so careless with it?"

Kale offered a halfhearted grin. "When we were drinking, we were. But you assume wrong. Billy had a good run of luck; I ended up borrowing three thousand from him and then ended up losing that. I only had eighty bucks on me when we left the casino."

"I was told you and Billy were betting against each other at the crap table, and the dialogue between you two got pretty heated."

"It was always that way," Kale said, waving his hand dismissively. "Billy and I were good friends. We always sat together in the sports book. We ate, drank, and gambled together, and usually drove to and from the casino together. But we had a friendly rivalry going most of the time. It livened things up. We both made good money betting the horses, but our strategies differ greatly. We seldom bet the same races, and when we did, we'd usually back different horses."

Snow leaned forward intently. "What sort of methods did the two of you use?"

Alice shifted her weight, crossed her arms, and frowned at her shoes.

Kale rested one ankle atop the other knee and leaned back. "Well, Billy was a wizard with probability. He was an ace handicapper to begin with, and very thorough about examining all of the factors in each race. He could break it down into percentages. He'd calculate his own morning line for each race he deemed playable by his standards.

"The standard strategy with most serious horseplayers is to find the best horse in a race and only bet on it if it's a standout. But you end up picking mostly low-priced favorites, and you can't make money on those because the odds are too low. The tracks take out anywhere from fourteen to twenty percent or more from the pari-mutuel pools, and then they round the payoffs down to the nearest twenty cents. So you need an extreme overlay to win money over the long run.

"Billy almost never bet the best horses. Sometimes he'd bet a horse he thought had only a ten percent chance of winning. That's nine to one—but the horse might go off at fifteen to one. That's a tremendous profit. Of course, he wasn't always right, but over the long run he was making a fairly consistent twenty percent profit.

"I don't spend as much time poring over past performances the way Billy did. I pick out the best three or four horses and study them in the paddock and post parade. You can tell a lot about a thoroughbred by watching him. Horses communicate with body language, and I concentrate on that."

"But you don't get much time to see them from off-track," Snow said. "Isn't that a disadvantage?"

"It is, somewhat," Kale allowed. "But I don't need that much time to get an impression of the horse's temperament, form, and level of confidence. A quick look is all I need. Most horses tell you the same thing: they don't want to be out there, or they're sore or tired, or all three. Very few of the cheaper horses love the competition of racing. The rest don't even want to go near the paddock, much less the starting gate."

"How did you learn all of that?" Snow asked.

"Eighteen years of working with thoroughbred race horses," Kale said. "I grew up in Victorville, California. When I was eighteen, I drove down to Pomona while they were racing there and wandered around the barn area, asking around about getting work. Mitch Michaels took me on as a stable hand. I started out mucking stalls, feeding and washing down horses, and walking "hots." I lived in tack rooms in his shed rows in the southern California circuit for a lot of years, making peanuts. But it was a fantastic way of life.

"Eventually Mitch Michaels promoted me to assistant trainer, and not long after that I got my stable of horses to train. I did pretty good for a while, but I never really had very many horses under my supervision. There's a lot of talented competition. Eventually I figured out I was better off wagering on them than training them. About ten months ago I gave it up and moved out to Vegas to try and make a living at it. And I've done pretty well. I try to pick what I think is the best-looking horse in the race, and it has to go to the post at better than three to one. I haven't been doing as well as Billy; my profit is only twelve percent so far. But it was higher at first. I've been having a bad streak for the last month or so."

Kale folded his hands in his lap and looked down at them, frowning. "It can be really frustrating when almost all of the horses I pick at less than three to one win, and the bets I make at the higher odds all lose. I've often considered changing my strategy to just betting everything regardless of the odds, but I know I wouldn't show a profit. I'd be lucky to break even." He looked at Snow. "Of course if I keep losing the way I have for another month, I'll only be breaking even overall. I'm worried about losing my confidence. It's a lot easier making a profit betting horses when you don't have to rely on it for income."

Snow's eyes narrowed. He nodded. "That's what happened to me," he said quietly. "I quit the police force to play poker full-time at the poker rooms on the Strip at Bellagio, Treasure Island, and Wynn. I won consistently for two and a half years. Then I had a bad run that lasted six months. It destroyed me. I had to give it up."

Alice looked at Snow and cleared her throat, but said nothing. Clearly she was losing patience with Snow's chatty confession.

Snow got the hint, but pressed on. "The aspect of poker I hated the most was facing my opponents. When you're beating someone out of a lot of money—some of those guys feel like they'd like to kill you. You can see it in their expressions and the way they act, especially when they've had too much to drink. I can imagine how you must have felt being in the thick of losing your shirt while your buddy was hauling it in."

"Sure, it was aggravating," Kale said. "But when you're a pro, you have to be able to handle the ups and downs. Billy was like a brother to me. I'd never even imagine any harm coming to him."

Snow fixed his gaze on Kale's face for a moment. He nodded. "Of course, horse racing's different than poker. You don't have to face the people you're betting against. I've always had an interest in playing the horses, but I never got serious about it because I thought it was impossible to make a profit because of the track take. Like you say, it's at least fourteen percent. In poker I found it impossible to make a profit when the rake was higher than three percent."

Alice crossed her legs and began bobbing her foot up and down.

Snow ignored it. "The only guy I read about who made his living betting horses was Pittsburgh Phil. But that was well over a hundred years ago. He kept his own notes on past performances. Now everything is documented so well in the *Form*. It looks like the best horses are always the favorites. Don't you think that's true?"

"Definitely," Kale said. "There's a lot of information out there for the betting public. That's why Billy and I came up with our own quirky methods to beat the odds. And Billy's method was ingenious. Who would think to bet the fifth best horse in a race when his odds are right?"

Snow nodded. "Are there others at that sports book making money at the tracks?"

Kale shrugged. "I don't know. I see a lot of the same people there day after day. A lot of old guys who are probably retired. I know some of them are placing hefty bets. But I've never had a conversation with any of them. Nothing beyond a greeting or a nod. I don't like to pry into somebody else's business."

"I know what you mean. Trying to dig information out of people bothers me sometimes—but that's what I do for a living." Snow studied Kale's face. "So, you haven't been back to the Boulder Nugget since the shooting?"

Kale shook his head. "I've just been sitting around here, doing a lot of reading and just thinking about things. But I need to get back into my old routine. The biggest problem is that it won't feel right with Billy gone. Just sitting next to that guy made me feel like a winner. I never met anyone who had so much self-confidence. He was brilliant, and a good guy all around."

"He must have had losing streaks."

"Oh, sure," Kale said. "He told me the worst streak lasted four months. But he came out of it with the best winning month ever. He was phenomenal."

The living room fell silent for a moment.

Finally Alice spoke. "Dean," she said, "is there anyone you can think of who might have wanted to harm Billy?"

Kale, scowling, shook his head. "Everybody liked that guy."

"What about his wife?"

"I've got nothing bad to say about Gina. She's a classy lady. They got along great together."

"But Billy and Gina were separated for four months," Alice pointed out.

"That was because of Billy," Kale said. "He took an interest in that slot technician at Boulder Nugget, and it got out of hand. I could only guess what it was he saw in her. But it didn't last long."

"Six months?"

Kale nodded. "I guess that's about right. It's amazing how that guy could keep his head and be so smart about picking horses but so stupid about picking women. It's one thing to get seduced into the hay with her, but to want to build a relationship with that woman—forget it."

"What's wrong with Cassie Lane?" Snow asked.

"Most of the time she's really sweet, but she can turn into a bitch at the drop of a hat," Kale said. "She would seldom leave Billy alone for more than a few hours at a time. She hovered around us in the sports book every chance she got, and she expected him home every night before she got off at six during the weeks she worked the day shift. So they could spend quality time together."

"What do you think attracted Billy to her?" Snow said.

"Frankly, I think it was her tits," Kale said, glancing at Alice and shrugging. "Gina's are not that prominent. She was a model. You know, they tend to run small in that profession. Some guys are fixated on big knockers, and I think Billy was that way. I have to admit, Cassie's boobs *are* appealing to the eye."

Snow nodded. "I'm told that you're seeing her now."

Kale nodded. "We've always gotten along pretty good. I guess I just sort of fell into it with her."

"You think there's any chance Cassie Lane shot Billy?"

Kale shook his head. "No. No way in hell. Cassie told me she hired you to find out who killed Billy. Why would she do that if she shot him? That wouldn't make any sense. She's got her mood swings and issues, and she can get worked up a lot of the time, but she doesn't seem like the sort who could go off the deep end. She's a little nutty, but I think all women are." He gave Alice another half-apologetic look. "I've been involved with a few who were a lot meaner and crazier than her over the years. And none of them ever killed anyone that I know of. Of course, had I married any of them, it might have been different."

"You've never been married?" Snow asked.

Kale shook his head. He leaned forward and rapped his knuckles on the tarnished wooden surface of the coffee table, then leaned back in his chair, crossing his legs at the ankles. "What about you, Jim?"

Snow nodded solemnly. "I'm a two-time loser. That was enough for me. After the first one I thought I had picked the wrong woman. After the second one I gave up."

Kale nodded grimly. "I think that's pretty common these days. Women aren't what they used to be. Present company excepted of course."

Alice rolled her eyes and shook her head.

"What about Gina's two brothers?" Snow asked. "Could they have been involved in Billy's murder?"

"I don't think so," Kale replied. "They're a couple of oddballs, but they seem harmless. I've never been bothered by them; I just humor them. Billy let them get under his skin. He was always complaining about them."

"Do you think the problem Billy had with them could have contributed to Billy's affair?" Alice asked.

"It's possible," Kale said. "But I'm convinced it was Cassie's knockers that wedged Billy and Gina apart temporarily."

"Who do you think shot Billy?" Alice said.

Kale reached up and ran his fingers thoughtfully over his chin and the side of his neck. His eyes narrowed. "I've thought about it a lot. I have to say I think it was somebody who lives down the street from Billy and Gina. They were probably familiar with Billy's routine. Almost every Thursday Billy and I shot craps till late. One of his neighbors probably knew that and knew Billy carried a lot of money. I think you guys should canvass the neighborhood. The cops probably did that—but they could have missed something a sharper mind would pick up on. I think you two are pretty savvy. That's the impression I get."

Snow grinned stupidly. "Thanks, Dean." He pushed himself up off the couch. Kale got up and they shook hands. "It's a rare pleasure to meet you," Snow said.

Kale smiled. "If you have any other questions, give me a call. Maybe we could do lunch some time and exchange views on professional gambling tactics. It's not often that I run into anyone who understands percentages."

"That sounds like a good idea," Snow said. "I'll be interested in finding out how you're doing a couple years down the road."

Alice stood up from the sofa. Holding her purse in front of her, with one hand folded over the other, she studied Dean Kale curiously.

CHAPTER 6

Alice and Snow spent the next couple of hours going door to door, talking to the neighbors on that quiet street in Henderson where a man had been shot to death a week earlier.

All the people they talked to were alarmed by what they'd heard, fearful that they might be the next victim. One resident opened his front door holding a handgun at his side. He told Snow he also had a shotgun leaning against the corner of the wall next to the door, in case someone attempted to kick his door in.

Some of them asked for identification, and Snow would obligingly present his private investigator license in front of the peephole.

No one had heard anything other than two gunshots and the one car driving away after the shooting. None of them suspected Gina of having a hand in the killing, though a few of them insisted they wouldn't be surprised to learn the brothers were involved somehow; both were openly hostile, frequently working on their dilapidated cars in the Ryan driveway, kicking, pounding, and yelling obscenities at their uncooperative vehicles.

The moving van stood parked on the street in front of a home in east Las Vegas, with the rear door rolled open. The name painted on the side read "Guys and Dollies Moving." Two men were carrying a six-drawer dresser up the sidewalk toward the front door, with straps wrapped under the piece and over their shoulders.

Snow parked his Sonata on the opposite side of the street. He and Alice sat in the car and watched the men finish unloading the van. After the movers' last trip into the house, Snow and Alice got out and ambled across the street to the van.

One of the men had climbed inside the cab to fill out paperwork. The other stood leaning against the back of the truck, smoking a cigarette. He was twenty-nine, of medium height and weight, and wore his hair in an overgrown buzz cut. He watched Alice and Snow with a bored look on his face.

"Are you Damon Brown?" Snow asked.

The man took a drag on his cigarette, letting his hand fall to his side. He blew the smoke out. "Yeah," he said.

Snow introduced the two of them, and Damon Brown nodded his greeting.

"Nice day for moving," Snow said with a smile.

Damon took another drag on his cigarette and nodded. "It's okay."

"It must be brutal during the summer."

"I wouldn't know," Damon said. "I've only been doing this for a few months."

"How do you like it?"

"It's a job," Damon replied.

"At least you don't have to worry about working out after you get off work," Snow said. "It's built into your job."

"I wouldn't anyway," Damon said. "I'm not big on wasting energy—working out."

"Sorry to hear about your brother-in-law," Snow said.

"Not as sorry as he is," Damon said.

"You must feel pretty bad about that."

Damon Brown took another puff and shook his head. "I'm not glad that he's dead, but it's a relief knowing he isn't around anymore."

"The two of you didn't get along?" Alice chimed in.

"The guy was high and mighty. He thought he was better than everybody because he didn't have to work for a living. Just living the good life, hanging out at casinos every day. I don't know what Gina saw in him. She was a supermodel. She could have had anybody she wanted. Instead she married that prick."

"We were told they separated for a while. Were they arguing a lot?"

"No, they never argued," Damon said. "Gina isn't perfect, but she doesn't pick fights. She rolls with the punches. They got along okay. Billy got the urge for a little strange stuff, so he started banging a slot mechanic from the casino. I can't say as I blame him for that. She's got some giant coconuts hanging from her tree. Who wouldn't want to roll those babies around?"

Alice raised an eyebrow. "Your knuckles get sore, dragging on the floor?"

Damon frowned at her. "What's that supposed to mean?"

"So it was Billy's idea to move out?" Snow cut in.

Damon turned to him. "Yeah, he wanted that stuff full-time. Gina just let him go. After a while I guess he got tired of his new toy and came back home."

"How were they getting along after he moved back in?"

"Just like before. Like I said, he and Gina never argued. But I bet there was plenty of that going on with the slot woman."

"Cassie Lane is pretty volatile?"

"Yeah," Damon said. "Billy said she was a bitch. Always picking on him, bossing him around. In general, making his life miserable. I guess that took the bloom off her bazooms."

"Did that upset you, having Billy move back in with your sister and you?" Alice asked.

Damon Brown took another draw on his cigarette. "No, it didn't upset me. I was just disappointed. I was just getting used to not having the bastard around."

"How about your brother, Lance?" Snow asked. "How did he feel about the whole situation with Billy?"

"Same as me," Damon replied. "Billy was like a pile of dog shit on the sidewalk as far as we were both concerned. You just have to step around it so you don't get any on you."

"Did either of you make any sort of threats toward Billy?" Alice asked.

"Sure," Damon said. "We both did. A lot. But we were just fucking with him. The guy had no sense of humor."

"Do you have any idea who might have shot Billy?" Snow asked.

Damon took another drag. "I'd say it was the big-breasted slot slut. That's what I think." He let the smoke stream slowly out of his nostrils.

Lance Brown was working in the pit at the Drain & Lube on East Sahara Avenue when Alice and Snow arrived at the customer service counter, asking for him. He ascended the steps into the backroom and ambled through the short corridor, past the restrooms, into the customer lounge to meet with Alice and Snow. He resembled his younger brother, only a couple of inches taller, with longer hair and a bushy mustache. His company-issued gray pants and shirt with "Drain & Lube" stitched in red above the breast pocket were streaked with oil.

Wiping his hands with a dirty rag, he stopped in the middle of the room, looked at Alice, then Snow, and offered a nod. "You the private dicks?"

They stood up. Snow put his hands in his pockets. He glanced around the room at an elderly woman with two kids crawling around on the floor next to her, and a middle-aged man wearing a dark gray suit with a gold tie, reading a battered copy of *Motor Trends*.

"Why don't we talk outside," Snow suggested.

The three of them walked out to the parking area and stood in an empty space in front of an acacia tree.

"What do you think of this place?" Snow asked. "You recommend I get my oil changed here?"

Lance Brown shoved the rag into his back pocket and folded his arms. "Sure, it's okay. Why?"

"I've read stories about some of these oil change businesses charging for work they don't do," Snow said.

"That could happen anywhere," Lance said. "I paid to have a fuel filter replaced once at a dealership service department. I crawled under there to check it out after I got home; had to take my car back and complain to the service advisor. I threatened to write to their corporate office, so they replaced it and gave me a refund. I had a buddy who paid to have the oil changed in his differential at a dealership. The mechanic drained it but forgot to refill it. It seized up on the way home. My buddy took them to court and lost.

"But that's nothing. I had another buddy who worked as a dental technician. He told me he went out drinking on a regular basis with the two dentists he works for, and they confided in him one night that they usually don't drill cavities out all the way prior to filling them. That way they're guaranteed return visits for additional work in the future."

"I guess it's bad all over," Snow muttered. "I heard about a guy who checked into a hospital for a hemorrhoid operation and died of complications. He was only fifty-two."

"Shit," Lance Brown said. "That's why I always ask for extra lettuce on my cheeseburgers. It's good insurance."

"That's good thinking," Snow agreed.

Alice sighed and cut in. "We're investigating Billy Ryan's murder. We're interested in any information you could give us."

"I don't have any idea who killed him."

"Did you hear or see anything prior to or after the shooting?" she asked.

Lance shook his head. "Just the gunshots. Two of them. Woke me up from a dead sleep. Then I heard the car racing off down the street."

"Did you hear any voices outside at all?" Snow asked.

"No. Nothing. But I'm a pretty heavy sleeper."

"After the gunshots, what did you do?"

"I heard Gina and Damon going downstairs, so I went down too. We looked out through the front window and saw Billy lying there dead. They went out to check the body, and I went to call the cops."

"You think there might be any chance Gina or Damon might have had anything to do with it?" Snow asked.

Without hesitation Lance frowned and shook his head. "Nah, no way."

"What about you?"

"If I'd shot him," Lance argued, "I would have taken his money. He still had his bankroll on him when he died. And it would have been 9mm bullets that killed him instead of .38. And I sure as hell wouldn't be out here talking to you two."

"I guess that's true," Snow said. He clapped Lance on the shoulder. "Thanks for giving us your time."

"No problem," Lance said. "You seem like an alright guy. You want your oil changed while you're here? I can arrange a discount."

"Not today," Snow said. "I've still got another couple thousand miles worth on the old oil."

"Well, don't put it off too long," Lance said. "You should see the glop that oozes out of some people's crankcases. I see it every day."

"That's good to know," Snow said. "I'll try to keep my glop to a minimum."

CHAPTER 7

Julia Rice was sixteen, the same age as her late friend Brittany Wile, who had been run over by Billy Ryan's Nissan Altima in a crosswalk a week earlier. Julia had long black hair with bangs to the middle of her eyebrows. Though she wore no lipstick or facial ornaments, her eyes were covered with enough makeup to give her a ghoulish appearance. She wore a black cotton blouse, black leggings, and black knee-high boots.

She sat upright, with her arms crossed, in one of the client chairs in Alice James's office.

Jim Snow, sitting in his usual spot to the right of Alice's desk, began the interview: "We talked to your mother and Brittany's parents about the accident, Julia. They weren't able to give us much information. Brittany's mother and father weren't even aware that Brittany wasn't in her room that night. They said she must have snuck out sometime after everyone went to bed. And your mother told us she didn't get home from work until four thirty in the morning. She said her shift at Harrah's ended at two a.m., but she went out for drinks and an early breakfast with a friend after she got off work. She said she checked on you and your brother and you were both in bed, asleep, at four thirty. I'm hoping you can fill us in on Brittany's activities between the time her parents went to bed and when she was struck by the car."

Julia tipped her head to the side and blinked. "Okay. Brittany showed up at my house around eleven thirty. My brother, Dustin, got home from work fifteen minutes later, and we watched TV together for an hour; then we all went to bed."

"All three of you went to bed? Where did Brittany sleep?"

Julia uncrossed her arms and folded her hands together in her lap. "Usually Brittany slept in my room in the extra bed. I have two twin beds. But that night she was in Dustin's room."

"How old is Dustin?"

"He's nineteen."

"We were told that Brittany was three months pregnant," Alice said. "Did you know about that?"

"Yes, she told me."

"Did she tell anyone else that you know of?"

"She told Dustin a couple weeks ago. It was one week before she died."

"Was it Dustin's baby?"

"Brittany told me Dustin was the only guy she slept with. So it had to be."

"How did Dustin react when he found out?"

"He was upset. They started arguing about it as soon as she told him. He was pretty worried and didn't know what to do about it." Her eyes welled up with tears. "But I mean, he didn't kill her. He would never do that."

"Did they argue the night Brittany was hit by the car?" Snow asked.

"No, not at all. They only argued when she first told him she was pregnant. He just reacted to it I guess, but he calmed down pretty quick. My brother doesn't have much of a temper usually."

"After Brittany told him, did they discuss it further, that you know of?" Alice said.

"No. They just didn't think about it anymore. I mean, Brittany never mentioned it again to me. And Dustin never said another word about it that I know of. I think they just wanted to forget about it."

"I understand," Alice said. "Do you know what time Brittany left your house?"

Julia shook her head. "I was asleep. My mother woke me up around five thirty that morning to tell me what happened to Brittany."

"How far did Brittany live from your house?" Alice asked.

"It's about three-quarters of a mile, I think."

"And how did she usually get to your home?"

"She walked. She had her driver's license, but her parents didn't let her drive much."

"Did she always take the same route?"

Julia nodded. "She took Wampler Street."

"And that took her about fifteen minutes or so?"

Julia nodded. "It's not far."

"Do you know why Dustin didn't drive Brittany home that night?" Snow asked.

Julia shrugged. "He said he was still asleep when she left. She didn't want to wake him up, I guess. So she must have just gotten dressed and walked home. It's not that far," she repeated. "But if Dustin had woken up while she was getting dressed, he would have driven her. He usually drove her home—unless they were fighting."

"You say they weren't fighting that night," Alice said.

"I didn't hear anything," Julia said.

"But you were asleep."

"Yes, but when they had an argument it was loud enough to wake me up."

"They would yell at each other?" Alice suggested.

"Yes," Julia said.

"I thought you said Dustin doesn't have a temper," Snow said.

"He doesn't," she said. "Everybody argues, though."

"But you say Dustin and Brittany didn't argue at all between the time she told him she was pregnant and the accident."

"That's right," Julia said. "They didn't that I know of."

"But before Brittany got pregnant they argued quite a bit?" Alice said.

"No. Just occasionally. Not that much."

"What did they argue about?"

"Stupid things, like the way Brittany dressed. Dustin didn't like her dyeing her hair black. And she wanted to get her nose pierced. Stuff like that."

"Was Brittany a Goth?" Alice asked.

"No," Julia said. "And I'm not either. We don't follow anything. We just like black. We dress the way we want to dress. There's no deep meaning to it."

"What about Dustin? Is he Goth?"

"No," she said. "He thinks it's stupid. He likes sports. He was a quarterback in high school. He made All-American his junior year. But he screwed up his knee when he was a senior. So he couldn't even get a scholarship. But he's got a good job."

"What does he do?" Alice said.

"He's a shift manager," Julia said, her eyeliner spreading down to her cheeks from the tears. "He works at Grandpa Gene's Pizza on Stephanie."

There were two other couples in line in front of Alice and Snow at Grandpa Gene's Pizza parlor. It was 7:30 p.m. and half the tables in the restaurant were occupied. A tall and slender young man with boyish good looks, a thick head of short brown hair, and a friendly manner stood at the counter, taking orders. The nametag pinned to his red, short-sleeved Grandpa Gene's shirt read "Dustin Rice."

After waiting on the customers in front of Snow, Dustin turned his eyes to Snow and smiled.

Snow gave the boy a nod. "We called," he said. "I'm Jim Snow."

Dustin's eyes widened. "Oh. Right. Okay."

"Is this a bad time?" Snow said. "Or can you give us a few minutes?"

Dustin Rice glanced around the restaurant at the empty tables. "Now is okay," he said. "Where?"

"How about your office?"

"The owner is back there doing paperwork," Dustin said.

Snow turned and looked around. He pointed to a table in the far corner. The nearest customers were seated three tables over. "That one should be okay," he said. "And actually, we'd like to order a pizza while we're here. We can talk while it's baking."

"Okay. That's cool. What would you like?"

"I'd like a medium Meat Lover's Supreme and a medium lemonade." Snow turned to Alice.

"I'll have a small Veggie Delight and a bottle of water."

Dustin rang up the order, took Snow's money, and followed Alice and Snow to the table in the corner.

"This is a nice place," Snow said, surveying the layout after the three of them had been seated. "I'd never heard of it. Are there more of these restaurants in Vegas?"

Dustin shook his head. "It's the only one."

"Business must be pretty good, it looks like."

"Not bad, I guess," Dustin said. "The pizzas are pretty good. We don't hold back on the toppings like some of the chains."

"Have you been working here long, Dustin?" Alice asked.

He nodded. "I worked part-time while I was in school my senior year, after I recovered from my knee operation. And I went full-time after graduation. I don't know what I want to do yet. I had planned on going to college with a football scholarship, but now that's out the window."

"We heard about that," Alice said. "That must be hard for you."

Dustin nodded. "Football was my whole life. Now it's pizza. Mr. Samuelson, the owner, tells me Grandpa Gene's is a team and I'm the quarterback, but that's so lame. I made first team All-American my junior year, and now I sell pizza. Any idiot can sell pizza."

"I think Mr. Samuelson is just trying to cheer you up," Alice said.

"I know," Dustin said, solemnly. "He's a nice guy. At least I don't have to work for a jerk."

"Just give yourself time," she said. "You'll find something else to capture your interest."

"I thought I did," he said. "And now she's dead."

"You're referring to Brittany?" Alice asked.

Dustin nodded.

"How long were you involved with her?"

"I don't know. She and my sister had been hanging out together since they were in kindergarten. So I've always known her. It was a gradual thing. I guess it was about a year ago she started showing interest in me. She was too young for me, so I just treated her like another little sister. But after she turned sixteen, she changed dramatically. She started to seem a lot older, and I started having trouble ignoring her. One thing led to another, and before I realized how involved we were, I was in trouble with her. I can't believe I was so stupid, but I got carried away."

"All it takes is one time," Snow agreed.

"Well," Dustin said, "there were a lot more than that."

"Do you realize the trouble you could have caused yourself?" Snow asked.

"Yeah, sure," he said. "She was a minor and I'm not. But seriously, she grew up a lot during the last year. She was starting to seem like she was my age."

"I don't think the law much cares about how old the girl seems."

Dustin nodded glumly. "Yeah, you're probably right."

"What was your reaction when you found out Brittany was pregnant?" Alice asked.

"I was scared," Dustin said. "I didn't know what to do. There weren't many possibilities. Her parents are pretty conservative. I don't think they would have allowed us to get married. And Brittany wanted to stay in school. Probably she would have had the baby, and her parents would have helped her raise it."

"How was your relationship with Brittany's parents?"

Dustin shrugged. "I never saw much of them. They didn't know I was involved with Brittany. I think all they knew was that Brittany was best friends with my sister."

"They didn't know about Brittany being pregnant?" Alice asked.

He shook his head. "Brittany only told my sister—and me. She was planning to tell her parents sometime before it got to the point where they could tell by looking at her."

"That sounds like a good plan," Snow said, leaning forward. "Do you think Mr. and Mrs. Wile would have gone to the police after she told them?"

Dustin shook his head. "I don't think so. They're pretty nice people. They don't seem to be vindictive. I think they like to give everybody a break. I mean, if Brittany had been thirteen, it might have been something to worry about. But she was only three years younger than me. You know, when I'm thirty, she would have been twenty-seven. That's no big deal."

"Have you talked to them since the accident?"

"They stopped by my house afterward and wanted to know if I knew anything about how it might have happened. I said I didn't."

"Did they seem to believe you?"

"Sure. Why not?"

"What did they say about Brittany being pregnant?"

"They weren't happy about it, but that's obviously not an issue anymore."

"Have the police talked to you?"

He shook his head. "Why would they need to talk to me? I was home in bed."

"They cover a lot of ground," Snow explained. "I think they'll get around to you eventually, just as a matter of procedure."

"You said you were scared when Brittany told you she was expecting," Alice said. "What were you afraid of?"

"The responsibility of having a kid—and suddenly being stuck with Brittany. I mean, I cared about her. But I wasn't thinking about our future together. I was just always thinking about..."

Snow nodded, knowingly. "That's perfectly normal," he said.

"How did you feel when you found out what happened to Brittany?" Alice said.

"I was sick to my stomach," Dustin said. "After my mother told me, I felt like I was in a daze. It was like somebody hit me in the head and the stomach with a club at the same time. I couldn't even think at first. When I did start to come out of the fog, I couldn't believe she was gone. I still can't believe it. I miss her a lot, you know, the more it sinks in." He looked down at the floor, his face pale.

"Was Brittany sleeping in your sister's room just before she left your house?" Snow asked.

He looked up at Snow, met his gaze with red eyes. "No, she was with me in my room."

"What time did she leave?"

"I don't know," he said. "I was asleep. I didn't wake up until my mother came in my room and told me Brittany had been killed." He blinked rapidly a few times, his eyes filling with tears. He wiped at both eyes with the back of his hand.

"Brittany was hit by a stolen car," Alice said. "Do you have any idea who might have been driving it?"

Dustin shook his head. "A drunk driver, I guess."

"Was it you?" Snow asked.

He shook his head. "No."

"One of your friends?"

"No."

Snow studied Dustin's face. "I wonder if you could help us eliminate you as a possible suspect, Dustin," Snow said.

"Sure," he said. "What do you want me to do?"

"Could you get us a copy of your home phone and cell phone records listing all calls made beginning last Wednesday morning up until Thursday evening?"

"Sure," he said. "No problem. I don't have anything to hide. Anything else?"

"Would you be willing to submit to a polygraph test?" Snow asked.

Dustin's eyes widened. "Why would that be necessary?"

"It's just another step in the elimination process," Snow replied.

"I don't know," Dustin said. "I'm not crazy about the idea, but I want to cooperate. I guess it would be okay."

"Alright," Snow said. "We'll keep that in mind. We'll be in touch."

———

After dinner at Grandpa Gene's Pizza, Alice and Snow split up and spent an hour canvassing the homes surrounding the Rice residence. For the few who failed to answer their doors, Snow left a business card with a note asking the occupants to call him. Everyone they talked to had been in bed sleeping or at work during the early morning hours of Thursday, March 22, except for one person—a middle-aged woman who lived a couple doors down. She told Alice she remembered arriving home shortly before 4:00 a.m. that Thursday morning, after getting off work and shopping at a twenty-four-hour grocery store. She was sure she had seen Dustin Rice's Honda Civic parked on the street in front of his house. She said it was always there at that time of the morning.

At 9:30 p.m., Alice and Snow met at Snow's car. Alice told Snow what she'd learned from the woman who lived down the street from Dustin. "That takes care of your far-fetched theory that Dustin drove to Billy's home to steal his car to use to kill his pregnant girlfriend."

"He's a smart kid," Snow argued. "He may have left his car in front of his house and gotten one of his friends to help him. It's not as ridiculous as you make it sound. I'm not saying Dustin picked out Billy specifically as a carjacking target and drove straight to his house. His buddies and he could have been driving around looking for a victim. They see Billy's car drive past. They follow and don't have the opportunity to jump him until he gets home."

"Why would they shoot him in the back?"

"They didn't want to leave a witness."

"That's really a stretch," Alice said.

"I don't think so. If I were in Dustin's shoes and I wanted my pregnant girlfriend dead, that's exactly what I would do."

Alice studied Snow's face, thinking. "Tell me, have you ever gotten a girl in trouble?"

Snow sighed. "No." He rapped his knuckles on the dashboard. "But to be honest, I came close a couple times. It was a matter of timing that saved me. I've heard there's a very small window of opportunity with regard to the female cycle."

Alice smiled and stifled a chuckle. "They used to call that the rhythm method. I'm surprised you're aware of it."

"When I was young, dumb, and full of... beans, I was only aware of *my* rhythm."

"I'm glad you got lots of practice, but that's not something I need to know about."

"I didn't get lots of practice. Don't put words in my mouth. And what about you?"

Alice put her hand on his leg. "I'm a woman of color, Jim. I was born with rhythm."

"Uh-huh," Snow said. He started the car. "Well, I'm beat. I think we should call it a night." He turned his head to her and lowered his voice. "Your place or mine?"

Alice laughed.

CHAPTER 8

They were lying in Alice's king-size, four-poster bed after sharing an intimate encounter. Alice lay on her side, with her head on Snow's shoulder. She was nestled under her down comforter with it folded back over her. Snow lay on his back under the thin cotton sheet, his left arm curled around Alice.

It was beginning to turn numb from the weight of her torso.

"Jim," Alice murmured.

"Yeah," Snow said.

"I've been thinking about something that bothers me."

"Me?"

She snickered. "No. The investigation."

"What about it?" Snow asked.

"I think we're wasting too much time."

Snow grunted.

"I've been thinking about Dean Kale. He was the last person to see Billy Ryan alive. That makes him our most likely suspect."

"Dustin Rice was the last person to see Brittany Wile before she was killed," Snow argued.

"But she was the second victim," Alice said. "I think her death was an accident."

"I'm not so sure."

"What if Dean Kale's lying about getting out of the car at his home and letting Billy Ryan drive home alone? That doesn't ring true with me."

Snow slid his right arm under the sheet and scratched his stomach. "So, you're suggesting Kale drove Billy home and shot him? What's his motive? They were buddies."

"I don't know," Alice said. "I think we need to dig deeper and try to find a motive."

"Think about this, Alice," Snow said. "Nobody saw Kale driving Billy's car when they left the casino. And since there aren't any video cameras where they parked—they don't have that evidence. Why would he even admit to driving Billy's car at all?"

"Probably as a precaution," Alice surmised. "In case someone came forward later and told the police they saw him driving Billy's car out of the casino parking lot."

"That's conceivable," Snow said. "But it's improbable."

"I don't think so," Alice countered. "The more I think about it, the more probable it becomes in my mind. And Kale was the last person to see the victim alive. That's important."

"Well," Snow said, "further down the road we can follow up on it."

"I think we should focus on that angle now."

"Maybe after we finish our investigation of Dustin Rice."

"We don't have time for that," Alice said. "We've already used up an entire day. We only have four left."

"We're over halfway finished with Dustin Rice," Snow said. "I don't want to take our focus off him until he's eliminated."

"Why?"

"That's the way I always worked in Homicide," Snow said. "I'm comfortable with that procedure."

"But we're not in Homicide anymore, Jim," Alice complained. "We don't have unlimited time. We have forty hours total billable time available for this case, and I don't want to waste it chasing a flimsy lead down a dead-end street."

"Dustin Rice is not a flimsy lead," Snow muttered.

"He agreed to give us his phone records and take a polygraph test. And a neighbor said his car was home shortly after the hit-and-run."

"A lot of subjects have agreed to polygraphs and changed their minds after we arranged for them."

"I don't blame them," Alice said. "I wouldn't take a lie detector test. I don't think they're always accurate. They're just machines."

"We haven't even looked at that kid's phone records yet," Snow argued. "Like I said before, Dustin Rice could have easily gotten one of his buddies to help him commit a carjacking before he killed Brittany Wile with the jacked car. We need to see his phone records and talk to his friends. And I think the polygraph test would be a good thing. Then we can move on."

"But we hardly ever pay for a polygraph test. Why are you insisting on it this time?"

"I've got a gut feeling on it," Snow said. "I like to go with my gut."

"I know," Alice snapped. "That explains why we're always eating at buffets. By the time we do all of that, we won't have much time left. And I don't think Dustin Rice had anything to do with Brittany's death."

"Really? Where'd that come from? Feminine intuition? Alright, look, you investigate Dean Kale; I'll finish with Dustin Rice."

Alice pulled her head back and sat up, glaring down at Snow. "Our client is paying for us to work together. It's what she wants. It's what we agreed to."

"Jesus," Snow muttered. "Alright, we'll do what you want. You want to lead the investigation, so be it. I don't care." He rolled over onto his side, slapped his pillow twice, and laid his head on it, with his back to Alice.

"No," Alice said. "We'll do it your way, if you feel so strongly about it."

"No," Snow growled. "We won't do it my way. You don't like my way. We'll do it your way."

"I don't want to do it my way. I was just presenting my opinion. I see now that was a bad idea. Whenever I do that, it upsets you. This isn't much different than when I was working with Mel Harris in Homicide."

"Don't bring that guy into this," Snow said. "Forget about it. Let's just get some sleep. In the morning we'll flip a coin."

"Flip a coin?" Alice said. "That's no way to run a business."

"Okay, then we'll roll some dice. You like that better?"

Alice lay back down on her back, staring up at the ceiling. "This conversation is getting ridiculous. Let's just drop it."

"Fine with me," Snow mumbled.

Alice rolled onto her side, away from Snow.

Snow sat up. "I'm going home," he declared.

Alice turned her head. "Why?"

"I can't sleep here," Snow said.

"Why not?"

"Because now I'm pissed," Snow replied. "And this damn comforter is hotter than hell. It's seventy degrees in here. This thing's made for Minnesota in January, sleeping outside in a tent. It's spring and we live in a desert."

"It might be spring on the calendar, but it's been getting down into the forties every night."

"Outside. Not in here," Snow argued.

61

"You don't have to have to have the comforter on you," Alice suggested. "Just fold it over on me. I'm okay with that."

"I know. But with just the sheet, I wake up cold in the middle of the night. So I put the comforter on me and get too hot. Then I put one leg out from under it, and that's still too hot. So I throw it back off, and it gets cold again."

He got out of bed and began to dress.

"I guess we should have spent the night at your place," Alice said.

"We still can," Snow said. "You can come with me if you want."

Alice laughed. "This is silly. Why don't you just get back into bed?"

Snow snorted and shook his head.

He pulled his clothes off and slipped back under the sheet. Alice kissed him and turned off the light.

CHAPTER 9

Cassie Lane was seated in the client chair opposite Alice's desk, with her arms and legs crossed, her lips compressed, and her eyebrows drawn together.

"What do you have so far?" she asked.

Alice rested her forearms on the edge of her desk and interlaced her fingers. "We've interviewed Gina Ryan and her brothers. We've talked to her neighbors. Also, we've spoken with the closest friend of the hit-and-run victim and the friend's brother, who was the victim's boyfriend. Afterward we spent an hour knocking on doors in that neighborhood."

Snow was sitting to the right of Alice's desk, with his fingers interlocked behind his head. Cassie gave him a brief look of disgust, then turned her glare back to Alice. "Did you learn anything?"

"Nothing substantial," Alice said.

"Any suspects?"

"Not yet."

Cassie sighed and nodded. "Well," she said, "you're both fired."

Alice exchanged a bewildered look with Snow, leaned back in her swivel chair, and studied Cassie's face. "You just hired us yesterday. You can't expect results in one day. In fact, a week isn't usually enough time."

"I'm sure it isn't," Cassie said. "You must need the money desperately. Otherwise you'd be able to hire a receptionist. I can't believe I hired a team of investigators who have a cardboard cutout of Betty Boop in their lobby."

"You thought it was a clever idea yesterday," Snow said.

"Well, I was just being nice," Cassie said. "I think it's stupid. Now that I've had time to think about it, I realize you're both morons. So I'm taking you off the case. I'd like a refund for what's left of my retainer."

"Okay," Alice said. "We'll send you a check as soon as your funds clear our bank."

"I'm just wondering," Snow interjected, "why you didn't take the time to think about it before you hired us?"

Cassie turned her gaze to Snow and cocked an eyebrow. "I did. But now I've had more time and realize I made a mistake. Besides, I talked to the police yesterday, and they told me they have suspects in custody, and I didn't have to pay them anything for them to accomplish that."

Snow propped himself up with his elbows against the arms of his chair. "Who are their suspects?"

"Two young men who they caught driving a stolen car. They think they can tie them to several other robbery/carjackings over the last month, including Billy's. The detectives said they're working on the girlfriend of one of the suspects. They're confident they can break her down."

"Going after a wife or girlfriend, that's usually a fruitful strategy," Snow said. "I'm glad to hear you've gotten such quick results. You should be pleased."

"I'm very pleased," Cassie Lane said, "but not with you."

She scowled at Snow with dead eyes. Staring into them, Snow felt a chill run up his spine.

CHAPTER 10

"There are two things I'm aware of that are effective in combating depression," Snow said as he gazed at the breakfast menu. "Exercising to exhaustion and consuming a big stack of waffles. I don't have the energy for the former, so I'll have to go with the latter."

"I've never known you to require an excuse to order waffles," Alice said. "You order them every time we come in here."

"That's not true," Snow argued. "Only for breakfast. For lunch and dinner I order something different."

"Yes, I know. A double cheeseburger and fries." Alice opened her napkin and set it on her lap. "What are you depressed about, Jim?"

"Losing a client for no good reason always makes me glum."

"At least we didn't shoot this one," Alice said.

"There's a bright side to everything," Snow agreed. "But that's not the ray of sunshine I was looking for. I've gone over in my head everything we said to her, and I can't figure out why she suddenly turned so hostile. The only explanation that comes to mind is that she may be the sort who suffers badly from the onset of her menstrual cycles."

"Oh, good Lord," Alice said, pressing the tips of one thumb and forefinger to her eyes. "I have never met a man more obsessed with menstruation."

"I have my reasons, believe me," he said.

A rangy, Nordic-looking man in his mid-forties with a full head of thick brown hair stopped beside their table. He wore gray slacks, a white shirt, and a blue-and-white-striped tie.

"Hey," he said, smiling. "What have you two been up to? Anything interesting?"

"Just struggling to get by like everybody else, Eddie," Snow said.

"I know what you mean," Eddie said. "Every time I see Charles Barkley sitting there with his cohorts looking bored as he analyzes those basketball games, it makes me wonder if he'd like to change places with me. Let him see how much fun it is running a restaurant."

"I think he'd rather trade places with somebody who's shooting craps," Snow said. He took a sip of coffee.

"Me too," Eddie said. "I guess you haven't figured out a way to make a living doing that yet?"

"Nah, I've never been any good at telekinesis or precognition, and that's what it would take. Most of the time I can't even find my ass with both hands."

"That's from all that running you do," Eddie said. "Cut back on that and eat more of my waffles, and it'll be easier to locate."

"Thanks for the tip," Snow said.

Eddie turned his head to Alice. "Keep this guy out of trouble, will you, Alice?"

"I've been trying."

"Okay. See you guys later." Eddie gave a short wave and walked away.

"He complains a lot about it," Alice said, "but he seems to enjoy what he does for a living."

"I'm not so sure," Snow said. "I think Eddie might be one of those quiet-desperation types. He keeps it hidden to prevent scaring off the customers."

"What gives you that idea?"

"He's got a wife and four teenagers," Snow said.

"I read that married men are the happiest of anyone."

"That's because when they responded to the poll for that article, their wives were standing over them with a raised rolling pin."

Alice shook her head and chuckled. She drank some coffee. "So, what do you want to do today, Jim? We've got a whole day in front of us with no pending cases."

"Isn't that a switch? It's nice to have the time off, but now I wonder if the phone will ever ring again." He sighed. "I don't know. What do you want to do?"

"We could take in a movie," Alice suggested.

"That's an idea," Snow said. "Or we could go to the zoo. The weather's perfect for it."

"Las Vegas has a zoo?"

"Of course."

"You mean The Mirage or Circus Circus?"

"The Las Vegas Zoo," Snow said. "It has nothing to do with a casino."

"That's amazing."

Snow shrugged. "Not really. It's pretty small. You could drive right past it and miss it. I think they should demolish downtown and move it there. Make it bigger. They could train the monkeys to deal blackjack, and people could ride elephants up and down Fremont Street. That would be more fun than a helicopter ride over the dam."

Snow's phone chirped. He leaned back, reached into his front pants pocket, and pulled it out. After checking the number he put it up to his ear.

"Jim Snow here," he said.

The voice was soft and low, barely audible above the background noise in the restaurant. "Mr. Snow, this is Cassie. Is this a bad time?"

Snow leaned forward, putting his elbows on the table. "No, it's okay, Cassie." He cocked an eyebrow at Alice.

Cassie sighed. "I need to talk to you and Alice."

"What about?"

"I'd rather not discuss it over the phone."

"I'm afraid Alice and I wouldn't be interested in discussing an investigation that we're not under contract for."

"I don't understand," Cassie said.

"You took us off the case," Snow said.

There was no response. Snow waited.

"Cassie?" he said.

"Okay. I'd like to put you back on the case."

"Why?"

Another sigh. "I'd prefer not to talk about it over the phone. I could come to your office."

"When?" Snow asked.

"As soon as possible."

Snow considered this. "This conversation is a little hard to believe, Cassie," Snow said. "After our last discussion—"

"I'm sorry," she said.

"Alright. How about if we meet you at our office an hour from now?"

"Thank you. I'll see you there."

"Just a reminder that we have a four-hour minimum. So that starts over again."

"That's fine," she agreed.

"Okay. We'll see you in an hour." Snow ended the call and slipped the phone back into his pocket.

"What was that all about?" Alice asked.

"Apparently we're back on the job."

"She just fired us less than two hours ago," Alice protested. "And insulted us in the process."

Snow shrugged. "Maybe she went out and had her hair and nails done, and now she feels better."

"Fickle," Alice said.

Snow took a sip of coffee. "Well, it's another four hundred bucks, at least. The client is always right."

"Half the time," Alice said.

CHAPTER 11

Cassie's complexion was ashen, her eyes swollen and gray. She appeared to have aged since they'd seen her earlier that same morning. Resting her elbows on the armrests of the client chair she had seated herself in, she interlocked her fingers and squeezed them as though she were praying desperately.

"I'm so sorry," she said. "I should have told you everything when I hired you, but it's so embarrassing. To be honest, I'm ashamed of it, and afraid."

Snow fell into his swivel chair at the end of Alice's desk. "What are you afraid of, Cassie?"

"Everything," she said. "And now I'm really in trouble."

"With who?"

"I don't know," she said.

Cassie picked her purse up off the floor and opened it. She reached inside and pulled out a folded sheet of printer paper. Opening it, she smoothed it out on the desk in front of Alice.

Alice leaned over it. Snow got up and did the same.

Across the top half of the paper, hand-lettered neatly in thick, black ink, it read: *KEEP YOUR MOUTH SHUT, BITCH!*

"Where did this come from?" Alice asked.

"I don't know," Cassie said, her wide eyes filled with terror. "I found it on the floor of my vestibule, near the front door, just before I called you. Apparently someone slid it under the door. Or..."

Alice and Snow seated themselves.

"Or what, Cassie?" Alice asked, but Cassie only shook her head.

"What is it this person expects you to keep your mouth shut about?" Snow asked.

Cassie put the fingers of both hands over her mouth. Shaking, she began to sob, tears streaming down her cheeks, her gaze fixed on the sheet of paper. She said nothing.

"Did you report this to the police?" Alice said.

She shook her head. Through her fingers, her voice sounded muted. "I can't."

"Why not?"

Cassie wiped at the tears on her cheeks. Alice brought out the box of tissues and slid it across her desk toward her.

Cassie pulled two of the tissues out and dabbed at her face. Calming slightly, she took in a breath and let it out. "I should start at the beginning," she said. "I never told you this because I was sure you wouldn't handle my case. And I wouldn't blame you."

"We've never refused an assignment yet," Snow said, "and I don't think we'll start now."

"Don't be so sure of that," Cassie said. "I'll bet you've never had a client who was a crazy woman."

"I don't know," Snow said. "The definition of crazy is subject to interpretation. What makes you think your mental state fits into that category?"

Cassie fixed her gaze on Snow, her eyelids half closed from the weight of what she was about to say. "I've been diagnosed with dissociative identity disorder—DID," she confessed.

"I've never heard of that," Snow said. "What is it?"

"They used to call it multiple personality disorder," she said.

Snow arched his eyebrows. "Like in those movies—*The Three Faces of Eve* and *Sybil*."

"Something like that," Cassie said. "But my condition isn't as dramatic. My therapist has told me it's more subtle. And she suspects that's why she is the only person who knows about it. The people I work with don't even know."

"How many personalities do you have?" Snow asked, wondering if he'd worded it inappropriately.

"Two others that my therapist and I know of," Cassie said. "I'm told, Claudia is my age, and Chelsea is five. My therapist has met both of them. She's spoken with Claudia extensively, but Chelsea rarely comes out."

"Have *you* met them?" Alice asked.

"No. I'm not even aware of either of them. I have these periods of amnesia, I'm told, whenever one of them comes out and takes control. I don't see or hear anything either of them does or says. It's like I go into hibernation when that happens."

"You don't remember coming in here and terminating our services earlier this morning?" Alice said.

Cassie shook her head. "I thought you were still working for me until I talked to Mr. Snow on the phone."

"You can call me Jim," Snow said. He spread his hands in front of him. "So apparently we met Claudia this morning when she took us off the case."

"How did she act?" Cassie asked.

"Angry and hostile," Snow replied.

Cassie nodded. "Yes, I'm told that's how she is: angry, mean, rude, ruthless, demanding... My therapist tells me Claudia has a lot of issues."

"Is Claudia the reason you and Billy Ryan split up?"

"Yes. She's the reason I've never been able to form a lasting relationship with anyone. And I'm sure Chelsea hasn't helped at all either. I know that one time Chelsea came out after Billy and I had finished making love. Apparently she jumped out of bed and started screaming at him to leave her alone, then ducked back inside, and I had to come out to deal with the results of her tantrum. Billy was in shock, and I couldn't tell him the truth."

"What did you tell him?" Alice said.

"Nothing. I just apologized, and nothing more was said about it. But that was the turning point in our relationship."

"How long have you known about this disorder?"

"Only a year," Cassie said. "I began to realize there was something wrong with me when I was twenty-two. Six years ago. So I went in for counseling and was diagnosed with depression. After two years I wasn't showing any improvement, so I found another therapist, who diagnosed me as bipolar. But I think she suspected there was something else wrong with me, because she referred me to the therapist who's treating me now, Dr. Dawn Rodgers. She's wonderful; I love her. She diagnosed my condition after just a few weeks. By that time she'd already met both Claudia and Chelsea. She prescribed medication, and I see her twice a week."

"Are you making progress?" Alice said.

"It's slow," Cassie said. "But Dr. Rodgers says DID is highly curable, and it's just a matter of time and hard work."

"That's encouraging."

"Yes, it is … except now there's this additional problem with what happened to Billy and that poor girl who was run over. And this note."

Neither Alice nor Snow spoke. They waited.

"I'm afraid Claudia may know something about the two deaths," she continued. "The last thing I remember the night they happened was being at work, talking to a customer about a malfunctioning slot machine. The next thing I knew, it was a quarter to four, Thursday morning, and I was two blocks from my home, walking along the sidewalk. But I wasn't coming from the direction of the bus stop on Boulder Highway. I was coming from the opposite direction. I was walking home from the direction of where the police had found Billy's abandoned car."

"Did you tell the police about that?" Snow asked.

"No," Cassie said.

"Why not?"

"That's obvious, isn't it?" Cassie said. "Because I'm scared to death that Claudia might have killed Billy."

"Why would she do that?"

"I don't know," Cassie said, her voice hoarse with emotion. "Retribution maybe. Other than what Dr. Rodgers tells me, I don't know her. She's a part of me, but I have no idea what she's capable of—or what she's done. That note was written with a fine point permanent marker. I know that because I have one in my desk at home that matches the printing on the note."

"Have you checked your phone records for calls that might look suspicious?"

"Yes. I'll give them to you, but there's nothing there. Just calls to a couple of friends of mine, including Dean Kale. But I made no calls at all the night of the shooting."

"What about text messages or emails?"

"Nothing suspicious."

"You told us that you're now romantically involved with Dean Kale. How well do you know him?" Alice asked.

"Mostly through Billy," Cassie replied. "He's always been a good friend to both of us. He's a nice guy. And I'm sure he cares about me."

"What about Dean and Claudia?" Snow asked. "How do they get along?"

"I have no idea," Cassie said. "But there doesn't seem to be a problem yet."

Snow could feel his jaw muscles tightening. He struggled to exude an air of control and confidence, though he knew he was wandering around in uncharted territory. "Cassie, you mentioned the bus stop. Do you normally take the bus to and from work?"

"No," she said. "My car was getting some work done on the transmission. They had it in the shop for that whole week."

"What time did your shift end that night?"

"Two a.m.," Cassie said. "Sometimes I get something to eat somewhere and then go home."

"At the casino?"

"Sometimes," she said. "Their coffee shop is open twenty-four hours."

"Do you usually pay with a credit card?"

"Sometimes," she said. "There's nothing on my online statement. But other times I pay cash. There's no way to be sure if I ate there or not."

"Where else might you have stopped after your shift ended?"

"A lot of different places," she said.

"Any place in particular, more than the others?" Snow asked. She shrugged. "Denny's."

"Would it be alright if we talk to your therapist?" Alice said.

"Of course," Cassie said. "I can call and arrange it, if you like."

"That would be helpful, I think."

"If there's anyone else you'd like to talk to, just let me know."

"I think it would be worthwhile for us to get together with Claudia again. Do you think that might be possible?"

"I don't have any control over that," Cassie said.

"What if she takes us off the case again?" Snow interjected.

"Tell her I said no. I'll continue to pay you."

"Do you think Claudia wrote this note?"

"It's possible."

"How did you feel about Billy moving back in with Gina?" Snow asked.

"I was very upset about it. But it didn't surprise me. We started having problems as soon as Billy moved in with me. And I can't even be sure as to the extent of the damage Claudia and Chelsea did, because I only find out about it secondhand."

"Did you communicate with Billy at all after he moved out?"

"I talked to him on the phone a few times about making arrangements for him to move his stuff out of my home. And I dropped off his mail. He submitted a change of address with the post office, but there were a few pieces of mail that never got forwarded, so I took them over and dropped them off."

"Did you make any attempt to rekindle your relationship with him?"

"No," Cassie said. "I knew it would be useless."

"You didn't go over to his residence to talk to him about getting back together with you?"

She hesitated. "I didn't. But I don't know what Claudia did. I don't even know for sure how well Claudia got along with Billy. I do know that she had sex with him, because I found out about it later. Sometimes immediately afterward I would come out. It seemed like she wanted me to come out, so I would see that he had slept with her. Like she wanted to flaunt it. And there had been times in the past, before I met Billy, when I would wake up in some strange man's bed completely naked and not know how I got there or what I had done with him."

"Do you and Claudia have some sort of rivalry going?" Alice asked.

"I don't know what I have with Claudia," Cassie said. "She's a mystery to me. I feel like she controls me, and there's nothing I can do about it."

Alice nodded. "I understand. Is it possible Claudia may be a threat to your safety?"

"I don't think so," Cassie said. "Claudia has never harmed us, but that doesn't mean she never will. And I don't know who that note came from. I don't feel safe. It's possible Claudia may have seen something—or she might have been involved in Billy's death. I've been thinking about hiring a bodyguard temporarily. At least somebody to guard my front door."

"Can you afford that?" Alice asked.

"Not really. Although I could borrow it from my retirement fund."

Alice looked at Snow. He shrugged and nodded.

"If you like, Cassie," Alice suggested, "you can tag along with us while we're working on this assignment at no extra charge. But you'll have to keep out of the way; we can't let you listen in at all when we're interviewing people. I have a spare bedroom you can use while we're on the case."

Cassie brightened. "That's very kind of you, Alice," she said. "I'll try not to be any trouble for you. I just hope the same can be said of Claudia and Chelsea. But they each have a mind of their own."

"What about your job? How do you plan to deal with that?"

"I've arranged for time off until this situation is resolved. I have a lot of vacation time built up."

"Cassie," Alice said. "If we find that Claudia was involved with Billy's murder somehow—what will you expect to happen next?"

Cassie pressed her lips together and swallowed hard. "I've already resigned myself to that. If you come up with evidence tying us to the crime, just let me know first. Then your final task in this case will be to accompany me down to the police station, where we'll explain to them everything we know. And if it comes to that, then they can lock me up."

CHAPTER 12

Dr. Dawn Rodgers practiced her profession in one of four offices in a suite located on West Charleston Boulevard in Las Vegas. Her office was simply furnished with an inexpensive sofa, two easy chairs, a floor lamp, two hanging spider plants, and a collection of framed nature paintings on the walls.

Alice and Snow left Cassie Lane in the waiting room, reading a paperback, and followed Dr. Rodgers into her office. They seated themselves next to each other on the sofa, with Dr. Rodgers across from them in one of the easy chairs.

Dr. Rodgers appeared to be in her late forties. She was a short woman with small eyes behind wire-rimmed glasses. She had a square jaw and large teeth, and wore her blonde hair cut short. Wearing a blue knit blouse and black pants, she sat with her knees together and her forearms resting on the wooden arms of her chair.

"I talked to Cassie on the phone this morning, and she asked me to tell you anything you want to know. She said you're investigating a murder that she may or may not have information about, and she seems very anxious about it, so I'm hopeful you can find out who was involved and why."

"Thank you, Dr. Rodgers," Alice said. "And thanks for seeing us on such short notice. Cassie speaks very highly of you, and she mentioned that you're her third therapist in six years. Is that unusual?"

"Not at all," Dr. Rodgers said. "Many of my clients received therapy for over a decade before their disorders were finally diagnosed correctly. Cassie was misdiagnosed for five years, with depression and then bipolar disorder, before being referred to me. I have many years of experience dealing with dissociative identity disorder, and I've studied it extensively. Surprisingly, even with all of the advances that have been made in the field, many clinicians still refuse to acknowledge its existence. Others are skeptical and know little about the condition and wouldn't know how to recognize the symptoms, much less treat it. I was able to diagnose Cassie's disorder within two weeks of her initial session with me. I met both of her alternate personality states very quickly. They were eager to present themselves.

"In fact, she began switching states right in front of me near the beginning of therapy. Cassie manages the transition as smoothly as a car changing gears. It's barely noticeable and usually only takes less than a minute."

"Does she show any visible signs when that happens?" Alice said.

"She usually gets a severe headache. Though she doesn't always complain about it, I can tell by the pained expression on her face. She also gets quiet and appears to go into a light-headed, trancelike state," Dr. Rodgers replied. "Sometimes it looks as though she's about to faint. On rare occasions she'll tap the heel of her foot rapidly on the floor. When the tapping stops, I can be sure the switch in alters—alternate personalities—is complete."

"How long have you been treating her?"

"A little over a year," Dr. Rodgers said.

"Has she made any progress toward recovery?"

"A little, I think. But with this type of disorder, it's never anything that occurs overnight. Usually it takes three to five years to achieve full integration into a single identity, but with proper treatment, combining therapy and medication, the prognosis is quite good. DID is a highly curable condition. And it's quite common. One percent of the population is afflicted by the disorder."

"Is it congenital?" Snow asked.

"No. It's a result of continual early childhood trauma, usually repeated abuse. Young minds are very fragile during development and they aren't able to cope with the overwhelming effects of recurring trauma, so the memories of it are hidden away. Dissociation is actually a normal, self-protective defense mechanism. Alternate parts of the internal system are created to deal with the harmful memories.

"Cassie and her brother suffered a great deal of abuse from their parents. Claudia, who is the same age as Cassie, is the most dominant of Cassie's three identities. She remembers the details of all of the childhood trauma, as does Chelsea, who is only five. But Cassie remembers none of it. So she is isolated and unaffected by it. As a result, she's kind, friendly, and warm, while Chelsea is usually in a frenzied state, and Claudia is most often openly hostile. Claudia is the typical product of an abusive childhood environment who goes on to abuse nearly everyone she comes in contact with during the expanse of her adult life."

"Are any of the three personalities conscious of the others?" Alice asked.

"Only Claudia," Dr. Rodgers said. "She's very intelligent and alert. She sees and hears everything that takes place with all of the identities. No matter which personality you're conversing with, you can be sure Claudia is taking all of it in. She doesn't seem to miss anything. But Cassie and Chelsea are not aware, firsthand, of their alternate identities. They experience amnesia during the times they aren't in control. They only see the evidence of the actions of the alters after the fact. And as I'm sure you can imagine, it can be quite disturbing."

"It sounds like you're telling us that Claudia is the dominant personality."

"Yes. There's no doubt about that. But Cassie is the host. To Cassie, Claudia is like an unwelcome guest who refuses to leave."

"You mentioned Cassie's brother and her parents," Snow said. "Do you know where they are now?"

"Her brother committed suicide when he was sixteen," Dr. Rodgers said. "Her father is a prominent attorney. Her mother does high-profile charity work. They're both alive and well, living here in Las Vegas—"

"I'm sorry," Alice cut in, "but are you saying neither was punished for the abuse of their children?"

"That's not unusual, sadly. It's never come out. Her father warned her as a child that if she told anyone, someone would kill her."

"So that creep is out living among us?" Alice said.

"And thriving," Dr. Rodgers said. "His threat worked. Claudia and Chelsea won't tell anyone about the abuse they endured. And Cassie doesn't remember any of it."

"But Claudia and Chelsea have told you about it."

"Yes. But it wasn't easy getting it out of them. I had to promise not to inform the authorities. So I need to ask you to keep it to yourselves."

"Certainly," Alice agreed. "So, you were about to tell us about Cassie's relationship with her parents, I believe."

"Just that Cassie never communicates with either of them in any way."

"That's not surprising, I guess," Alice said, "since Cassie doesn't even communicate with herself."

Dr. Rodgers smiled. "That is the biggest hurdle. But I'm confident the day will come when her three selves will want to join together as a team for the good of all of them and start sharing information and memories with each other. That's when real progress can be made toward recovery."

"Are any of the other identities a potential danger to Cassie, do you think?"

"I don't believe so," Dr. Rodgers said. "Cassie herself is very passive, and Chelsea only needs to be comforted in order to calm her. All she does is cry and wail and push people away. And while Claudia is ferocious and brutal, she has never harmed anyone physically that I'm aware of, including herself."

"I'm having trouble wrapping my head around all of this," Snow said. "You don't think Claudia is capable of murder?"

"No, I don't believe so. But she's very cunning and secretive, so I can't be absolutely certain."

"You say Cassie's brother committed suicide," Alice said. "And that he endured the same sort of abuse as Cassie. I would imagine that likely drove him to take his life?"

Dr. Rodgers shrugged. "I think that's quite likely, yes."

"Why wouldn't you believe Cassie is capable of doing the same thing?"

"Cassie and her brother were two different individuals."

"But so are the three identities residing in Cassie's mind. Isn't that true?" Alice asked. "Couldn't one of them be just like Cassie's brother?"

Dr. Rodgers's face began to flush as she pondered this, smiling uncomfortably. "Yes, but I never had the opportunity to meet Cassie's brother. I've gotten to know Cassie and both of her alters very well over the last year."

"How do we get Claudia to talk to us?" Alice said.

"The best way I know of is to just ask her to come out and speak with you. She may not be the dominant personality when you inquire, but she's always paying attention, and she can come out whenever she wants. I'm convinced of that. Like I mentioned, Cassie is the host, but Claudia is very bright and forceful. She has a strong, influential personality. She just needs to realize she's not doing herself any good by ignoring Cassie and Chelsea. She needs to get the three of them to band together."

"All for one, and one for all," Snow quipped. "Like the Three Musketeers."

Dr. Rodgers gave Snow a perplexed look, then gave her head a little shake and asked, "Do you mind my asking about the specifics of this murder you're investigating? Cassie told me she hired you, but she didn't tell me anything about it or how she might be involved."

"That's because she doesn't know whether she *was* involved," he said. "She told us her memory is blank during the hours leading up to and immediately following the crime." Snow gave Dr. Rodgers a quick summary of the details as reported by the police, and told her about the note Cassie found on the floor in front of her door.

Dr. Rodgers clasped her hands together. "Oh my, that is troubling. It sounds like Claudia may be hiding something. That doesn't surprise me; she's good at that. It may be that she's afraid to say anything due to threats from the author of that note. This is exactly how Claudia has dealt with her childhood memories of abuse."

Dr. Rodgers sighed. "Well, is there anything else you need to know?"

Snow shifted his weight in his chair. "This stuff is all new to me. It's really fascinating. I'm just wondering about these three identities Cassie has developed. Were they all manifested at the same time?"

Dr. Rodgers tipped her head back slightly and gave Snow a trace of a smile—a condescending look he had seen many times, during his formative years, from teachers who had been unsuccessful in their attempts at molding his mind.

"That's difficult to determine," she replied. "Probably not. It's actually unusual that Cassie has so few alters. In the majority of cases, there are many more. Possibly a dozen or more in some patients. New personalities can form at any time."

Snow nodded. "Can you be sure Cassie doesn't have more than the three personalities that you're aware of?"

Dr. Rodgers lowered her head and peered at Snow over the top rim of her glasses. "I'm sure," she said. "I've worked with a lot of DID cases over the years. I know how to gain the trust of my patients and cajole them into revealing all of their identities to me. I can assure you, Cassie only has the three identities."

Alice and Snow exchanged a glance. Snow shrugged.

"I guess that's it for now," Alice said. "Thank you for seeing us, Dr. Rodgers."

"I'm happy to help in any way possible. If you need to speak with me anytime, feel free to call my cell phone and leave a message if I don't answer. I try to return my calls between sessions, so it shouldn't take more than an hour to get back to you."

Alice and Snow stood up and shook hands with Dr. Rodgers.

Back in the lobby, Alice and Snow noticed the chair Cassie had been sitting in was vacant. She was nowhere to be seen.

The receptionist was a plump young woman with shoulder-length black hair and plastic-rimmed glasses. Alice asked her about Cassie.

With wide eyes, she shrugged and shook her head. "I don't know where she went," she said. "We were having a pleasant conversation about this and that, and I got up to go to the restroom. I was only gone for a few minutes; when I came back to my desk, she was gone."

"Maybe she stepped outside to get some fresh air," Alice suggested.

"That's probably where she is," the receptionist agreed. "It's gorgeous outside."

"Yes, indeed. A beautiful day in the neighborhood," Snow intoned.

The receptionist giggled.

Alice James rolled her eyes.

CHAPTER 13

"I was reluctant to say anything when you offered to take Cassie under our wing," Snow muttered, "but I was pretty sure it was a bad idea. I was afraid this would happen. As soon as Claudia came out—she'd skip out on us."

They had left the building and were standing on the sidewalk in front of Snow's Sonata, glancing around for any sign of their wayward client.

Alice sighed. "I don't see any reason not to offer our protection if she wants it. If Claudia rejects it, that's her prerogative."

"Jesus, this is the weirdest shit I've ever dealt with. I still can't believe it." Snow shoved his hands into his back pockets. "Imagine meeting somebody like that in Vegas while you're in party mode, thinking you hit the love jackpot, and tying the knot. And a couple days later you find out you're stuck with two of them—one's the woman you adore, and the other is a horrific bitch." He shook off the image and sighed. "Far as that goes, it's somewhat of a relief that Cassie's gone. I wouldn't be able to sleep at night with her in the next bedroom. Cassie's not a problem, but her other half might get the urge to murder us in our sleep."

"I don't think so," Alice said. "Claudia might be hostile, but I don't think she's dangerous. You heard what Dr. Rodgers said. She should know."

Snow snorted. "Yeah. Maybe she does, maybe she doesn't. She gets paid a lot of money to make informed guesses. That's my opinion."

"She's a trained, experienced professional, Jim."

"So were the first two therapists Cassie went through," Snow said. "You heard what the good doctor said. They both misdiagnosed her for years. Why should she be the one who gets it right? Most people are incompetent at their chosen professions, and I don't think doctors are any different. I don't know much about shrinks, but from the stories I've heard, medical doctors are nothing more than licensed drug pushers. All they're interested in is taking blood pressure and getting lab tests done, so they can prescribe as many chemicals as possible. The drugs cost a fortune and don't even make you feel good. Instead, they make people look and feel like zombies."

"Where did you get that information?" Alice said.

"My own experience, and stories from friends, friends of friends, and acquaintances. I see what they go through. The poor bastards. One old guy I knew was taking almost two dozen medications. Every new prescription he got caused side effects that required another prescription to counteract them. He ended up dead from heart failure."

Alice frowned. "How old was he?"

"Eighty-seven."

"That's pretty old."

"He'd have had another five to ten years without the meds," Snow said. "He was that sort of guy."

"What about you? When was the last time you visited a doctor?" Alice said.

"Six or seven years ago," Snow said. "I had a sore throat that lasted a week. I figured it was strep, so I found some guy with good reviews on the Internet and went to see him. I think his friends and relatives wrote the positive reviews. He was a smoker, fifty pounds overweight. He told me I had a flu virus and there wasn't anything he could do about it."

"Did he take a culture?"

"No," Snow said. "He just looked at my throat. But I don't think he could see very well; he wore trifocals that were almost an inch thick. So then he tried to take my blood pressure. He put the cuff on too tight with the tube hanging out of the wrong side, and tried to tell me my reading was too high. He wanted to start me off with some diuretics and beta-blockers. I showed him how to put the cuff on the right way. He pumped it up again, and it was normal.

"The dumbshit didn't even know how to take my blood pressure, so how could I be sure I didn't have strep throat or mono? I picked out another doctor and got a second opinion. He told me I had the flu and a heart murmur. He wanted to send me to a cardiologist for an echocardiogram. I was forty years old. No other doctor had ever detected a heart murmur my whole life. So I went to another doctor, one my sister recommended. He told me I had the flu and no heart murmur, but my blood pressure was a little high. I told him my blood pressure was high was because I was on the verge of a physician-induced anxiety attack.

"Anyway, the next day the sore throat went away, and I started coughing and sneezing, so apparently it was the flu. So the first fat, cigarette-smoking doctor got it right. Blind luck. I haven't been to a doctor since. Now I just use the Internet to diagnose myself. If it's something serious, requiring hospitalization, I'll just get my gun out of the attic and shoot myself."

"You're forty-seven, Jim," Alice said. "At your age anything can happen. You could be a ticking time bomb. You need to get regular checkups. I'm happy with my doctor," Alice said. "Why don't you try her?"

Snow raised an eyebrow. "A female doctor? Is that kosher?"

"Women have male doctors," Alice pointed out.

"I don't know," Snow said. "What does she look like?"

Alice frowned. "What difference does that make?"

"If she's attractive, my blood pressure's liable to elevate up out of the normal zone temporarily. Especially if she expects me to drop my drawers, turn my head, and cough. And what if I get an erection?"

The sound of a cough came from the corner of the medical building.

Alice and Snow turned toward it and saw Cassie on the sidewalk, strolling toward them. "Did you find out anything useful in there?" she asked, hooking her thumb toward the entrance.

"We thought you'd wandered off," Alice said.

"Nah. I just had to get out of there. I couldn't stand listening to the lame conversation Cassie was having with that receptionist. I hate being a captive audience to stuff like that."

Alice and Snow exchanged a look.

"You're Claudia, I take it," Alice said. "So we meet again."

"Wrong guess. I'm not Claudia."

Alice's eyes narrowed. "Who are you?"

Cassie came to a halt in front of Alice, produced a lopsided grin, and put her hands on her hips. "I've been eager to meet you, Alice. You can call me Chad. What do you say we get a drink? I could use one. I know a bar not far from here."

CHAPTER 14

At half past one in the afternoon, the Velvet Villa on East Sahara Avenue was bustling with an energetic young crowd lining the bar and scattered among some of the tables bordering the small, vacant dance floor. It was an elegant bar with an abundance of hardwood and crystal chandeliers.

Snow escorted Alice and Cassie/Chad to a corner table farthest from the bar and slid two chairs out for them on one side of the table before he seated himself across from them.

He leaned back and surveyed the bar, noting that most of the patrons were female, some quite lovely, others not so much. After further scrutiny, however, Snow came to realize that the male customers were actually women dressed and barbered to appear masculine. It gradually dawned on him that he was the only man on the premises.

Chad folded his arms and leveled a devilish grin at Snow. "Have you figured it out yet?"

"It's a gay bar," Snow said, meeting Chad's gaze with an amused smile. "Is this the liquid lunch crowd or an early start on the Friday night revelry?"

"A little of both," Chad said. "I think some of them come here for lunch and neglect to go back to work. It must be nice to have a job that provides that leniency…and, yes, it is a gay bar of sorts. For women only." She raised an eyebrow. "Do you feel uncomfortable here, Mr. Snow?"

Snow shrugged. "I wouldn't come here by myself, but I don't mind. What about the patrons? You think any of them might object to my presence?"

Chad chuckled. "I'm pretty sure all of them have an open mind. They won't bother you." She turned her head to Alice. "How about you, Alice? Would you like to go someplace else?"

Alice smoothed out her skirt and put her hands in her lap. "I'm fine with it," she said without smiling.

"I'm glad to hear that," Chad cooed. He leaned in closer. "I love your perfume. It's very subtle."

"It's soap," Alice said. "I seldom wear perfume."

Chad slipped an arm around Alice's waist. "It's wonderful," he said, moving even closer.

Alice stood up and strode around to the other side of the table. She sat down next to Snow.

"Quite an interesting place," Snow observed. "Do you come here often, Chad?"

"That's a tired pickup line," Chad countered. "Are you trying to flirt with me, Mr. Snow?"

"Just curious," Snow said. "I can't think of any other way to ask it."

"Actually, no," Chad said. "I don't get out much."

"Socially?" Alice said. "Or are you referring to your control over your mind?"

"Both, unfortunately. Life is hard enough playing a minor part in a group of four. On top of that—can you imagine what it's like being a man inside a woman's body—and having to share it with two women and a child?"

"No," Alice said. "I'm afraid I can't."

"I'm confused enough as it is, with just me inside my head," Snow said.

After a brief pause while a waitress took their order, Alice asked Chad why he thought it was that his therapist had no knowledge of him.

Chad unfolded his arms. "I don't like her. She's cold, pretentious, and arrogant."

"Have you talked with her?"

"Oh, yes," Chad said. "I've been out during some of the sessions. But she doesn't know it's me. I pretend to be Cassie or Claudia. I have a lot of fun with it because that bitch can't tell the difference." He emitted a deep, sinister laugh.

"Aren't you interested in getting better?" Alice asked.

"How?"

"Combining your alternate selves into one unified personality. Isn't that the objective of therapy?"

"I'm not so sure that would happen," Chad said. "I would most likely cease to exist. Cassie might live happily ever after, but I wouldn't."

"Don't you care about Cassie?" Snow asked.

"Not really," Chad replied.

"What about the future?"

"Nobody has a future," Chad declared. "We all end up dead. All I can hope for is the opportunity to have some fun and get out as much as possible."

"How do you manage that?" Alice asked.

"Fun? I'm doing that now. Having a few drinks and fucking with your heads."

"But how do you gain control of your conscious mind?"

"I honestly have no idea," Chad said.

Snow leaned forward. "Is there some sort of dispatcher inside your mind that determines which personality comes forward and runs the show?"

Chad shrugged, smiling. "I don't know. I wish I did."

The waitress returned with their drinks. Snow paid her and she left.

Snow poured some of his beer into his glass and drank from it. Alice took a sip of her wine.

Chad drained the double shot of bourbon in front of him, chasing it with a sip of his draught beer. He wiped his mouth with the back of his hand and belched softly. "Anything else you want to know? You're paying for the drinks."

"It goes on Cassie's tab," Snow said.

"Seriously?"

"No," Snow said. "I'm kidding. You want another shot?"

"I'm fine for now," Chad said. "I guess I should apologize for my behavior. I get a little rambunctious when I'm bored."

"Don't worry about it," Snow said. "All we ask is that you're honest with us. If there's anything you'd rather not tell us, just say so. Okay?"

Chad took another swallow of beer. "No problem. No sense wasting Cassie's money. She works hard for it."

"What about you?"

"I seldom come out at work. I'm mostly into having a good time."

"What happens when you do come out while she's on the job?" Alice said.

"Usually it's because somebody's giving Cassie a hard time. I guess she can't handle it."

"But you can?" Snow asked.

Chad nodded confidently. "I can handle anything."

"What about Claudia?"

"She's tough as nails," Chad said. "But she gets carried away. She tends to be rash."

"So you're the enforcer," Snow said.

Chad grinned. "That's me. But if you can't have fun along the way, there's no sense making the trip."

"Are you aware of what your alternate personalities say and do?" Alice asked.

"Bits and pieces," Chad said. "It's like drifting in and out of consciousness. There are lots of long gaps that are missing, but sometimes I feel like I'm in a trance, that somebody else is doing the talking and I'm just witnessing it."

"Did you witness the murder of Billy Ryan?" Snow blurted.

Chad shook his head and drank more beer.

"What about the hit-and-run of that teenage girl in the cross-walk on Greenawalt Road?"

He shook his head again. "Don't know anything about that either."

"What about Claudia? You think she knows anything about the murder or the hit-and-run?"

"I don't know," Chad said. "You'd have to ask her."

"She's aware of everything the four of you say and do. Dr. Rodgers told us that. Is that true?"

Chad shrugged. "I don't know. Ask Claudia."

"Will she talk to us?"

"I don't know. Again, why don't you ask her?"

"Alright," Snow said. "Claudia, would you like to come out and have a drink with us?" He winced, realizing how ridiculous this sounded, as though they were conducting a séance.

Chad chuckled. "While we're waiting, I think I'd like another double shot of Wild Turkey and a beer."

Snow caught the waitress's eye and raised a finger. She nodded at him and continued to her immediate destination with her loaded drink tray.

Chad picked up his beer glass and drained it. Setting the empty glass down on the table, he frowned at it, wincing. He lowered his head and touched his fingertips to his forehead.

Alice leaned toward him. "Are you alright?"

Chad moaned. "I have a headache," he said. "I get these sometimes when I drink too fast." He leaned back in his chair, his eyes closed. Then he stood up. "I need to use the restroom. I'll be back."

"Would you like me to go with you?" Alice said.

Chad released a pained laugh. "More than anything—but no, I'm okay. I just need to pee. The headache will pass—it always does."

"Would you still like me to order you another drink?" Snow asked.

"Yes. Please. I'm okay." With that, Chad headed unsteadily toward the ladies' room.

After she'd gone, Alice took a sip of her wine and looked at Snow. "She's switching states."

Snow nodded, staring after her. "Maybe. Then again, I imagine it might just be a regular headache women have whenever the moon changes phases."

"You know what I can't imagine?" Alice said.

"What's that?"

"You as a psychotherapist."

Snow took a drink of his beer. "Would you like my professional opinion on this situation?"

"Let's have it."

"I don't think Chad is all there."

"So, you've taken to psychoanalyzing each of Cassie's alternate identities? Isn't that digging a little too deep?"

"A homicide detective can never dig too deep," Snow insisted. "Why should it be different for a shrink?"

"Cassie on the whole has been diagnosed with a mental disorder, so it should go without saying that all of her personalities are out of whack."

"I'm not so sure," Snow said. "It seems logical to me that Cassie's complete mind exhibits one disorder, while each individual personality could have other disorders of different types. Paranoid schizophrenia, possibly."

"I don't know," Alice said. "What are the symptoms of paranoid schizophrenia?"

"Nuttier than a fruitcake," Snow said. He took another drink of beer.

The waitress appeared. "Would you like another round?"

"Sure, why not," Snow said. "If whoever comes back from the ladies' room doesn't want what Chad's having—I'll drink it."

"No more for me, thank you," Alice said. "I may end up driving—again."

"You're alright with that?" Snow asked.

"Why shouldn't I be?" Alice said. "I spend more time driving your car than mine."

The waitress finished scribbling, picked up Chad's empty glasses, and moved on to the next table.

"I think Chad's just a little immature," Alice said. "How could he not be? He's barely had any experience. He acts like a playful puppy."

"I think maturity is a myth. It's what happens to people after they've been worn down to the point where all they look forward to is their next nap."

"That's very sad," Alice said.

"Not really," Snow insisted. "It's the perfect ending to a good beer buzz." He took another drink of beer, looking thoughtful. "Remember Gina Ryan mentioning that she ran into Cassie at a grocery store and invited her over for coffee?"

"Yes."

"Well, Cassie doesn't seem to like Gina at all. That means it was either Claudia or Chad that Gina had coffee with. And judging by the way Chad has been attracted to you, I'm thinking it might have been Chad who Gina met in the store."

"I don't know," Alice said. "Chad seems pretty unrefined. Gina probably would have been disgusted by him."

"She's a former hooker," Snow said. "And he might have been on his best behavior to try and get in her pants."

"I guess that's possible."

"I wonder if he was successful."

"That sounds like something you'd wonder about," Alice said.

———

Ten minutes later their client walked out of the ladies' restroom. She had a confused expression on her face. She stopped and glanced around the interior of the bar, noticed Alice and Snow waving to her, and proceeded at a brisk pace toward their table.

She stopped beside the table and stared at the double shot and beer. "Who was sitting there?" she asked.

"Chad," Alice said.

She turned her wide eyes to Alice. "Who is Chad?"

"You don't know Chad?" Alice asked.

She shook her head.

"Who are *you*?" Alice said.

"Cassie." She pressed her lips together and swallowed. "Who is Chad?" she asked again.

Alice stood up and touched Cassie's arm with her hand. Softly, she said, "Why don't you sit down, Cassie."

Cassie's eyes turned back toward the shot glass. "I was drinking that?"

Snow reached over and picked up the shot glass with one hand and the draught with the other and set them down in the middle of the table. He said nothing.

Cassie stepped around the table and fell into her seat. She put her face in her hands and wept silently, her shoulders shaking.

Snow picked up the shot glass and knocked back the bourbon.

Alice opened her purse and brought out a travel pack of tissues and set it down in front of Cassie. They waited.

A few moments later the sobbing subsided, and Cassie removed her hands from her face and sat back. She plucked a tissue from the tiny packet and blotted the dampness around her red eyes. "So, now there's Chad?" she asked.

Alice and Snow both nodded.

"Now there are four of us? And one is a man?"

"I'm afraid so," Alice said.

"Is he straight or gay?"

"I suppose," Snow interjected, "that depends on how we would define Chad's gender."

Cassie threw her hands out in front of her. "Chad is a man! Right?" she squealed.

"That would mean he's straight," Snow said.

"Oh, my god!" Cassie wailed. "This just keeps getting worse." She interlaced her fingers into a double fist and touched her knuckles to her lips, staring down at the table.

"It's not so bad," Alice said. "Your disorder is not as complex as most. Dr. Rodgers told us most people suffering from DID have many more identities than you do."

"That's right," Snow agreed. "Four isn't bad. That's not even enough players for a basketball team."

Cassie looked at Snow. "What is Chad like?"

"Spirited," Snow said. "Honest and forthright."

"I just wonder why it is that Dr. Rodgers doesn't know about him. I have to find out about him in a bar?" She glanced around at the patrons. "What kind of a place is this?"

"Something different, that's for sure," Snow said. He noticed a woman at another table staring at him. She had a buzz cut and wore jeans and a tank top. She looked familiar. She was sitting with another woman sporting a short Mohawk.

The woman staring at him smiled and waved. Snow waved back, wondering whom he was waving at.

"Who's that?" Alice asked.

"I have no idea."

The woman got up and crossed toward him. She stopped next to their table and shoved her hands into her front pockets, with her thumbs sticking out like horns. "Jim Snow," she said, smiling. "It's been a long time. How are you?"

"Fine," Snow said. "You're looking good." His eyes went to the tattoo of a snake on her upper arm.

The woman laughed. "You don't remember me, do you?"

Snow chuckled. "I need to get around to sorting out the filing in my head one of these days. Help me out a little."

"Rhonda Kifer," she said. "We dated for a couple weeks—I guess it was twelve years ago. My hair was a lot longer then. You called an hour before you were supposed to pick me up and canceled the date and broke up with me. You did it with a voicemail message."

Snow arched his eyebrows and opened his mouth in recognition. "Oh, I remember now. You didn't answer your phone when I called."

"I was in the bathroom," she said. She wasn't smiling now. "I never understood why you didn't leave a message for me to call you back. Instead of just leaving me a voicemail message—like I was nothing!"

Snow shrugged. "We'd only been dating a short time."

"You told me you thought we were soulmates!"

"Was that the night we had all those margaritas?"

Rhonda shook her head, exasperated, then set her jaw. "I'd slap you right now, but I don't want to make a scene with my friend watching. I don't want to lower myself to that. So. I just stopped by to say hi and wish you the best." She nodded vehemently with wild eyes, baring her teeth.

"Well, thank you," Snow said. "It was nice seeing you again, Rhonda."

Rhonda turned and stormed back to her table.

All three of them watched her leave.

"After you broke up with her," Alice said, "she turned into a lesbian?"

"I seem to have that effect on some women," Snow muttered.

CHAPTER 15

George Carver was the head of security at the Boulder Nugget Hotel Casino. He was barrel-chested, six five, in his late forties, with a thick head of black hair combed straight back. Snow estimated he was probably sixty pounds overweight, but he wore it well under his gray, department-store suit.

Carver was standing outside of the railing that separated Burger King from the main casino floor. Snow approached with a nod and a handshake.

"How's your father-in-law doing?" Snow asked.

"Good," Carver said. "He's out of surgery and recovering nicely. He's a tough old guy. Three heart attacks in one year, and he's still chugging along. They said he was plugged up worse than I-15 with a jackknifed big rig on a holiday weekend."

Snow nodded. "Sounds pretty bad."

Carver nodded too. "Quadruple bypass." He folded his arms and surveyed the banks of slot machines in front of them, looking for trouble. "Maggie says he looks pretty good though. He's got more color in his cheeks than a kid who just farted on his first date."

"That's a lot of color," Snow agreed. "Maggie still back there?"

"Yeah. She wants to stick around until he's up and walking around. She's still worried about him. Actually, she's been talking about us moving back there, but I'm not up for that idea."

"I don't blame you," Snow said. "I've never been to Cleveland, but from what I've heard about the place, it doesn't sound like paradise."

"It's a shithole," Carver said. "That's why we moved out of there. Though we had it pretty good back there after I made detective. Working robbery was no picnic, but it was okay. Maggie was the one who wanted to move to Vegas. It was all she talked about before we got here. So we did it. Now it's been seven years, and all she talks about is moving back. The kids are there, her folks are there. All the rest of her family is there. What a mess."

"I can imagine," Snow said.

"And we're pretty much stuck here now," Carver continued. "We bought our house near the peak of the housing boom, so we're upside down big time. I'd have to come up with a couple hundred thousand or work out a short sale to get rid of the place. What a mess," he repeated.

"You've got a lot of company. I hate thinking about what my house is worth."

Carver unfolded his arms and sighed. He shook his head. "Well things could be worse."

"That's a good way to look at it, George," Snow agreed. "Then, when things do get worse, you'll be ready for it. That's worked well for me."

"It pays to maintain a positive outlook. Even if it's based on bullshit."

"That's the best commodity to invest in. It never stops rising."

Carver burst out laughing and clapped Snow on the arm. "You're always good for a laugh. Cheers me up every time you stop by, you son of a bitch."

"Gotta hold onto your sense of humor," Snow said. "Once you lose that, your gall bladder's next."

Carver chuckled. "You got time to have a few brewskies with me later on?"

Snow shook his head. "No time. I'm tied up with this case we're working on, and I'm having a hell of a time getting the knots out of it. I'll have to give you a rain check."

Carver nodded. "Where's Alice, by the way? I haven't seen her with you for quite a while. You two still getting along okay?"

"Sure, great," Snow said. "She's babysitting our client. They're over at Starbucks, drinking something expensive. What did you manage to find out about Cassie, George?"

"I checked the video footage like you asked for—Thursday, March 22, starting around one in the morning. And Cassie Lane stopped by the crap table Billy Ryan and Dean Kale were playing at twice and whispered something to Kale.

"At two a.m., when her shift ended, she went to the main bar, ordered what looked like a double shot of tequila and a beer, and sat down at a table alone. She was on her third round when Kale approached her a few minutes before three a.m. They had a brief exchange of words, and he continued on to the restroom. She finished her beer, got up, went to the ladies' room, and left the casino at five after three.

"Meanwhile, at the crap table Billy Ryan and Dean Kale colored in their chips, went to the cashier's cage, where Billy Ryan cashed in. At 3:10 a.m. they left the casino together, using the same exit Cassie had used five minutes earlier.

"Outside the casino, all of them took the same exact route to the southeast corner of the parking lot. Our video coverage doesn't extend that far. That was the last I could see of them on video. So, either they all three drove off together, or their cars were parked near each other."

"Cassie's car was in the shop that night," Snow said. "If she went home alone, she would have gotten a cab at the front entrance of the casino or walked toward the bus stop on Boulder Highway."

"So she apparently drove off the lot with one or both of them."

"Looks that way," Snow said. He clapped Carver on the back. "Thanks a lot, George. I owe you one."

"Just doing my job to help out one of Nevada's best investigators."

"When you see him," Snow said, "tell him I said hi."

They both laughed. Snow gave a wave, turned, and walked toward Starbucks.

When he got to Starbucks, Snow found Alice sitting at one of the little tables alone, with a half-empty cup in front of her. Lining the inside of the cup above the milky tan remains of her drink was a brownish foam residue that looked like some sort of chemical waste.

Snow sat down in the empty chair. "Where's Cassie?"

"She left."

"Where to?"

"I don't know," Alice said. "She switched from Cassie to Claudia right in front of me. I just happened to look away from her for a few seconds. When I looked back, she was staring at the table with a pained, dazed expression. A moment later she looked at me and started insulting me. Then she got up and left. The good news is that she agreed to an interview."

"How did you talk her into that?" Snow said.

"I told her she's a suspect. And I also told her, if she didn't work with us, we'd start working with Homicide with a view toward getting her locked up as soon as possible—for first-degree murder."

"What did she say to that?" Snow asked.

"Her tone got a little friendlier, and she said she'd call one of us to schedule an appointment for an interview."

Snow looked at his watch. "When?"

"She didn't say. I won't be surprised if she doesn't call. What did *you* find out, Jim?"

Snow told her.

"So that was Chad sitting in the bar after Cassie got off work," Alice said. "That's my guess."

"Sounds that way."

"Why would Chad be interested in leaving with those two men?"

Snow pondered this for a moment. "Either Chad is bisexual, or he switched to Cassie or Claudia before Dean Kale came up to her in the bar. Maybe Claudia drinks like Chad, and that was her sitting in the bar. Or maybe Chad or Claudia was planning to murder Billy Ryan."

"With the help of Dean Kale," Alice suggested.

"But why?" Snow asked.

"That's something we need to figure out. To do that, I think we need to turn our investigation to Dean Kale. We can't put it off any longer. We're running out of billable hours."

CHAPTER 16

"Do you still keep up with the horse racing scene, Mr. Michaels?" Alice asked.

Mitch Michaels chuckled amiably and shook his head. "I shouldn't admit this, but I wasn't keeping up with it the last five years I was working in it. You start getting close to retirement, and it's hard to stay interested."

Alice and Snow were seated in Mitch Michaels's living room in San Bernardino, California. The sixty-nine-year-old former horse trainer sat across from them, stretched out in an easy chair. At just over five feet, with a slender build, Michaels appeared to be the picture of health.

"Horse racing used to be touted as the leading spectator sport in the country," Michaels continued. "But that was based on attendance figures. I don't think it's ever been much more than a vehicle for gambling. How many people would want to watch a bunch of horses run if they couldn't bet on them?

"Training horses is like any other profession. It's a means of making money to put food on the table. There's really nothing much to follow in the sport. It's not like baseball or football or tennis. Does a retired garbage collector still follow the trash? Maybe that's a bad comparison..."

"What do you do to keep busy?" Alice said.

"This may sound odd, but my wife Linda and I travel around the country running marathons," Michaels said. "We've been married now for forty-two years. Linda was always a runner, and when I retired seven years ago, she got me interested in it too. I used to run the mile in high school, but never ran another one until the age of sixty-two. And I'll tell you—I've learned a lot about physical conditioning that I never really understood until I started training myself for these marathons."

Snow smiled and leaned forward slightly. "I got into that for a while myself. I've always been a runner, but I could never run a marathon. I always got injured once I got past thirteen miles for my weekly long run."

Michaels nodded. "You're pretty big. You lift weights?"

"Yeah," Snow said. "That's probably part of the problem. So, now I just run half marathons now and then. That works out okay for me."

"That seems to be the most popular distance," Michaels agreed. "I'm a featherweight, but twenty-six miles is still pretty tough. I don't know how those ultra-runners can go a hundred miles up and down a bunch of mountains. It's amazing what the human body can endure." He turned his eyes to Alice. "Are you also a runner, Alice?"

"No," she said. "I play tennis a lot and hike with Jim."

"Tennis is a sport I could never get interested in," Michaels said. "I tried it—too much like Ping-Pong. There's nothing to do but hit the ball back and forth. I also tried golf, but couldn't get interested in that either. Linda is obsessed with bingo. That's where she is tonight. I go with her once in a while to keep her company, but she's an addict. She can't get enough of it."

"We considered taking up golf," Snow said. "But the cost is prohibitive. And we aren't partial to early tee times."

"True," Michaels said. "Now that I'm retired from training horses, I like to sleep in as much as possible."

"How did you get started in that career?" Snow said.

"Similar to the way Dean Kale got his start working for me," Michaels said. "Same age too. I was eighteen, just out of high school. I was five two, a hundred and twenty pounds, and decided I could get rich working as a jockey. So I started out mucking stalls, walking hots, and eventually got the chance to ride pony horses and start galloping horses in the morning, along with schooling races. I lost fifteen pounds and got some mounts on cheap horses as an apprentice.

"I was never one of the top riders, but I made enough to support myself riding the southern California circuit for twelve years. I took a lot of spills, the worst of them the time I broke my collarbone going down aboard the favorite. She broke down in the stretch of a sprint race, and I crashed through the inside rail. That was it for me.

"Luckily, one of the trainers who gave me a lot of mounts took me under his wing, and I became an assistant trainer. When he retired, I took over. I did all right over the years. Though I went through some rough patches where I was down to only a few horses. Times like that, I always thought about getting into something else—like becoming a jockey agent—or anything to make a living. But it always picked back up again. All in all, I did okay for myself. No regrets."

"When did you first meet Dean Kale?" Snow asked.

"Just like me, he was eighteen and had recently graduated from high school. If I remember correctly, it was September 1994, the LA County Fair meet at Pomona. I saw myself in that kid when he walked down my shedrow looking for work. We were shorthanded, so the timing was perfect, and he was eager. So I put him to work doing the same chores I endured when I was starting out on the backstretch. I gave him a tack room to bunk in, and he seemed genuinely happy with the daily routine. He was a bright kid, a real charmer. Everybody liked him, including me."

"Did his parents know where he was working?" Alice asked.

"That was the odd thing about the situation," Michaels said. "Dean's father had been killed just days before in a botched robbery attempt. I didn't find out about that until a couple days after I hired Dean, when the cops came nosing around, asking Dean questions."

"How was his father killed?" Snow asked.

"Shot to death."

Alice glanced at Snow, then turned back to Michaels. "What about Dean's mother?"

"Dean told me she passed away from cancer when he was ten."

"Did they find the perpetrator of the shooting?"

"Not that I know of," Michaels said. "The police only came out the one time. I never saw them again. I know it was tough on the kid; he seemed deeply troubled by it. But he worked through his grief in the barns. He turned into one hell of a talented horseman.

"I promoted him to assistant trainer, and eventually he went off on his own. He did really well for years. He was a genius with claimers. Dealing with those horses is like a big outdoor poker game. Everybody is always trying to fool everybody else. Dean Kale would enter horses that had been off for long periods, below their previous class levels, out of shape, wearing front wraps when they didn't need them. He'd race the horses into condition at those lower levels, instructing the jockeys to let them run easy and take the overland route. After two or three races, he'd move the horses up in class and win. Well, nobody's going to pay a higher price for a horse that can't run close to the front in the cheaper races."

"Nobody caught on to what he was doing?" Snow asked.

"Sure they did," Michaels said. "But Dean was a good poker player. Sometimes he bluffed. He'd bring horses to the track that were washed up and enter them at low prices with front wraps and they'd get claimed and the new owners would find out the horses really did need the front wraps and couldn't win at any price. They never knew what they were getting with the guy."

"What about when the horses started winning?" Snow asked.

"He'd keep moving them up in class to make them pay a decent price. Some of them did get claimed. But usually after, they were off form and needed a six-month rest.

"Dean Kale was also a pro at claiming horses. That guy could judge horses just by looking at them. He was especially good at claiming horses that would spit out the bit in a sprint. He'd move them up in class at a mile, and they'd lead wire to wire at big odds."

"Was he betting on them?"

"I heard he was betting hundreds on horses going off at ten-to-one or more."

"Was he just betting his horses?"

"I think toward the end he was betting on anything that would make money for him. Though I'm sure he had someone going to the betting windows for him."

"What do you mean by 'toward the end'?"

"He got into big trouble. The problem with Dean was, he didn't have patience. He was always looking for the quick ways to win races and cash bets. I didn't realize until later on how ruthless he was. And it got him into trouble with the California Racing Board."

"What sort of trouble?"

"Medication violations. Some of his horses tested positive for illegal drugs. They found loaded syringes in one of his tack rooms. They were building a case to have his license revoked. He went to one of the board members and asked him if they'd suspend their investigation if he voluntarily gave up his license. The board agreed to that, and it saved Dean a hefty fine. It was a sad ending to what started out as a brilliant career.

"That was a year ago. I heard he left California, but I have no idea what he's doing now."

"He's betting the horses from a sports book in Las Vegas," Snow said. "He says he picks the horses by just looking at them on the monitors in the paddock and post parade. Is that possible?"

Michaels laughed and shook his head. "Well, if anybody could, it would be Dean."

CHAPTER 17

They met Detective Daniel Miller at a restaurant in San Bernardino, near the freeway. He was the detective the sheriff's office had referred Snow to when he called to get information on the murder of Samuel Kale, Dean Kale's deceased father. Detective Miller had called a few minutes later from his cell phone. He said he was familiar with the case. Miller had recently been promoted to detective reporting to the Homicide Detail. He'd been assigned to work on the cold case files of San Bernardino County to get his feet wet. He said he had reviewed the files for the Samuel Kale murder only a few weeks ago.

Detective Miller was in his mid-thirties, of average height and build, with a crew cut. He looked sharp in his black dress slacks, a short-sleeved white shirt, and a red and blue tie. He was standing outside the restaurant's front door, next to the newspaper racks, when Alice and Snow walked up to him from their car.

They shook hands and Miller asked to see some ID. "Sorry, but I need to be sure who I'm talking to."

"No problem," Snow said.

He and Alice produced their Nevada private investigator licenses. Miller studied them and nodded. They went inside and were seated at a booth.

"What do you recommend here?" Snow asked, scanning the menu.

"Everything here is excellent," Miller proclaimed. "I like the liver and onions. They prepare it really tender, and my wife never makes it. She said she grew up on the stuff and she's sick of it. Her mother used to serve it once a week and fried it until it was tougher than shoe leather."

"My mother made it the same way," Snow said. "I think she was afraid if she didn't cook it long enough, we'd all get worms."

Miller laughed. "I don't know. I tried making it a few times before I got married, and it always turned out tough."

"How long did you cook it?" Alice asked.

"Fifteen, twenty minutes."

"That's the problem," she said. "It only takes three minutes on each side."

"I guess I would have known that if I'd ever bought a cookbook."

"That's the last thing you'll find in a bachelor's bookcase," Snow said. "In fact, I never even got my first bookcase until I was thirty-seven."

"It's not very big," Alice told Miller. "It has three shelves. The bottom one for his phonebooks, the middle one has books on weight training, running, and fishing. The top shelf is empty. That's where he sets his beer while he's vacuuming."

Miller burst out laughing. "I can relate to that. I've got three locations where I set mine when I'm vacuuming: the dresser, the kitchen counter, and the top of the bookcase in the living room. If I set it anywhere else, I won't be able to find it."

"My old man always set his beer cans on top of the TV," Snow said. "That was back when televisions came in cabinets. He put everything on the TV: cigarettes, matches, keys. My sister told me he used to set me on the TV while he was changing my diapers."

"That's probably what's wrong with you," Alice said. "All that static electricity going into your head."

"It's probably why most of my hair fell out."

Miller looked at Snow's head and nodded, smiling.

The waitress showed up and took their orders and the menus.

Snow took a sip of his water. "So, Daniel, what can you tell us about the Samuel Kale murder?"

Miller shifted his weight and rested his forearms on the table. "Not much," he said. "There's very little in the file. He was shot in the chest in the living room, near the front door, after he got home from work around six in the evening."

"Were there any witnesses?" Alice asked.

"None."

"Do you know what he did for a living?"

"The report says he drove a bread truck. Friends and neighbors said he was a hardworking guy, didn't have any known enemies. Wife died of cancer years before, so he was raising his two kids alone. He was an ex-Marine; served four years. Fought in Vietnam. Neighbors said he was friendly and honest. He was a bit of a redneck and strict with his kids."

"Any suspects?" Snow asked.

Miller shook his head. "The evidence at the scene was consistent with a burglary turned deadly. The house had been ransacked. His wallet, a few hundred dollars cash that he kept in his underwear drawer, and two handguns that he kept in a drawer of his nightstand were all missing. There was nothing else of value in the house."

"What was he shot with?" Alice asked.

"9mm. Two rounds: one to the chest, the other to the side of the head after he was on the floor."

"Were any shell casings recovered?" Snow asked.

Detective Miller shook his head.

"What sort of guns were stolen?"

"A Glock 9mm and a Smith & Wesson snub-nose .38, Model 36. Both guns were registered, so we've got the serial numbers."

Snow frowned. "I suppose neither of them has ever turned up."

"No, they haven't."

"I wonder if the 9mm was the murder weapon," Snow postulated.

"That's entirely possible," Detective Miller agreed. "The perpetrator might have been unarmed at the time of entry into the house and found the guns before the victim got home, and panicked, and decided to use one on him."

"That's the problem with keeping loaded guns lying around," Snow said.

Miller nodded. "They do come in handy to unarmed criminals."

"Was there any sign of forced entry?"

"Back kitchen window was broken out completely."

"What about the son, Dean Kale?"

"He was eighteen at the time," Miller said. "He had graduated from high school and was still living at home with his dad. People who knew him said he couldn't decide what to do with his life. Samuel wanted him to join the military—specifically the Marines. But Dean wasn't interested in that. Personally, I think it would have been a good choice."

"You were a Marine?" Snow asked.

Detective Miller straightened. "Yes. It was a decision I never regretted. I can't say I enjoyed every minute of it, but it has paid off for me. The self-discipline and pride it instilled in me will last a lifetime. It got me the job I have now."

Snow nodded. "I had a job like yours," Snow said. "I threw it away to play poker for a living."

Miller produced a knowing smile. "Perhaps you should have been a Marine?"

Snow shook his head. "I think Alice may be right. It probably has something to do with having my diapers changed on top of the TV while *Hogan's Heroes* and *Gomer Pyle* were blasting out of it."

Miller chuckled. "Gomer Pyle was a Marine—right?"

Snow nodded. "He was one of the reasons I never joined. So, what about Dean Kale? Was he ever a suspect in his father's murder?"

"No. I expect there was some tension there between father and son, but Dean had an alibi. The day of the murder was one of his days off. His sister says he was staying with her in Pahrump, Nevada. At the time of the murder, they were sitting in her living room, drinking wine and beer with two of her friends. The two friends confirmed it. They even went so far as to say that Dean drank so much he vomited around seven p.m."

"That's what happens when you mix wine and beer," Snow said.

Miller nodded knowingly. "Especially when you're only eighteen."

CHAPTER 18

"Like I told you on the phone, I can only give you a few minutes," Mary Kale said. "I need to be at work by ten."

She was standing in the doorway of her home in Pahrump, Nevada. A petite blonde in her late thirties, with a pixie face and large eyes, she wore khaki slacks and a forest-green polo shirt with "Pump & Jump Fitness" stitched in yellow above her left breast.

"That's fine," Alice said. "We'll try to keep it brief."

Snow stood next to Alice, with his hands in the pockets of his thin jacket. It was a brisk forty-eight degrees outside, with a chilly breeze. On mornings like this he wondered if he should invest in some sort of stylish hat to keep his balding head warm.

"I didn't want to meet you at work," Mary continued. "I don't want anyone getting the idea I'm in some sort of trouble. You look like cops." She studied Snow for a moment and then Alice. "And I'm not inviting you inside. You could be anybody. This could be a pretext for a home invasion for all I know."

Alice and Snow produced their Nevada-issued licenses.

Mary studied them. "Those look real enough, I guess. But I'm still not letting you into my house. I feel safer out here where the neighbors can call the cops in case you try something and I have to scream."

"That's fine," Snow said. "We could talk in the car, where it's warmer."

"I'm not getting in your car with you," she snapped. "I'm not stupid."

"Wouldn't you like to put on a jacket? It's a little on the cool side this morning."

She gave Snow an icy stare. "The cold doesn't bother me. And I don't plan on standing here very long. I wouldn't even have agreed to talk to you except that I'm curious what this is about. On the phone you said it concerns my brother. Is he in trouble again?"

Alice fastened the top button on the coat of her business suit and folded her hands in front of her. "What sort of trouble has he had in the past?"

Mary scowled up at Alice. "Just that fiasco with the horse racing board. But he didn't do anything wrong."

"We heard about that," Snow said.

"From Dean?"

Snow shook his head.

"Well then, you've heard one side. It was a crock."

"What happened?"

"They made some baseless allegations about him drugging his horses. They wrote up some phony reports to try to get his trainer's license revoked."

"Why would they do that?"

"He refused to kiss their butts. It all started after he declined to enter any of his horses in races they had no chance of winning. You didn't hear about that, did you?"

"This is our chance to get it from you," Snow said. "What happened with that?"

"Apparently the racing secretaries have trouble filling their race cards after they've written conditions favoring horses owned and trained by their buddies. So they put pressure on the other trainers to enter their horses. Dean always flat-out refused. So they went after him. He finally had enough and quit."

"That's a shame," Snow said. "But he seems to be doing pretty good with his new career."

"Dean's very bright and energetic," Mary said. "He could be successful at anything he put his mind to."

"That's the impression I got."

"So you've talked to my brother?"

Snow nodded.

"What's this about?"

"A friend of Dean's was murdered, and Dean was the last person to see him alive. So we need to eliminate him as a person of interest. We're investigating the murder and just following our usual procedure."

"I haven't been questioned by the cops. Neither has Dean, that I know of."

"They have their own methods—and, apparently, different leads," Alice replied.

"I don't understand what you hope to get out of me. I don't know anything about the murder, other than what Dean told me."

"What did he tell you?"

Mary Kale narrowed her eyes at Alice. "He said they were in the casino till late. Billy Ryan was drunk, so Dean offered to drive him home."

"In whose car?"

"Billy's car," she said. "Dean said they drove to the casino together that morning in Billy's car."

"And did Dean do it?" Snow asked.

"Do what?"

"Drive Billy Ryan home from the casino."

"Dean said he drove as far as his place and that Billy insisted on driving the rest of the way himself."

"Doesn't that seem strange to you?" Alice said.

"What's strange about it?"

"Dean realized Billy was too drunk to drive. If it were me I would have ignored Billy's protests and just driven him all the way home."

"I've talked to my brother about it," Mary said. "And believe me, he wishes he had done that. His judgment wasn't a hundred percent."

"He'd been drinking too," Alice said.

"That's what he told me. But he was the more sober of the two."

"Too bad there wasn't someone else available to drive both of them."

Mary shrugged. "When someone has been drinking, it's usually not them who decides they need someone sober to drive them."

"That's true," Snow said. He studied her face and considered his next question. "It sounds like you and Dean stay in touch on a regular basis."

Mary offered the first hint of a smile. "We've always been very close. It was just us two kids growing up with my father, and that was no picnic. We formed a bond to help us deal with him. He was a bit of an authoritarian. That's a nice way of putting it."

"My sister and I grew up in a similar situation," Snow said, "and she's also a few years older than me. We were never very close, though. And our father wasn't overbearing. He drove a dump truck for a living. All he seemed to care about was sucking down some cold ones after work. Now that I'm older, with reduced expectations, I realize that's not a bad goal to have in life."

Alice gave Snow a sidelong look of disapproval. Snow grinned at her.

Turning back to Mary, Alice said, "Dean told us he's been in a losing streak lately."

"He told me about that. He'll pull out of it. I remember him telling me about a fifty-two-race string of losing entries he had while he was working as a horse trainer. He came out of it by winning eight out of his next ten starts. He understands the ups and downs of horse racing."

"How's he fixed for money?"

"He's never been in short supply of that."

"I'm sorry to hear about what happened to your father, Mary. It must have been difficult to deal with. Did he leave you and Dean with anything when he passed away?"

She gave Alice a smirk. "We each got half of a twenty-five-thousand-dollar life insurance settlement. We were surprised to learn that he even had a policy. We used a large portion of it for the funeral expenses." She paused for a moment, then sighed and crossed her arms. "That was a long time ago. It's ironic. Our mother passed away when I was thirteen. I never realized the pain she endured near the end; she was good at hiding it from us. I think about her every day. She was a wonderful woman—always put her own needs and wishes behind ours. I never could figure out what she saw in my father. When we were kids, we used to wish he were dead, even though it would leave us without parents. Yet after our father was murdered, Dean and I were both devastated. My father's personality left a lot to be desired, but we still missed him greatly after he was gone."

"How did it happen?" Alice asked.

"My father had just gotten home from work. Cops believed it was a robbery gone bad, because the house had been broken into and gone over pretty well."

"That had to have been a terrible shock," Snow said. "And now Dean's best friend's been killed in much the same way." He shook his head.

"Yes," Mary said. "He's having a tough time of it, I think."

"What was reported missing when your father was killed?"

"Two guns," Mary said. "Also my father's billfold and three hundred dollars he kept hidden in a drawer."

"No jewelry, watches, or anything like that?"

"My father wore a watch with a plastic crystal that he bought at a drug store. That was his only jewelry. He was cheap."

"Who else was living in the house at that time?" Snow asked.

"Only Dean."

"Do you know where he was at the time of your father's murder?"

"With me," Mary Kale said. "He had a couple days off from work. So he drove up to spend the time with me. He did that a lot. We were very close."

"You were off from work too?" Alice said.

"Yes. At that time I was working as a sales associate in a sporting goods store. Everyone was flexible. I was usually able to switch shifts to get the same days off as Dean. And Dean was always good about letting me know in advance when he was coming up to stay with me."

"On the day of your father's murder," Alice said, "what were you and Dean doing?"

"We had some friends over for drinks."

"Your friends or Dean's?"

"My friends," Mary said. "Dean didn't know anyone in Pahrump other than me. All of Dean's friends lived in Victorville. That's where we grew up."

"Anyone in particular who Dean hung around with the most back then?" Snow asked.

Mary Kale hesitated. She cocked an eyebrow at Snow. "Do you usually go to this much trouble? All of this was so long ago."

"We like to be thorough," Alice chimed in.

Mary shifted her gaze to Alice. "Well, I suppose there's no good reason not to give you the name of my brother's best friend from high school. I'm sure you could find that on your own anyway."

"That's true."

"His name is Henry Brierschmidt," Mary Kale said. "I heard he's a minister in Bakersfield. I don't have his phone number, but I'm sure that will pop up in any search engine on the Internet."

CHAPTER 19

Reverend Henry Brierschmidt was a pudgy man with a thick head of brown hair neatly trimmed and combed back. He wore a white shirt, open at the collar, with the sleeves rolled up and black pleated slacks.

He greeted Alice and Jim at the front door of his unassuming clapboard home next door to the church where he gathered his congregation every Sunday. His handshake was firm yet gentle, as was his demeanor.

Leading them into his study, he seated them in matching padded chairs surrounded by books lined up on shelves and in bookcases. After easing himself into his high-backed executive chair, he rolled it up to his aged wooden desk and smiled solemnly.

"There seems to be a sudden interest in Dean Kale and the passing of his father. A homicide detective stopped by this morning asking questions. Is this just a coincidence, or are you working with him in some way?"

"If it's Detective Miller you're referring to," Snow said, "we had dinner with him last night and discussed the investigation of Samuel Kale's murder. That may have spurred some additional interest, since it's one of the cold cases he's looking into."

"I see," Reverend Brierschmidt said. "I didn't know it was common for the police to share evidence with private investigators."

Alice crossed her legs and smoothed out her skirt. "Law enforcement agencies share information with each other and anyone they believe can help them solve a case. It works both ways."

"I'm curious why you're investigating Samuel Kale's murder."

"We aren't. We're investigating another murder, more recent. The victim was a friend of Dean Kale. We're interested in knowing what you can tell us about Dean."

Reverend Brierschmidt blinked several times and swallowed. "I see. So, you think Dean was involved in this second murder?"

"All we can do is guess at this point," Snow said.

"And you're looking for a character reference from me."

"That's right."

"I haven't seen or heard from him since we were eighteen. I have no idea what sort of person he is now."

"People don't change much over the years," Snow insisted.

"I disagree," Reverend Brierschmidt said. He raised his hands in front of him, pointing his fingertips toward his chest. "I'm an extreme case in point."

Snow leaned forward. "How so?"

"I've always been willing to share my story with anyone who's interested. For many it provides hope in their own lives." He leaned back in his chair and interlaced his fingers across his abdomen. "I was confused and weak in my younger days, Mr. Snow. I lived only for the moment. And Dean was the same way. We were impetuous."

"In what way?"

"Like many misguided youngsters, we were into drugs. Not heavily, but we smoked a lot of marijuana. Dean was dealing it and I was his best customer. It wasn't until I was twenty-one and couldn't hold a steady job that I took a step back and assessed my situation.

"I decided to give up on reefer at that point and turn to the Lord. With the help of our family's pastor, I fought through my addiction and broke through to the other side, clean and at peace with myself for the first time in my life."

Snow nodded, though he raised an eyebrow. "I heard pot isn't addictive."

"Anything that makes you feel good can be addictive," Reverend Brierschmidt said.

"All it ever did for me was to make me paranoid," Snow confided. "I never liked the stuff."

"I see," Reverend Brierschmidt said, regarding Snow with a somewhat puzzled expression before giving his head a small shake and continuing. "At any rate, it was soon after that I got the call."

"From who?"

"To do the Lord's work."

"Oh, right. That's good. Congratulations. But I wonder: Do you ever get the urge to smoke the stuff anymore?"

Reverend Brierschmidt's eyes narrowed. "Every day I think about it. But I've never given in. That is my salvation."

"That's great," Snow said. "But what about Dean Kale? What was going on with him back then?"

"Nothing good, I'm afraid. I'll tell you the same truths I revealed to Detective Miller. And to be completely honest, the lies I told to the police back then have always haunted me. But I was trying to protect my best friend—and myself."

"What sort of lies?" Alice asked.

"I need to explain the entire situation for you to understand why I covered up the truth. The day before Dean's father was murdered, Dean told me his father had discovered his stash in his bedroom closet. Apparently he had become more and more suspicious because of Dean's behavior, so his father performed a thorough search of Dean's room and found the weed.

"When Dean got home, his father confronted him and gave him an ultimatum: he could enlist in the Marines—or he could go to jail. He told Dean, if he chose the former, on the day he shipped out to boot camp, Samuel would flush the drugs down the toilet. If Dean refused, he said he would take the pot down to the police station and tell them where he found it.

"Dean was in a panic. The last thing he wanted was to spend four years in the military—especially the Marines."

"What was his plan?" Alice asked.

"He was intent on telling his distributor what happened and that he couldn't get the stash back from his father. He thought maybe his distributor could strong-arm his father and coerce him into giving up the drugs."

"Is that what he did?"

"I don't know. He wouldn't tell me. He said it was better if I didn't know and that I should forget everything he told me. I saw him just a couple hours before his father was killed." Alice and Snow straightened in their seats and exchanged a look. The Reverend didn't appear to notice. "We smoked some reefer together in his car," he went on, "in a grocery store parking lot, of all places. Usually that would mellow him out, but it just seemed to make him more agitated and confused. And that was the last time I saw him. He just left town after the cops interviewed him. Somebody said he joined a carnival. Somebody else said he was in Mexico. Later I found out that he was working as a groom at the racetrack. Last I heard a few years ago was that he was doing quite well as a horse trainer at Santa Anita and Hollywood Park."

"What did you tell the police back then?" Alice asked.

The Reverend swallowed, and then looked directly into Alice's eyes. "I lied to them," he said. "I don't know why I did it. Dean didn't ask me to. But it just rose up in me and I did it. I told them I didn't know anything and I hadn't seen Dean in a week."

"What do you suppose happened?"

"I heard the police wrote it up as a robbery/murder and had stopped investigating because they had nothing to go on."

"Do you think Dean had his father killed by this drug distributor he talked about?"

The Reverend shook his head. "No, that sounded far-fetched to me."

"Do you know who the distributor was?"

"No. Dean would never tell me that. I think he was afraid I'd get into the business and compete with him."

"Do you think Dean murdered his father?" Snow pressed.

Reverend Brierschmidt took in a breath, held it for a beat, and let it out slowly. "I'd rather not give my opinion on something like that."

"Do you think Dean Kale is capable of murder?"

He folded his arms across his chest, his face beginning to flush. "Again, I don't believe it's my place to provide that sort of opinion."

Snow nodded. "Well, in an indirect way, you just did."

CHAPTER 20

Highway 58 eastbound from Bakersfield. Jim Snow at the wheel of his Hyundai.

"It looks like you were right about Dean Kale," he said. "His sister was obviously lying. And she got her friends to lie for him too. She may have been in on it. I think he shot his old man with the 9mm. He may have disposed of that gun or maybe even both of them. Or he could have kept the .38 or even both handguns. He may have shot Billy Ryan with his old man's .38."

"That would be too easy for us," Alice said.

"No it wouldn't. Because he probably had sense enough to dispose of the gun after killing Billy. We'll never find it. And even if he still has it, there isn't enough probable cause to get Metro to move with a search warrant."

"For once we agree," Alice said.

"That's a step in the right direction," Snow declared.

"Which direction?"

"Me getting a roll in the hay once we get to my place."

Alice blinked at him. "You certainly know how to get a girl in the mood," she said.

"We could pick up some wine," Snow suggested. "Get you drunk."

"The old ways never seem to die," Alice said.

"We could light a fire."

"You don't have a fireplace."

"I have that set of emergency candles I keep in the pantry for electrical outages. We could light a couple of those and put on some music."

"Bon Jovi doesn't work for me."

"I'll let you pick this time. Or we can download something slow and romantic, like that number Pink released after she finally got a new boyfriend."

Alice laughed. "So, what's our next move with this case? What do you think?"

"What do you want to do?"

"The only reason you're asking me is because you don't have a clue."

"I may not have a clue, but I have a gut feeling."

"What's that?"

"I think one of Cassie's personalities was in Billy's car with Dean when Billy was shot. Somehow we need to get Claudia or Chad to open up about that."

"How do we do that?" Alice said.

"If we can prove that Cassie was in Billy's car after he and Dean left the casino, we can threaten to present that information to Homicide if Claudia or Chad doesn't tell us what he or she knows about the murder."

"I can tell by the eager tone in your voice, you've been giving that a lot of thought."

"I have," Snow said. "Whenever we've been out on the town and you've had to drive me home—what happens?"

"Nothing," Alice said. "You're usually too intoxicated to get the little guy to stand up."

"I'm talking about on the way home."

"We always stop at McDonalds, because you're hungry and it's the only burger place open."

"That's right," Snow said. "It's a guy thing. Maturity brings with it the knowledge that it's bad to go to bed after drinking on an empty stomach."

"I always thought you were just hungry."

"That too," Snow said.

"We could talk to Gina. Ask her if there was any place Billy and Dean liked to stop on their late-evening travels from the Boulder Nugget."

"You said she can't be trusted."

"Sure, but what reason would she have to lie about her late husband's eating habits? He wasn't poisoned; he was shot."

Snow grinned. "I love the way your mind works. Clear and logical. That's what I find attractive—along with your curvy gams."

Alice put her hand on Snow's thigh. "Now *that* kind of talk might just get me into your bed."

Inside her purse Alice's phone rang. She retrieved it and checked the number, then put it to her ear. "Hello, Cassie," she said. "I'm putting you on speaker." She pressed the button and held the phone up above the center console.

"Okay," Cassie said. "Hi, Alice. Hi, Jim."

"We haven't heard from you in a while," Alice said. "Are you okay?"

"Physically, I'm fine," Cassie said, her voice sounding strained. "Mentally, I'm a wreck."

"What's wrong?"

"I'm just getting more and more paranoid, I guess," she said. "I'm afraid to go home because someone might be there waiting for me, so I spent the night in a motel, and I hardly slept all night. I've spent the day driving around and hanging out in public places like department stores and museums. I came out of the Clark County Museum—which is really cool, by the way— and fell asleep after starting my car. I only closed my eyes for a minute and woke up an hour later with it still idling in park. I'm a complete wreck. I was wondering if I could hang out with you guys. I'd feel safer."

"Of course," Alice said. "Though we tried that before, and your alternate parts didn't seem up for the idea. So if you wander off again, there's nothing we can do about it. We can't hold you hostage."

"I know, I know," Cassie said. "I understand that and I'm sorry. I wish I could control them, but, you know, I'm not even conscious of what they do."

"I understand," Alice said. "I downloaded two books on DID last night and read through them both, so I have a better understanding of your disorder. I find it quite remarkable. I explained some of the high points to Jim before we went to sleep, so he's up to speed too."

"You read through two books in one night?" Cassie said. "That's incredible."

"Not really," Alice said. "Most of it was filler and repetition that I was able to skim over. It didn't take long to read through the meat of the material."

"Well, thank you for doing that. I'm impressed."

"Research is part of our job, Cassie," Alice said. "Where would you like us to pick you up?"

"I could meet you at your office."

"Okay," Alice said. "We should be there shortly after eight. I'll give you a call when we're thirty minutes out."

"All right," Cassie said. "Thank you. And I wonder if we could stop by my place and pick up some clothes and things."

"That won't be a problem," Alice said.

"Maybe we could get a chance to talk with Claudia sometime this evening," Snow suggested.

"She hasn't cooperated with you about that yet?" Cassie asked.

"She's pretty stubborn," Snow said. "But I think she'll do the right thing for you eventually."

"I sure hope so," Cassie said. "I'm not sure how much longer I can deal with this."

CHAPTER 21

"Cassie," Alice asked, "when was the last time you saw Dean Kale?"

They were seated in Alice's living room, Alice and Cassie sitting across from each other holding a glass of white wine. Snow sat next to Alice on the couch with a bottle of beer resting on his thigh.

"I saw him at the casino while I was on my way to a malfunctioning slot machine the night Billy was murdered. I guess it was around five or six, but I didn't speak to him because I was busy."

"And before that?"

"Two days earlier," she said. "I woke up around four a.m. in Dean's bed. I don't know how I ended up there, or how much of the evening we'd spent together. I was off the previous day, but it was all a blank."

"Have you spoken to Dean since the shooting?" Snow asked.

She shook her head.

"You haven't thought about calling him?"

Her eyes widened. "Oh, I would never do that. I don't like seeming clingy. And I never know what Claudia has done. She may have already spoken with him, seen him, or even slept with him, for all I know."

"That must be difficult to deal with," Alice said.

Cassie took a sip of wine and sighed. "I don't know," she explained. "I can't say that I'm really interested in Dean. I try to be friendly toward him. I expect that Claudia must see something in him, because it looks to me like she spends a lot of her free time with him."

"Have you ever been intimate with him?" Alice asked.

"No. Never. There have been a few times when he started making advances and I'd suddenly get a terrible headache, so I would excuse myself and go to the bathroom. I always remembered going into the bathroom. I don't ever remember coming back out."

"I see." Alice drank some wine and studied her glass. "It sounds like Dean and Claudia have been having the relationship, and you're the third wheel."

"That's usually the way it happens," Cassie said. "It was different with Billy. Billy approached me—and we got along great. We seemed to be very compatible. I don't recall many memory gaps with him. I think Claudia spent very little time with him."

"You said Claudia was the reason you and Billy split up," Alice said.

"Yes. I think Claudia only came out to start trouble. I was only able to witness the aftermath of her arguments and shenanigans with Billy."

"Did Billy or Dean ever carry a handgun?" Snow asked.

"I'm fairly sure Billy didn't. Dean..." She paused, wet her lips, then pressed them together. She gazed down at her hands, gripping her wine glass. Her eyes welled up with tears. "Earlier today I started to get this vague image of him taking a gun out of a holster that was strapped to his lower leg. But it seemed like more of a memory of a dream I had than anything that actually happened. It was surreal."

"Where did this happen?" Alice asked.

"I'm not sure. It might have been in his bedroom. It was like he was in the process of getting undressed for bed."

"What happened after he withdrew the gun from the holster?"

"That's all I remember, and it was so hazy, it was like an indistinct portion of a childhood memory. It may have been a dream I had—or maybe I'm beginning to hallucinate. I hope I'm not becoming schizophrenic on top of everything else."

"Is that possible?" Alice asked.

"I don't know," Cassie said. "I'll have to ask Dr. Rodgers at our next session."

Alice and Snow exchanged perplexed looks.

Alice turned her gaze back to Cassie. "It seems to me it's possible you're starting to remember things that happened to Claudia."

"What did the gun look like?" Snow asked.

"It was a revolver," Cassie said. "Bluish black–colored, with a short barrel."

"A snub-nose," Snow said.

"Yes," Cassie said. "That's what it was. And the holster was strapped to the inside of his left leg."

Snow studied Cassie's face. Her eyebrows were drawn together, her jaw clenched.

"That's interesting," he said. "By the way—while we were waiting for you to pack your overnight bag, I checked your front door. The weather stripping is so tight around it, there's no way anyone could slip a sheet of paper under the door or anywhere around it. That note you showed us was placed on the floor from inside your house."

CHAPTER 22

Jim Snow was having his usual nightmare where he'd become aware that his billfold was missing from his left rear pocket and he couldn't find it anywhere. As he searched for it, he began to notice the pressure building in his bladder and began looking instead for the restroom. He was wandering around the inside of a strange building with no money, no identification, and no place to relieve himself. After a desperate search down several corridors, he noticed the sign for the men's room and rushed inside—only to discover there were no commodes or urinals—only multiple rows of potted plants.

He was in the process of deciding whether to water a begonia in a five-gallon nursery pot, when he awoke, glanced around the room, and realized he was lying safely in Alice's bed, with his back to her and his wallet on top of her dresser, next to his cell phone and keys.

Snow climbed out of bed and padded toward the bathroom door, stopping halfway there, turning his head, and staring at the open doorway to the bedroom.

When they'd gone to bed, the door had been closed and locked.

Now it was wide open.

Snow turned and stared back at the bed. In the faint light of the neighbor's outside security lights filtering through the blinds, Snow noticed two figures on the bed. Two women. Alice lay on her side near the far edge of the bed with her back to him. Lying next to her, holding on to her like a bear climbing a tree, was Cassie.

Snow padded to the light switch and flipped it on.

Both women stirred and winced from the light of the bedside lamp. Alice lifted her head off from her pillow and glanced down at the arm around her, then sat up and gazed in disbelief at Cassie.

With her eyes wide, Cassie scrambled backward to the far side of the bed, away from Alice, and stumbled out of bed.

"Oh, my God, I'm so sorry!" she squealed, putting her fingertips to her mouth. She turned and rushed out of the room, the back of her nightgown trailing behind her.

Alice swung out of bed, wearing a purple baby-doll nightie, and trotted across the room, with Snow following behind.

Down the hall they found the door to the spare bedroom closed. Alice rapped lightly on it with her knuckles.

"I'm getting dressed!" Cassie sobbed from inside the room.

"It's okay," Alice said. "No harm done, Cassie. It was probably Chelsea, got scared and wanted to get in bed with someone."

"No, I'm leaving!" Cassie said.

"You don't have to."

"I know, but I want to," Cassie countered.

A moment later the door swung open, and Cassie emerged, wearing jeans, sneakers, and a T-shirt. She hurried down the hallway and hustled down the stairs. They heard the front door open and close, and she was gone.

Alice and Snow stared at each other in silence.

"I was afraid something like that would happen," Snow finally blurted. "Only much worse. I think hiring a bodyguard for her would be a better idea than letting her stay with us."

"Well," Alice said, "that's her choice."

"Besides," Snow said, "she's got her own live-in bodyguard: Chad. That's who was in bed with us, spooning you. Chelsea didn't come in there; the door was locked... but I wonder how Chad got it open?"

Alice padded down the hallway to the open doorway of her bedroom. She reached above the door to the top edge of the jamb and retrieved a slotted pin with a loop at the end. She held it out to Snow. "She found this, I guess."

"Why do you keep it above your door?" Snow asked.

"That's where it was when I bought the place. So I just left it there. There's one above the hall bathroom door too. You don't have any of these in your house?"

"Well, sure," Snow said. "But I keep them in the top drawer of my nightstand. So nobody can get into my bedroom when the door's locked."

"What if you accidentally lock yourself out of your bedroom?" Alice said.

Snow considered this. He shrugged. "I have a reciprocating saw in the garage. It's good at cutting holes in stuff."

Alice shook her head and put the key back on the ledge of the doorjamb. "Well, I'm going back to bed. Why don't you go downstairs and lock the front door. I'll leave the bedroom door unlocked, so you won't have to cut a hole in it."

CHAPTER 23

Nine thirty, Sunday morning.

When they were two blocks from the Ryan residence in Snow's Sonata, a familiar car passed them, traveling in the opposite direction. The driver was Cassie—or one of her identities. She kept her eyes trained straight ahead, appearing not to have noticed them.

"Jesus," Snow muttered. "Who the hell was that?"

"I'll give you two guesses," Alice said. "One of them is bound to be right. It looks like she's coming from Gina's home. I wonder what she was doing there."

"Maybe she and Gina went to church together," Snow suggested. "We know she didn't spend the night, since we were hosting that fiasco."

"I wonder where she's headed now."

"We could find out," Snow said. "I don't believe she saw us. What do you think?"

"Let's do it."

Snow watched Cassie's car in his mirror. She made a turn. After her car was out of sight, Snow hit the brakes and executed a three-point U-turn. He followed at a distance down Greenawalt

Road, onto Boulder Highway. A few minutes later she turned off and parked on the street near the residence of Dean Kale.

A block behind her, Snow pulled over and watched Cassie swing out of her car and stride toward Dean Kale's front door, removing her keys from her purse as she went. Without knocking, she unlocked the door and went inside.

"What I wouldn't give to be a fly on the wall in there right now," Snow said. "You know what I'm thinking?"

"All three of them were in on the murder," Alice said.

"All three of whom?" Snow said.

"Claudia, Dean, and Gina."

"Right," Snow agreed. "What's the motive?"

"The half-million dollars Billy kept on hand."

"Split three ways? I don't think so. That wouldn't last long. Why would Gina kill her cash cow for such a small payoff? Billy was bringing home a lot of money."

"I've been thinking about it a lot," Alice said. "Why would someone as strong willed as Gina allow a man back into her life after he rejected her for someone else? With her charm and looks, she could find a more lucrative romantic investment. And I'm not so sure she isn't still plying her profession here in Las Vegas."

"Why did she reconcile with Billy?"

"I haven't figured that out yet," Alice said. "But I'm pretty sure it had something to do with money."

Gina Ryan looked radiant in a yellow sundress when she answered the doorbell. Her eyes were clear and bright, her cheeks rosy.

"Alice James and Jim Snow," she said. "It was great to get your call. Come in. I just made a fresh pot of coffee for you."

She led them into the dining room and offered them seats at the granite-top dining room table.

"Cream and sugar?" she asked.

"Black for me," Snow said.

"Just a little of both, thank you," Alice said.

Gina went into the kitchen and came back a minute later with a serving tray holding three ceramic mugs of coffee. After placing the cups on the table, she set the tray aside and seated herself, smiling at Snow.

"Back for more questions," she said. "You must be making progress."

Snow shrugged. "Forward or back, we're always moving in one direction or the other."

Gina laughed. "Your honesty is refreshing... Do you have a suspect in your crosshairs?"

"No one specific."

"The police tell me they're confident they have the case solved," Gina said. "They have two men in custody. But they can't get them to talk. Only one of their girlfriends, and she insists they never harmed anyone. But according to her, she was never with them when they committed the crimes, so it's all hearsay."

"Sounds promising," Snow lied, shaking his head.

"Did you learn anything more from Cassie this morning?" Alice asked.

Gina took a sip of coffee and set the cup down. "How did you know she was here? Have you been following her?"

"We passed her on the way here," Alice said.

Gina maintained her smile. Without blinking, she said, "In the last three days I've learned a lot about Cassie. We've spent quite a bit of time together, talking. She's a very secretive, complicated, and fascinating person. Once I got her to open up, she told me a lot about herself."

"How did you manage that?"

"By showing an interest in her and listening. I asked her why she hired you. At first she didn't want to tell me, but she seems to trust me. I think it's because I have a tendency not to judge people. I think if I hadn't been a model, I would have done well in the field of psychiatry."

"What did she tell you?" Alice asked.

"She said she has a condition called dissociative identity disorder. She said you know about it. That she hired you to find out who killed Billy, because she's afraid her other identity might have done it. But she didn't."

"How do you know that?"

"Because I've spent a lot of time talking to her about it—the other identity—Claudia. She had no reason to murder my husband. She told me Cassie was the one who was interested in the affair with him. That she, Claudia, had been trying to break it up, because she was interested in Dean. And she couldn't pursue him as long as Cassie was involved with Billy. She drove them apart so she could go after Dean."

"Why didn't Claudia let Cassie know about that?" Snow asked.

"Because they don't like each other. They stay completely away from each other."

"That's pretty obvious," Snow said. "What about Chad and Chelsea?"

"Who are they?" Gina asked.

Snow raised an eyebrow. "Nobody. Never mind."

"Who are they?" Gina pressed.

"I assumed she told you about them," Snow replied. "It's not my place to say. They're not important."

Gina stared at Snow.

"So," Alice said, "this was the Claudia identity you've been getting together with? Never Cassie?"

Gina turned her head to Alice. "I can't be sure. But yes, I think at least most of the time it was Claudia I was conversing with."

"How could you tell the difference?"

Gina pondered this for a moment. "I'm not sure. I mean, I didn't want to keep asking her who I was talking to. Their voices and inflections are the same."

"Yes, they are," Alice agreed. "Was she drinking at all?"

"Night before last she was," Gina said. "We went out to dinner and had a wonderful time. We both had a lot to drink. We ended up taking a cab."

"What was she drinking?"

"We both started out drinking gin martinis," Gina said. "After a few of those she switched to gin and tonic, and I nursed a glass of wine."

"Where did you go after dinner?" Snow asked.

"We went to her place for a nightcap. We had some brandy. And that was when she told me everything about her condition, her abusive parents, and her multiple years in therapy that was going nowhere. She really opened up to me. I was flattered that she wanted to reveal so much to me. But I wasn't shocked by it or judgmental; I just listened intently. I think she liked that. It seemed therapeutic for her. We talked all night. We made a strong connection on multiple levels."

Alice and Snow exchanged a glance.

Snow took a drink of coffee and settled back in his chair. "Gina," he said, "you mentioned some money that Billy kept on hand as a bankroll for his wagers."

"Yes."

"Where did he keep that?"

"Why?" She raised her eyebrows. "Are you planning to rob me?" She let out a mock laugh.

"I'm just wondering if anyone knew about it and where it was hidden."

"He kept it in a heavy-duty safe in our walk-in closet. It's bolted to the floor from the inside. It would be nearly impossible to walk off with, and someone would end up blowing up the house trying to get into it. I don't know if Dean knows about it—or Cassie. I never told anyone about it.

"When Billy and I broke up and he moved in with Cassie, he took all the money out of the safe and rented a safe deposit box. That tells you something about the trust he had in me that he didn't have with Cassie. When he moved back in with me, he put the money back in his safe in the closet."

"Do you have the combination for the safe?" Snow asked.

"Of course. If something happened to Billy, he knew I would need that. So he gave it to me. We trusted each other. After his death I took all of the money down to the bank and put it in a safe deposit box. I don't want it sitting around here. And I can't very well put it all into a savings account without it being reported by the bank."

"What do you plan to do for income?" Alice said. "Have you entertained any thoughts of getting back into your old profession?"

Gina grinned. "That's always a possibility. Maybe I could start my own modeling agency. But there's no rush."

"Did Claudia tell you where she was the night Billy was shot?" Alice asked.

"She said she was working until two a.m., and afterward she went straight home, heated up some leftovers, and went to bed."

"How did she say she got home?" Snow asked.

"She didn't," Gina said. "I imagine she drove her car home."

Snow nodded, frowning. "Did she ever get a ride home with Billy and Dean?"

Gina shook her head. "I can't say. I suppose it's possible Billy dropped Claudia off with Dean at his place on his way home."

"Did Billy and Dean ever stop to eat on the way home from the casino?"

"Sometimes they'd eat at the café inside the casino or the buffet."

"What about when it was late and they'd been shooting craps and drinking all night, long after the buffet was closed?"

Gina nodded. "There's a gas station named Beaver's Oasis that they stopped at for hot dogs sometimes, on Boulder Highway. It's just the other side of Sunset Road. Dean apparently has never been a big hot-dog fan, but Billy loved them. He was always raving about them. They're all-beef, kosher, and they're only a dollar each. I think the station uses them as a loss leader."

CHAPTER 24

Beaver's Oasis was a fairly new independent gas station and convenience store in Henderson, two miles south of the Boulder Nugget Hotel Casino. Snow remembered four years earlier seeing the various stages of demolition of the previous aging structure, the excavation of the lot, and new construction of the colorful building and pumps.

The station's gas prices were equal to the lowest in that area of Clark County, but Snow had never stopped there because he couldn't be sure of the quality of the gas. He had no idea where it came from.

Snow parked his Sonata in front of the store, and he and Alice went inside.

The man working the counter, in his mid-thirties, wore a faded black T-shirt with "Beaver's Oasis" stenciled in white above the tiny breast pocket. To his left, behind a glass sneeze guard, a couple dozen glistening hot dogs and polish sausages rotated on a large, stainless steel hot-dog roller.

Alice and Snow took their places in line behind an old man with a twelve-pack of beer and a young woman waiting to pay for her gas.

Snow studied the hot dogs with longing. It was still an hour and a half till lunch, but the peanut butter sandwich he'd consumed for breakfast was long gone from his stomach.

"They look pretty good," he whispered to Alice.

"Yes, they do," Alice said. "They've added just the right hue of coloring to trick your indiscriminate palate. What if they made them green?"

Snow considered this. "That would look tasty with mustard and relish."

Alice laughed. "Are you hungry already?"

"I ran six miles this morning," Snow said.

"Doesn't that make you want to eat something healthy?"

"Like what? Lettuce and a bowl of fruit? That just makes me hungrier. Or tofu? That sets in my stomach like cement."

"You like chicken."

"I'm sick of the taste of it," Snow complained. "Nearly every-thing tastes like chicken—even crawdads and frog legs."

"You don't have a refined palate, Jim," Alice said. "I think that's from drinking a six-pack before every meal."

"I don't drink a six-pack before every meal," Snow insisted. "Every other meal. And only dinner. I never indulge in alcohol before four p.m."

"I've seen you drinking at six thirty in the morning."

"Yes, but I didn't start before four the previous afternoon."

At the cashier's counter now, Snow displayed his private eye license. "I wonder if you could help us with some information."

"I don't know much, but I'll try," the cashier said.

Snow pulled three sheets of folded paper out of his shirt pocket. He unfolded them and showed them to the cashier. "We need to know if any of these three people were in here around 3:15 a.m. on Thursday, March 22."

The man looked down at the photos. "I wouldn't know. I work eight to four during the day."

"Could you tell us who was working the cash register during that time?" Snow asked.

"Mr. Beaver works at night," the cashier said.

"He's nocturnal, I guess." Snow chuckled. "No kidding. There's actually someone who works here with that name?"

"He's the owner," the man said. "You want to talk to him? He's in the office in back."

"Sure," Snow said. "We'd appreciate it."

The cashier locked his cash register and crossed to the short corridor next to the beer cooler. He stopped in front of the first door on the left and knocked. Snow heard a voice from inside. Then the cashier opened the door and leaned inside.

Some words were exchanged. Afterward the cashier strode back behind the counter. Following a short distance behind was a short, hefty man in his fifties, with dyed black hair and a matching goatee. He had a round face with an overbite.

He marched over to Snow and stuck out his hand. Snow shook it.

"I'm Willard Beaver," the man said. "What can I do for you?"

Fighting the urge to chuckle at the fitting name, Snow introduced Alice and himself and repeated what he'd said to the cashier. Beaver studied the three photos.

"All three of them look familiar," he said. "I've seen them in here before, I'm pretty sure, but I can't say when. March 22—that was over a week ago."

Snow looked up at the security camera bolted to the ceiling near the corridor, aimed toward the middle of the store. He turned his head and noticed another one above the cashier pointed down toward the counter.

"Those cameras work?" he asked.

"Sure do," Beaver said.

"Do you have the video archives for around 3:15 a.m. March 22?"

"Two weeks at least," Beaver said. "That's how long we hang on to the archives. So you're in luck. If you want to look through it, you can come back to my office."

Snow thanked him, and he and Alice followed Beaver into his office.

The room was small, with a battered metal desk, a four-drawer file cabinet in a corner, and a circular metal wastebasket. Hung on the paneled wall above Willard Beaver's swivel chair was a framed cartoon of a cross-eyed beaver.

Willard Beaver pointed at it as he entered the room and said, "That's a portrait of my grandfather. He was a carpenter." He let out a deep-throated laugh. "Actually my wife gave me that as a Christmas present one year. I think she was pissed off about something. But I like it—great conversation piece." He swept his gaze from Snow to Alice and back again. "I know what you're thinking. You figured Beaver was my nickname. Everybody does. But you can guess pretty easily what the other kids used to call me in school."

"The Beave?" Alice said.

Willard Beaver chuckled. "Even my closest friends weren't that kind. Everybody called me Bucky of course. Kids can be unsparing in their sense of humor—but Mother Nature had a hand in it. Well, anyway—" Beaver clapped his hands together, then leaned over and turned his computer monitor ninety degrees. He pointed at the two guest chairs. "If you move those chairs over around near the end of the desk here, you can get a good view of this thing."

Snow moved the chairs while Beaver booted up his computer. He pulled open the top side drawer and looked through a stack of DVDs. Finding the one he needed, he waited for the computer to finish its mechanics, then opened the program and inserted the DVD.

They spent twenty minutes watching the video footage of the cashier's counter near the front of the store, beginning at 3:10 on the morning in question. None of the three subjects appeared in the footage.

Alice and Snow got up to leave. Snow slid the chairs back to their original positions. They shook hands with Willard Beaver and walked out.

On the way out the front door of the store, Snow glanced upward and noticed another security camera, this one mounted under the eaves and aimed at the exit from the lot onto Boulder Highway.

He stopped, put his hands in his back pockets, and stared up at it.

"What?" Alice said.

"This camera," Snow replied. He looked in the direction it was pointing and then back at the camera. "It's aimed at the exit, but it looks like it could have a view of the southbound lanes of Boulder Highway."

He turned his head to Alice. Her eyes were wide with interest.

"Okay," she said. "It's worth a try. Let's go back inside."

Reseated around Willard Beaver's desk, all three of them stared intently at the monitor. All of the southbound lanes of Boulder Highway were well lit and visible. Beginning with the 3:10 a.m. footage, they watched cars passing the station at lengthy intervals.

At 3:17, a red Nissan Altima came into view.

"That's it!" Snow said.

Beaver paused the video. They leaned forward, staring at the car. It was traveling in the middle lane, with the windows down. Two male passengers were seated on the right side of the car, in the front and back seats.

"Can you advance it a little?" Alice said.

Beaver jogged it until the car was in the middle of the screen, then zoomed in.

The image was fuzzy, but Dean Kale was visible sitting in the front passenger seat. Billy Ryan was in the back seat directly behind him. Both of their heads were turned toward the driver of Billy's car, as though they were involved in a conversation.

The driver's hair looked familiar. They studied the features of the face.

"Well," Snow muttered. "That's Cassie driving the car."

"Or Claudia," Alice put in.

"Cassie and Claudia. Those two women look alike?" Willard Beaver asked.

"Or it could be Chad," Snow said.

Willard Beaver's eyes narrowed, and his brows furrowed. Snow saw him look away to his desk, where the calendar was opened to Sunday, April 1, today's date. Returning his gaze to Snow, Beaver searched his face for any indication that this might be a joke.

CHAPTER 25

"This is Alice James. I'm with Jim Snow. Who am I speaking to?"

The voice coming through the tiny speaker of Alice's cell phone sounded uneven and strained: "This is Cassie, Alice."

Alice held her cell phone above the center console of Snow's Hyundai. They were on Boulder Highway, heading toward their office.

"Cassie, it's imperative that we speak with Claudia. We can't wait any longer. We have new information, and if Claudia won't cooperate with us, we'll need to suggest that you accompany us when we go in and talk to Homicide."

There was a pause on the other end. Cassie's voice sounded faint. "What information do you have?"

"We know that you were driving Billy Ryan's Nissan after you, Billy, and Dean Kale left the Boulder Nugget," Snow said. "Only ten to fifteen minutes before Billy was shot."

"I don't remember that," Cassie said.

"We understand that," Alice said. "Obviously it was either Claudia or Chad who was driving the car."

"If it was Chad, wouldn't you need to talk to him?"

"Of course," Alice said. "But Claudia is supposedly aware of everything that happens to you, isn't that true?"

"Yes, that's what Dr. Rodgers has told me."

Alice looked at her watch. "It's almost eleven now," she said. "We're on our way back to our office. Jim and I are hoping Claudia will stop in and talk to us—say in a half hour or so?"

"You know I don't have any control over that," Cassie pleaded.

"I know, Cassie. I know. But that's just a message from us to Claudia. She's only causing trouble for all of you—especially herself—if she doesn't speak with us about what happened the night Billy was shot."

A pause, followed by a sob, barely audible. "What if Claudia did it? I mean, the way she's acting, I'm beginning to suspect, more than ever, that she might have."

Alice sighed and looked at Snow. Their eyes met.

"I don't think she had anything to do with it," Alice said. "But I'm pretty sure she saw something she doesn't want known."

Cassie sniffed. "Maybe."

"Have you spoken with Dean Kale at all in the last few days?" Snow asked.

"No. Not at all."

"Have you checked your call record on your cell phone?"

"Yes. There aren't any recent calls to Dean listed. The only calls listed that I didn't make were to Gina Ryan."

"Have *you* spoken with Gina lately?"

"No. Not at all. But it looks like somebody has, quite a few times."

"Alright," Alice said. "Call us anytime, Cassie. Okay?"

Barely audible, Cassie said, "I will. Thank you."

Alice disconnected the call.

"Jesus, what a mess," Snow muttered.

CHAPTER 26

Dressed in black chinos and a white cotton blouse, Claudia slouched down in one of Alice's client chairs. She crossed her legs and folded her arms, frowning.

"So, what's up?" she asked.

"That's what we're trying to find out," Alice said.

She was sitting erect at her desk, with her hands together and resting on top of it. Jim Snow sat quietly in his swivel chair to her right, studying Claudia.

"You having any luck?" Claudia said.

"A little. But we'd prefer not to rely on that. It would be better if we could get some straight answers from those who can provide them."

"And you think I can do that?"

"All we ask from you," Snow said, "is to tell us what you know about Billy Ryan's death."

"I don't know anything about it," Claudia said. "That's the truth. May I go now?"

"Why don't you give us a summary of your activities on the night Billy was murdered? Could you do that?"

"All right, but it won't be of any help to you. I'm sure of that."

"Maybe not," Snow said. "But it's best if we figure that out for ourselves."

Claudia shrugged. "Why should I be helpful when the two of you are so rude to me? I'm pretty sure I'd get better treatment from the police."

"How are we being rude to you?" Alice asked.

"You haven't offered me anything to drink," Claudia said. "I might be thirsty."

"Would you like some water?"

"I was thinking of something with more kick to it."

"What would you like?"

"What do you have?"

Alice reached into her bottom desk drawer, brought out a half-empty bottle of Old Whiskey River, and set it on the desk. "This is the only liquor we have on hand. But one of us can make a quick trip to the liquor store."

Claudia uncrossed her legs and straightened in her chair. She rested her forearms on her armrests. "I love bourbon," she said. "I didn't know you were such a heavy boozer, Alice."

"I'm not," Alice said. "This is left over from another case. Someone brought it in as a gift."

"Do I get a glass, or do you want me to drink it out of the bottle? Not that I mind."

Snow got up and left the room. He came back with three small plastic cups filled with ice and three bottles of water. He passed them out, poured some whiskey into Claudia's cup, then sat back down.

Claudia lifted her cup and drained the bourbon from it. Setting the cup back down, she poured more whiskey, nearly filling it. Leveling her gaze at Snow, she said, "I should be careful with this. If I drink too fast it gives me a headache." She let out a sinister laugh.

"That sounds familiar," Snow said.

Claudia took a sip of her fresh drink and leaned back. "You're very observant, Mr. Snow," she said. "Chad told you that, if I remember correctly."

"Yes, he did," Snow said.

Claudia cocked an eyebrow and smiled. "Or maybe it was me, pretending to be Chad."

"Maybe you're Chad pretending to be Claudia," Snow said.

"That's certainly possible, isn't it?" Claudia shifted her gaze to Alice and winked at her. "You look lovely today in your little business suit, Alice. I love the way you attempt to look so professional. I find it sexy."

Alice met her gaze but said nothing.

"I'll bet you've been wondering who sneaked into your bedroom last night and curled up with you."

"I'm pretty sure it was either you or Chad," Alice said.

"Why do you assume that?"

"Cassie wouldn't have done anything like that. And the door was locked. Chelsea is only five; she couldn't have figured out how to get the door open."

"Would you like to hear a secret that only I know about?" Claudia took another sip of bourbon.

Snow said nothing. Alice waited.

"There is no Chelsea," Claudia confessed. "I invented her."

"Why?" Alice asked.

"For fun. I enjoy fucking with Dr. Rodger's head. She's such a complete moron, she embraces everything I tell her. I get a kick out of acting like a five-year-old in front of her. I can throw fits, scream and holler—act like a complete brat—and she just sits there and takes notes. I can also do a pretty good impersonation of Cassie. But she's too easy. She has very little personality. Anybody can act sweet and innocent."

"Why do you dislike Cassie so much?"

"She's a coward. If anything stressful happens, she hides from it. She leaves me to deal with every bad moment in her life. I'm really getting sick of it."

"Have you tried to communicate that to her?"

"She can't deal with confrontation. And she doesn't pay any attention to me. When I come out, she runs away. I'd have to write her a letter."

"Like the one you left her near the front door?" Snow interjected.

Claudia looked at Snow. "Yeah. That scared the crap out of her, didn't it?"

"Why did you leave her that note?"

"I was trying to get her to shut up, but I guess that didn't work."

"Shut up about what?"

"Nothing." Claudia took another sip of whiskey, then topped off her drink from the bottle.

"Claudia," Alice said, "you're obviously the strongest of the three of you. Why don't you try to get everyone to work together? If you don't like Dr. Rodgers, find someone you respect. Try to pull together."

"Like a team?"

"Yes."

"That sounds like a pep talk to a bunch of department store sales associates," Claudia said.

"Don't you want to get better?"

"Of course I do," Claudia snapped. "But not if it means letting Cassie run the show."

"What about integrating? Isn't that possible? What if you kept a diary of your daily thoughts and activities so the others could read it and begin to understand you? Each of you could keep a diary. What about that?"

"I don't want anything to do with that bitch. I certainly don't want her privy to my thoughts. Just considering the idea of a diary she would have access to makes me gag."

"I thought you said she was sweet and innocent."

"She's a sweet, innocent bitch," Claudia said.

Alice shook her head. "Why are you so hostile?"

Claudia glared at Alice. "If you were carrying around the memories I have, you'd be bitter too."

"Would it help to confront your parents about what they did to you?" Alice said.

"Bad idea. They'd both end up dead, and I'd go to prison for murder," Claudia insisted.

"I was never abused, but I used to feel that way about my father for abandoning me," Alice said. "But I finally did get the chance to talk to him about it."

"What came from that?"

"Nothing good," Alice admitted.

"Then why do you want me to try it? If I accused my parents of abusing me, they'd only deny it. I couldn't prove anything in court—they're both respected citizens—pillars of the community. I'd only put myself through more turmoil and aggravation, and embarrass myself. I've had enough. I need to minimize it."

"Why don't you find another therapist?" Snow asked. He unscrewed the cap to his water bottle and drank from it.

"Rodgers is the third one," Claudia said. "The first two were clowns. How does anyone even go about finding a top-notch psychotherapist? It's a crapshoot. You just pick one and hope you get lucky. And I really don't want a therapist, anyway. I think it's a waste of time. Cassie's the one who's sold on the idea of therapy."

"How else do you plan to recover from your disorder?" Snow said.

"I don't have a plan," Claudia said. "If I could, I'd get rid of Cassie. But that doesn't seem to be possible without throwing her off a bridge and taking me with her in the process."

"What about Chad?" Snow asked.

Claudia sneered at Snow. "There is no Chad," she said. "I was just fucking with you because I realized you two idiots are as dumb as Dr. Rodgers."

"Chad was just an act?"

"That's right."

"How do we know you aren't really Chad pretending to be Claudia?"

"What's in a name? I call myself Claudia because I like that name. You can call me whatever you want," Claudia said. "What I'm telling you is that there is only the two of us: Cassie and me."

Snow sighed. "Well, that's good news. You just eliminated one of our suspects."

"And now there's just me?"

Snow drank more water. He screwed the lid back on. "Claudia, or whoever you are, would you mind running through your movements with us for the night of Billy's murder?"

"It won't do any good."

"Why not?"

"You'll just assume I'm lying."

"Based on what you've told us so far," Snow said, "that would be a pretty good assumption. Don't you think?"

Claudia grinned.

"Would you be willing to take a polygraph test?" Snow asked. "That way we'll be fairly certain what you tell us will be useful information, and it might provide some leads."

"I'd have to think about it," Claudia said.

"While you're deciding, would you mind telling us what you were doing the night of March 22?"

Claudia drank more bourbon. She topped off her cup again, then settled into her chair, and crossed her ankles. She fixed her gaze on her drink.

"I ran into Dean at the casino. He wanted to know if I was interested in spending the night with him. I guess shooting craps makes him horny. I told him I wasn't sure. I didn't want to spend most of it waiting for him to lose all of his bankroll at the crap table."

"You were aware he was losing?"

"He said he was having a terrible run. He didn't think he'd stick around much later than the end of my shift. He wanted to know if I'd drive him and Billy home. They were both pretty well soused. I said I would. Told him I'd wait for them in the bar after my shift until they were ready to go. But I wasn't interested in waiting all night. So I got off work, changed my shirt, and waited in the lounge."

"You had quite a bit to drink as well," Snow suggested.

"I had a few," Claudia said, taking another sip of her bourbon. "So, around three, Dean came by on the way to the bathroom and told me they were ready and they'd meet me out at Billy's Nissan in their usual spot. They always parked in the same place out near the corner of the lot, where there were hardly ever any cars, because Billy was always concerned about someone coming out of the casino drunk and bumping into his car. I guess he figured everyone was like him."

"Like him in what way?" Alice asked.

"A lush," Claudia said. She drained her drink and refilled it.

"Billy drank a lot?"

"Several times a week," Claudia insisted.

"What about Dean?"

"He could put the sauce away," she said, "but he's not a lush."

"What's the difference?"

"I love Dean," Claudia said. "I hated Billy's guts." She laughed and slapped the table. "I'm sorry. That's an old joke and I think I fucked it up."

Snow smiled. "So Billy and Dean met you out at Billy's Nissan in the corner of the parking lot…"

"Right," Claudia said. "I got there a few minutes before them. When they showed up, right off Billy started protesting about me driving his car. He didn't want me driving it."

"Why not?"

"He never liked me," Claudia said. "He was in love with Cassie. He adored her. He hated my guts. Of course, the feeling was mutual."

"Did Billy know about your disorder?"

"No. So he thought it was Cassie he had come to hate. The dumb bitch didn't have the guts to tell him about me. I think if she had, he would have stayed with her. Maybe not, but at least she'd have had a chance with him. With me jamming up the relationship, she had no chance of keeping that jerk around."

"What was it about Billy you didn't like?" Alice asked.

"He was arrogant and sanctimonious. He was convinced he was one of these people who was placed on this planet for a purpose. He didn't realize we all have the same purpose here. We've all been created to provide food for bacteria. That's our purpose. We're nothing more than livestock."

Snow stared at Claudia for a moment. Then he reached for the bottle and poured some whiskey in his cup of melting ice.

"Don't mind me, help yourself," Claudia said. She chuckled and slapped the table again. "You're all right, Snow. I thought you were a stupid asshole at first. But you're not so bad."

"Thanks," Snow said. He took a slug of his drink. "So, what happened out in the parking lot? Was there an argument?"

"Not much of one," Claudia said. "Dean told Billy to watch what he said about me, because I was his squeeze now. That's what he called me. That was his term of endearment for me. I liked it—it's genuine. That's what I love about Dean. He's genuine. Like me."

"What happened after that?"

"We all got in the car. Billy gave me the keys, and I started it up and drove off the lot. We were about a mile down Boulder Highway when they started arguing about hot dogs."

"What was that all about?" Snow asked.

"Billy was hungry. He wanted to stop for hot dogs at Beaver's gas station. I was up for it too—they're fantastic hot dogs. But Dean didn't want to stop. He told Billy to find something to eat after he got home. Dean was pretty cranky—he'd lost a lot of money—and Billy always rubs it in his face when he wins and Dean doesn't. They started yelling at each other. I told them both to shut up; the racket was making my ears ring. Then Billy called me a bitch, and I gave him the finger. I was getting angry by the time we got to Beaver's, so I drove right on past. And the yelling got louder."

Snow leaned back and held his hands apart. "But wait a minute. Beaver's Oasis is past the turnoff to Dean's home. Dean told us he drove to his home and Billy drove the rest of the way home alone."

"I can't tell you about that, because I wasn't in the car when they got to Dean's—or Billy's house," Claudia said.

"You were driving the car when you passed Beaver's," Snow said.

"That's right. I was."

"You were planning to drive Billy home and then take his car to Dean's and spend the night. Was that the plan?"

Claudia thought about it. She took another sip of whiskey. "Yeah, that was the plan."

"So, what happened?"

"I got so fed up with the arguing that I stopped the car and got out. I walked the rest of the way home."

"Where did you get out of the car?" Alice asked.

"At the corner of Greenawalt and Kallem Avenue."

"That's only about a quarter mile from Wampler Street," Alice said. "Where the girl was run down."

"I guess that's right," Claudia agreed.

"What did they say when you got out of the car?"

"Dean was pleading with me to get back in the car. Billy told him to let me go. Then they started yelling at each other again. One of them got behind the wheel and the car drove off."

"Which direction?" Snow asked.

"East toward Billy's house."

"Who was driving?"

"I don't know. I didn't look back. I just kept on walking down Kallem."

"Did you notice anyone else around on the street?"

"No. But I wasn't paying attention. I just had my head down, walking as fast as I could."

"Why didn't you come forward before and talk to us about this—since you obviously have nothing to hide?" Alice said.

Claudia shrugged. "I don't want to get Dean implicated in this. He's a great guy. I love him."

CHAPTER 27

Dean Kale appeared to have aged ten years since Alice and Snow had last spoken with him three days earlier. They were seated on the sagging couch in his living room, with Kale in the ragged stuffed chair.

It was now 4:30 p.m. on this Sunday, April 1, and Kale had just returned home from the Boulder Nugget sports book. He wore tan cargo pants and a wrinkled burgundy shirt with the tails out and the sleeves rolled up. His face was pale and creased, with dark circles under his eyes. There was a tiny scab on his upper lip, where he had apparently taken a reckless swipe with his razor.

"Are you feeling alright?" Snow asked. "We could come back tomorrow."

Kale took in a breath and blew it out. "There's no guarantee tomorrow will be better," he said. "I'm just under a lot of stress, part of which you two seem to be causing. I heard you've been talking to people about me."

"Yes, we have," Snow admitted. "Standard procedure. Just part of our investigation. We work our way down a list of people of interest, eliminating them one at a time until we get to someone who appears to have motive, means, and opportunity."

"So, how's it looking for me right now?" Kale asked.

"Not so good," Snow said. "But I'm not referring to our investigation so much. It's the one centering on the death of your father. The sheriff's office has reopened the case, and it looks like your alibi has fallen apart."

Kale's eyes popped wide. "What are you talking about?"

"Your sister told everyone you were staying with her in Pahrump when your father was killed. But we spoke with Reverend Henry Brierschmidt yesterday. He told us—and the police, apparently—that he had originally lied for you, that he had actually been with you in Victorville smoking dope two hours before your father's murder. Now that he's a man of the cloth, he's interested in preaching the truth, and he can't change that strategy when he's away from the pulpit."

"Shit," Kale muttered. His eyes blinked three times, and he lowered his gaze to the floor in front of Snow's loafers. "That fucking hypocrite. Now I suppose the cops will be out here trying to pin my father's murder on me again because I was the closest relative still living with him." He looked at Snow. "That's what they do—right?"

Snow nodded. "Pretty much. They're just playing the percentages...so why did you lie?"

"If I hadn't, they'd have convicted me for my father's murder—and I didn't do it."

"What really happened?" Alice asked.

"I was dealing weed," Kale said. "I was just a stupid kid wanting to get high on a regular basis and make a little cash for myself in the process. My father got suspicious—probably from the vacant stare and silly grin on my face at the dinner table every night. He searched my room, found my stash, and threatened to turn it in to the police if I didn't join the Marines. That's the last thing I wanted to do. I'd have ended up dead or with a career as a cop after I got out. I'd have rather gone to jail."

"What did you do?" Snow said.

"Something stupid. I went to my distributor and told him about my father finding my stash and that he'd threatened to go to the cops. I suggested they scare him a little—thinking he'd turn the weed back over to them—and I'd be off the hook.

"Instead, I guess, they shot him. Because I got home and his body was still warm. He was lying in a pool of blood. It didn't even look like they searched for the dope at all. Nothing was stolen. Everything was just the way it had been before they got there. It looked like I had shot him.

"So I ransacked the place, busted out the kitchen window, took his wallet and cash and his two guns, got in my car, and drove to my sister's place. I told her what happened, and she said she'd vouch for me."

"What did you do with the guns?" Alice asked.

Kale ran his fingers over his chin. "I tossed them into a ditch as soon as I got out of town."

"Had your father's 9mm been fired?" Snow said.

"No," Kale said. "I checked both guns. They were fully loaded—didn't appear to have been touched."

"It would have been smarter to keep them," Snow said. "The gun that was used to kill your dad could be matched to the bullets. Since your father's 9mm hasn't turned up, it looks like that might have been the murder weapon."

Kale arched his brows and smiled. "In that case, maybe I didn't toss the 9mm in a ditch."

"You still have it?" Snow asked.

Kale shrugged, his face displaying an evil grin.

"What about the snub-nose .38?"

"That one I threw in a ditch," Kale said.

"Why one, but not the other?"

"I'm not crazy about guns," Kale said. "One gun might come in handy for protection. I was traveling light back in those days."

"It was a .38 that killed Billy Ryan," Alice put in.

Kale shrugged again, his smile gone. "I don't know anything about that."

"Do you know anything about Cassie Lane driving you and Billy home the night he was murdered?"

Kale stiffened. He took in a shallow breath and let it escape slowly. He said nothing in response.

"We saw the three of you drive by Beaver's Oasis on their surveillance video after leaving the Boulder Nugget the night Billy was shot with the .38. Cassie was driving."

Kale's jaw muscles tensed. He folded his hands tightly together in his lap and glared at them.

"Dean, what happened after the three of you drove past Beaver's Oasis?" Alice asked.

Kale narrowed his eyes and fixed them on Alice. "We'd been discussing stopping at Beaver's for hot dogs but decided against it. After passing Beaver's, a little farther up the road we made a U-turn and drove to my place. Cassie and I got out. Billy headed home—or maybe he stopped for hot dogs first, since he wanted them so desperately."

Snow shook his head. "Billy didn't stop at Beaver's that night. In fact, from what we saw of the video footage, his car never passed Beaver's in the southbound lanes again."

"Maybe he took another route," Kale said.

"There is no other route without backtracking," Snow insisted.

Kale spread his hands. "All I can tell you is what happened."

"How many versions would you like to give us?" Alice asked.

"What are you talking about?"

"Three days ago you told us it was just you and Billy and in his car. Now you admit that Cassie was driving."

"I forgot about her. I was drunk. She's a small detail."

"That's not how she feels about you," Alice said. "She's smitten with you."

Kale gave a single laugh. "Must be my boyish charm."

"I think the two of you mesh pretty well," Alice said. "That's the impression I get."

Kale chuckled uncomfortably. "I won't expound on that metaphor. But we do get along pretty well, most of the time."

"You both have a tendency to stray from the facts," Alice said.

"Why? What did she say?"

"She said the three of you were arguing in the car. She got upset and stopped the car near the intersection of Greenawalt and Kallem Avenue. Then got out and walked home. Is that true?"

Kale stared hard into Alice's face. "No. That isn't true. She's lying."

"Why would she lie about that?" Snow asked.

"I have no idea. You'll have to ask her."

"What really happened the night Billy Ryan was murdered?" Snow pressed.

"I just told you," Kale insisted.

"Did you kill Billy Ryan?" Snow asked.

Kale met Snow's gaze. His words came out even and without inflection: "No, I did not. I never killed my father. And

174

I didn't kill Billy. He was my best friend—I had no reason to want him dead."

"You'd been losing a lot of money that night. You were in a foul mood. Billy had been gloating about his winnings and goading you. You'd both been drinking heavily on empty stomachs. You must have gotten the urge to blow a couple of holes in him."

Kale's face twisted into a mask of silent rage. "You've worn out your welcome," he growled. "You two motherfuckers get the hell out of my house right now! I'm sick of this shit!"

Alice and Snow got up and headed toward the front door.

Out on the street behind the wheel of his Sonata, Snow said, "I think we blew it in there. He'll never talk to us again."

Alice pulled her seatbelt over her and clicked it into place. "I don't think we did anything wrong in there. He's just starting to come apart at the seams."

"The bad cop/bad cop strategy never works. It gets the subject hostile every time."

"Well, you had the chance to stick to your good cop routine like you used the first time we interviewed him. It would be inconsistent for me to switch from bad cop to good cop between interviews."

"I thought we had him on the run," Snow muttered.

"Apparently, you're no longer convinced of his innocence," Alice said.

"No. I think he experienced some sort of delirious frenzy and lost control when they got to Billy's residence. I wouldn't be surprised if he shot him with his late father's snub-nose .38.

Remember what Cassie told us about seeing him pulling it out of an ankle holster while he was getting undressed?"

"I was thinking about that too," Alice said. "Dean doesn't have a handgun legally registered. You think he might have been carrying his father's gun around with him all these years?"

"Sure, why not?" Snow said. "The 9mm was the weapon that killed his old man. I think he kept both guns. Maybe as souvenirs. Who knows what goes on in his twisted mind?"

CHAPTER 28

Gina Brown's brother Lance was in the middle lane on Sahara Avenue, heading for the start of his day at Drain & Lube, when he heard and felt the big bang.

He had eased on the brakes when the traffic light switched to yellow in front of him, and had just come to a complete stop at the red in his usual position, the front bumper two feet inside the crosswalk.

The sudden impact from behind slammed the back of his head into his headrest, and his truck lurched forward further into the crosswalk, his tires skidding on the asphalt.

"What the hell!" he exclaimed to the dashboard.

He fumbled free of the seatbelt and swung out of the cab of his Tacoma. As he stomped angrily to the back of his truck, he saw a tall, curvy, middle-aged woman with bleached blonde hair climbing out of the car behind him. Her car was an older model Ford Taurus, badly oxidized.

"What the hell were you doing?" he bellowed at her.

Wearing black stretch pants, three-inch heels, and a red, frilly blouse, the woman scampered to the front of her car, craning her neck to assess the damage.

177

"Oh, I'm so sorry!" she exclaimed. "I just turned my head for an instant and you were completely stopped in front of me."

The two of them stopped and peered down at the rear end of Lance Brown's pickup. That was when they noticed it lying on the pavement in the foot-wide space between the two crumpled bumpers.

It was a snub-nosed revolver with a blue-black finish and wooden grips.

Brown stared at it in amazement. "What the hell is that doing there?" he asked.

He walked over to it, picked it up, and turned it over in his hands, noticing the grind marks on the butt where the serial number should have been.

"What are you doing with that gun?" the woman shrieked.

Lance Brown turned his head and looked back at her wide eyes. Her hands were open and out near her shoulders, as though she were under arrest.

"It's not mine," Brown told her. "I don't know where the hell it came from."

"It fell off your truck," the woman said. With that she trotted back to her car and jumped inside, slamming and locking the door behind her.

Brown watched her punch some buttons on her cell phone and put it to her ear. A moment later she gasped into the phone: "I need to report an accident—and a man with a gun on Sahara Avenue and the intersection of..."—she looked up at the street sign—"the intersection of Burnham. Hurry! Please hurry! I hit a truck and the driver has a gun!"

"It's not my gun!" Brown protested. He looked down at it one last time, then opened the backdoor to his truck and set the revolver on the seat.

He slammed the door shut, shoved his hands in his pockets, and assessed the damage to his truck, muttering angrily under his breath.

In the lanes around him traffic crawled past, curious eyes scouring the scene, searching for any morsel of devastation to liven up their dreary commutes.

———

Three hours later Lance Brown stood at the door of the James & James Detective Agency demanding answers.

"I'm in deep shit," he told Snow after he'd opened the door. "Somebody is trying to set me up, and I think you're in on it."

"What are you talking about?"

"You know very well what I'm talking about!" Brown fired back. "That gun in my bumper. You probably put it there."

Snow stared at Brown, perplexed. "Why don't you come in, Lance," he said, "and we can talk about it."

Brown stepped inside, glaring at the cardboard cutout of Betty Boop as if she too had contributed to his dilemma. He followed Snow down the short corridor to Alice's office, where Snow pointed at one of the client chairs.

"Have a seat, Lance," Snow said.

"What's up?" Alice asked, leaning back in her chair.

"Lance has a gun in his bumper," Snow said, slouching into his swivel chair at the right end of Alice's desk. "He thinks we put it there."

"*In* his bumper? What are you talking about? What sort of gun?" She moved the laptop to the side and frowned at Brown.

"Stop playing ignorant," Brown said. "You know what sort of gun. You two put it there."

"Why would we do that?" Alice asked.

"Because you're working for that big-boobed, lesbian slot mechanic to help her cover up her murder of my brother-in-law."

"What makes you think Cassie Lane murdered your brother-in-law all of a sudden?" Snow asked, leaning forward.

"It couldn't be more obvious!" Brown insisted. "That dyke has been having weird, kinky sex with my sister."

"How do you know about that?" Snow asked with raised brows.

"I've heard them going at it in Gina's bedroom. I came home for lunch on Friday. Gina's bedroom door was shut. I could hear moaning and panting noises coming from inside there. At first I thought Gina was watching a video of some sort. So I got a glass, put it up to the wall in my bedroom, and listened through it. It was Gina and Cassie going at it, all right. Sounded like one of those old Jane Fonda exercise videos. I heard Gina calling her by name."

"Jane Fonda?" Snow asked.

"No. Cassie." Lance Brown shook his head in disgust. "What a hypocrite my sister is! She's never had anything but criticism for that woman—now suddenly they're like lovebirds in spring."

Snow nodded. "Well, these things happen, Lance. But it doesn't make either of them murderers."

"The hell it doesn't. Billy had a shitload of money sitting around the house. Now Gina has it. Gina and Cassie."

"Why would Cassie get any of it?" Alice asked.

"Well, you know," Brown said, "when you have the fire of lust burning, after a few months the only fuel that will feed it is money."

Snow and Alice stared at him a moment, then glanced at each other before facing him again. Snow wondered if he'd gotten that line from a country western song.

"You think Cassie and Gina murdered Billy?" Snow suggested.

"I think Cassie shot him," Brown said. "But I'm sure Gina was in on it. And now you've all screwed me by planting that gun in the bumper of my truck."

Snow put his hands up in front of him. "Look, Lance. This gun in your bumper is news to us. Believe me. Alice and I always work within the law. We're not about to risk losing our business and going to prison for a little extra money. We're not that stupid."

Brown stared at Snow, his teeth clenched, his face reddening. He nodded. "Alright. I'll have to trust you."

"Good. You trust us and we'll trust you. We've never had any reason to doubt anything you've told us so far, and we don't expect that to change. Now, what kind of a gun was it?"

"A revolver," Brown said. "Smith & Wesson .38 with a two-inch barrel. Blue steel, wooden grips."

Snow's eyes widened. "You say it was 'in' your bumper? How, exactly?"

"It was duct-taped into the rear bumper of my truck. Anybody could have done it. My truck is always parked in the driveway when I'm home."

"How did you manage to discover it?" Alice asked.

"It fell on the pavement when some woman rear-ended me on Sahara Avenue. She was driving an old junker. I'm sure she did it on purpose so the gun would fall out right there in plain sight. Then she right away called 911 and told them I was holding a gun."

"But you weren't holding a gun," Alice clarified.

Brown arched his brows and let his mouth hang open. "Actually I *was* holding the gun when she called 911."

Alice stared at him in disbelief. "I thought you said the gun fell onto the pavement."

"I picked it up," Brown admitted.

"Why did you do that?"

Brown shrugged. "I wanted to look at it." He pressed his lips together and nodded at Alice. "It wasn't until after I picked it up that I realized that was a bad idea."

"So, what did you do with the gun then?"

"I put it in the backseat of my truck," Brown said.

"What happened after that?" Snow asked.

"The cops came. A shitload of 'em. The woman that hit me jumped out of her car and told them about the gun, first off. One of the cops asked where the gun was, so I got it out of the backseat for him—almost got shot in the process.

"First thing he noticed was the ground off serial number on the butt. I told him it wasn't my gun, but he didn't believe me. The woman pointed to where the gun had lain on the pavement. One of the cops got down and crawled under the bumper. He said there was a strip of duct tape stuck to the bumper where the gun had been hidden.

"So they cuffed me and put me in the back of one of the cruisers. I was there for nearly an hour. A wrecker came and towed my truck away to the police impound lot as evidence. They let me go.

"So I called Gina to come and pick me up. I told her what happened. Right off, she's wanting to know if I put the gun there. My own sister, building a case against me right off. The bitch.

"Fifteen minutes after I got home, two homicide detectives showed up and started asking me questions about the gun. I told them I don't know anything about it. But they thought I was lying. Because it's the same caliber as the murder weapon that shot Billy. Now, I didn't like Billy. I won't lie about that. But I didn't shoot him."

"I believe you," Snow said. "What does your brother, Damon, say about all of this?"

"He knows about Gina and Cassie and their demented attraction. We've talked about it. We're on the same page. We're already looking for another place to live. I called him right away this morning and told him what happened with the gun. He's thinking the same way I am—that Cassie and Gina conspired to put it there.

"I apologize for accusing you two of being involved. But you can see how I jumped to that conclusion."

Alice nodded. "I can also see how you jumped to the conclusion that Cassie and your sister had anything to do with it, but I think that later on you'll find that you were wrong about that too."

"How will I find that out if I'm arrested and serving time for murder?"

"That won't happen," Snow said. "This incident with the gun in the bumper sounds staged. Those detectives have realized that, I'm sure. They'll be investigating this woman who rear-ended you. It sounds like someone is getting desperate. When criminals get desperate, they make stupid mistakes."

"What kind of mistakes?" Brown asked.

"Grinding off the serial number on a gun," Snow replied. "There is a procedure the lab uses to bring back the number that was stamped into that handgun. Most of the time it's successful. At the same time they'll check the rifling to see if the bullets used to kill Billy Ryan match that gun. It'll take a few days, but they'll do it." Snow leaned back in his chair and sighed. "You don't have anything to worry about, Lance." Snow looked at Alice.

"That's right," Alice said. "It's doubtful that Gina had anything to do with this—nor Cassie. But we have a good idea who did."

"Did you manage to get the contact information from the driver who hit you?" Snow asked.

"Yes, I did," Brown said. "I got her name, address, phone number, plus her driver's license number and the plate number on her car. The cops were standing right there, so she had no choice."

"Great," Snow said. "If you wouldn't mind giving that to us, we'll dig into this mess and see if we can't get to the bottom of it."

"That's good to hear. Am I going to have to pay you anything?"

Snow shook his head. "No. We're already compensated."

They all stood up. Brown handed Snow a folded slip of paper with the information from the accident. Snow scribbled it into his notebook and handed it back.

Hands were shaken all around. Then Snow escorted Lance Brown to the front door of the office and instructed him not to worry.

Back in Alice's office, Snow plopped down in his swivel chair and leaned back.

"Dammit, we should have put a tail on Kale," he said. "We'd have probable cause by now."

"Hindsight is always perfect," Alice said. "Give me that information, and I'll run a quick check on the woman, her car, and her background."

Snow leaned forward and slid his tiny notebook like a hockey puck across the surface of the desk toward Alice. She opened it up and looked at it. "You want to set up a meeting with the investigating officers from Homicide, Jim?"

Snow leaned back again. "No sense in that," he said. "Marcia Stevens is the lead detective, right?"

Alice nodded.

"I was partnered with her for the worst part of a year. She has no sense of logic."

"I agree," Alice said. "Lieutenant Bradley wanted to team me up with her after Mel Harris complained to him about me."

"I thought you were the one who complained about him?"

"It went both ways. Anyway, when the section chief suggested Marcia Stevens, I almost quit on the spot."

"Instead of waiting a few months," Snow added.

"Right."

"Okay, so now what?" Alice said.

"Well, we could sit around and wait for the results to come back from the lab on that gun. With that evidence, even a dipshit like Marcia Stevens should know how to move on it."

"Lesser miracles have happened."

"But since we're getting paid, we might as well forge ahead. Put the pressure on this woman and get her to cooperate and stay out of jail. She could even keep the money Kale paid her to stage the accident."

"I agree," Alice said.

"How long will it take you to look up everything?"

"Not long if you help," Alice said. "It's after eleven. We could try to set up an interview with this woman for one thirty."

"If she answers her phone. So ... where do you want to eat?"

"You really want me to pick?"

"Sure."

"Which buffets would you like me to choose from?"

"We don't need to eat at a buffet," Snow insisted.

"I know we don't," Alice said. "But I'm not in the mood to watch you stare at a menu like it's a script from a horror movie. We can eat at the Boulder Nugget buffet. And I'll buy lunch."

"That's a first. This is fantastic, Alice," Snow said. "And it's not even my birthday."

CHAPTER 29

"What have you got?" Snow asked, walking into Alice's office. He sat down in one of the client chairs and stretched out, lacing his fingers behind his head.

"Joyce Phillips," Alice said, reading from her notebook. "She's forty-five. Impressive background. MBA from UCLA. Worked for fourteen years in marketing, five of that as the marketing manager for a company in Compton, California, that makes auto accessories. She was laid off a little over three years ago when the company folded. And she hasn't held an honest job since."

"What's she been doing?"

"She's been arrested eight times for solicitation in Las Vegas in the last two years."

"Good to know she's putting those marketing skills to work," Snow said.

"Eight times isn't bad," Alice said. "That's about average."

"Has she done any jail time?"

"Not yet. A couple more arrests ought to do it."

"Right."

Alice leaned back and looked at Snow. "Did you have any luck?"

"It's been so long since I've had any of that," Snow said, "I'm not sure I'd know how to recognize it."

"Did Joyce Phillips answer her cell phone?"

"Yes, she did," Snow said. "But she promptly hung up on me after I told her who I was and what I wanted to ask her about."

"Maybe I should try."

"Good idea. Tell her she won something, and we need to make arrangements to deliver it to her."

"What would that be?"

"A case of beer," Snow said. "With any luck she'll let us help her drink it."

Alice smirked. "I'm sure that'll work."

"Actually it has, more times than you can imagine," Snow said. "But only with the middle to lower echelon of society or the unemployed." He brought his hands out from behind his head and leaned forward. "If you can't get Joyce Phillips to talk to you, I've got an idea. Turns out she'd only owned that car less than twenty-four hours before the accident."

"That's interesting," Alice said. "And were you able to talk to the seller?"

"Yes," Snow replied. "She said she'd had it advertised for over a week, and Joyce Phillips was the first prospect to contact her about the car. Joyce called her around nine thirty last night. She said the only thing Joyce seemed to care about was whether the car ran. She wanted to come right over and look at it.

"She got there fifteen minutes later. She started it up and drove it less than a mile down the street and back. She didn't even take it on a freeway. Never drove it over thirty-five miles an hour. Joyce gave her the nine hundred cash, and they filled out the title and notice of transfer. And that was it."

"Did Joyce Phillips have someone with her when she bought the car?"

"Yes, a black woman about the same age as Joyce. She was wearing a red miniskirt with black heels, so the other woman was probably one of her peers dressed for work. Joyce drove the Taurus home, and her friend drove her car—which apparently wasn't in much better shape than the Ford Taurus. Joyce told the seller she needed another car to use when hers was in the shop."

"Amazing that a car that's drivable can be bought for nine hundred dollars these days," Alice said.

"Yeah, they're popular for demolition derbies—or for ramming someone with a gun taped to his bumper on Sahara Avenue."

CHAPTER 30

At 7:30 p.m. Joyce Phillips emerged from her small, single-story home in a rundown area of east Las Vegas. She wore a pink miniskirt, matching heels, and a black leather jacket. For a woman in her mid-forties, Snow noticed her legs were still an attractive selling point, probably, he assumed, from all the walking and standing she did every night.

She got behind the wheel of an old Chevy sedan sitting in her crumbling driveway and backed it into the street.

Snow started up his Sonata and, with Alice riding shot-gun, followed Joyce Phillips to an area of Fremont Street surrounded by cut-rate motels where wandering tourists could treat themselves to a different sort of Fremont Street experience.

They watched the woman's car turn into the parking lot in front of a large abandoned building; then they drove past it, turned right at the next intersection, and parked on the street.

Snow cut the engine.

"Do you think it's safe to leave the car here?" Alice asked, glancing around at the empty lots. "There's nothing here. We're the only car parked on this block."

"I didn't want to be too obvious and follow her into that lot. Where would you suggest we park?"

"In the parking lot. She won't notice. And even if she does, what difference does it make? After we approach her and start asking questions, she'll know we followed her."

Snow started the car, made a U-turn, then a left, and pulled into the lot. There were a number of empty spaces near the entrance and Snow turned into one, parking next to a late model subcompact.

"Do you see her?" Snow asked, checking his mirrors.

Alice sat facing Snow, gazing through the back window. "She's down at the end of the lot. She's still in her car, putting on makeup."

"I thought women did that while they were en route to their destinations. Multitasking."

"It's safety first for Joyce," Alice said.

Snow nodded. "Probably makes all of her johns wear a condom."

"She looks pretty healthy for her age. She doesn't look like she's into drugs at all."

"Probably because she got a late start on this second career of hers," Snow suggested.

"Smart of Dean Kale to pick one who's lucid and dependable looking."

"She's not bad looking for her age," Snow said. "I didn't see any tattoos or piercings. I wonder how much she charges?"

"Probably less than you might think … here she comes," Alice said. "You want to talk to her here in the lot?"

"I don't want to startle her. She might run back to her car. Let's let her get out to the street. She might be more willing to talk if she's afraid of arrest for soliciting."

Alice turned to the front, pulled a paperback out of her purse, and pretended to be reading it.

Snow picked a map out of the slot in his door and unfolded it. He laid it over his steering wheel, pretending to be studying it.

He heard the clicking of the woman's heels approaching, watched her pass behind his car in the rearview mirror. Without giving them a look, she turned toward the sidewalk. She headed west along it, in the direction of downtown, striding with purpose, her gaze wandering along both sides of the street.

"Let's go," Snow said, folding up the map.

He shoved it back into the map holder in the door and climbed out of the car. Alice draped her purse over her shoulder and joined him at the back of the car.

They hurried out of the lot in the direction the woman had gone. They spotted her a block away, standing next to a covered bus stop shelter, with her hands clasped together in front of her.

She gave Alice and Snow a furtive glance as they drew near, then directed her view down the street as though she were watching for an approaching bus. Inside the shelter, sitting on the bench, two men and two women of various ages sat engrossed in their electronic devices.

Turning her head away from Snow as he stopped beside her, she sauntered around the back of the shelter to the other side with Snow and Alice following.

She stopped and folded her arms, staring across the street at nothing.

"How's business?" Snow asked. "Looks like you're the first to arrive on this block. You're quite an eager beaver. You must enjoy your work."

"What is it you need?" Joyce Phillips snapped, a scowl covering her face. It made her appear ten years older.

"Some answers," Snow replied.

"I don't give those."

"It might be worth your while to make an exception," Snow said.

Without turning her head, she said, "You're cops?"

"Private investigators," Snow said. "I'm Jim Snow." Tipping his head toward Alice, he said, "And this is my associate, Alice James."

The woman said nothing.

"We can just follow you around all night if you'd prefer that," Snow said. "I doubt it would be good for business, though."

"We're not investigating you or the accident you were involved in," Alice interjected. "We're investigating a murder. And you should be aware, if you knowingly help the perpetrator to hinder law enforcement from building a case for a murder charge against him, you *will* find yourself behind bars for acting as an accessory after the fact. But if you're an unwitting accomplice who decides to become helpful after the fact, that's different."

"I don't know what you're talking about."

"In layman's terms," Snow said, "you're in deep shit." He reached into his back pocket, pulled out a folded sheet of paper. He opened it and showed it to Joyce. It was a DMV photograph of Dean Kale. "Do you know this guy?"

She stared down at the photo, then gave Snow a perplexed look. "I've never seen that man before in my life."

"He didn't hire you to ram into Lance Brown's truck on Sahara Avenue this morning?"

"Definitely not."

"Who did?" Snow asked.

"Nobody."

By now the four occupants of the bus stop shelter were looking up at the prostitute, apparently having found the spirited exchange taking place next to them more interesting than their smartphones.

Joyce looked at them.

Alice reached out and touched the side of Joyce's arm with her fingertips. "Why don't we go talk in our car?" she said. "We won't take up much more of your time, and we won't go to the police with anything you tell us."

"Unless you killed a man with that gun that was hidden in the bumper of Lance Brown's pickup," Snow said. "Is that what happened? You shoot somebody with that gun? If you did, the crime lab will find your DNA all over it. People think all they have to do is wipe it off and the DNA disappears, but it's not that simple. It can hide in the cracks and crevices."

"I didn't kill anybody," Joyce said. "I don't know anything about that gun. That was the first time I saw it, after I rear-ended that truck and saw it lying on the road. The guy picked it up, so I called the police. Anybody else would have done the same."

"You would have called the police even if he didn't pick it up," Snow insisted. "Isn't that true? Wasn't that the plan?"

No response.

One of the waiting passengers inside the shelter turned his head to the left and stood up. The other three passengers did the same. Joyce turned her head in the direction of a double-deck bus easing to a stop near the shelter. She stepped away from it and began walking with Snow on one side and Alice on the other.

"Joyce," Alice said, "we know what you've been through. Believe me, the last thing we want is to make your life more difficult than it already is. But there is something you need to know."

"About what?"

"That gun you saw lying on the pavement," Alice said. "In two or three days, a couple of homicide detectives will come knocking on your door. And they won't be as amiable or accommodating as we are. They won't be willing to waste time following you around, hoping for an opportunity to talk to you. They'll take you down to Homicide and put you in a room. You could be in there all day—unless they get the answers they want—and at that point they probably won't believe them."

"Why don't we go talk in my car?" Snow said.

Joyce stopped walking and looked down at the sidewalk. She pressed her lips together, her eyes misting over; then she turned and began walking back to the parking lot.

At Snow's Hyundai he opened the passenger door for her. She slid onto the seat. Snow jogged around to the driver's side and got in. Alice climbed into the backseat behind him.

Snow spoke first. "The person who paid you to ram Lance Brown's pickup probably doesn't realize the gun that was confiscated by the police is traceable to the registered owner, but it is," he said. "The serial number was ground off, but the crime lab won't have any trouble getting it to show up. You see, when a gun is stamped with the serial number, the metal under the indentations for the numbers goes through a structural change and the lab people have a number of techniques they can use to reveal the number. While they're at it, they can match the gun to the bullets recovered from the victim."

Joyce sighed. "I don't know anything about that gun or what it was doing there. I just happened to look away for a moment and plowed into that truck."

"Did you step on the brakes at all?" Snow asked.

"I didn't have time to react. I just turned my head back to the front, and there was the rear of the truck right in front of me."

"The police say the damage to both vehicles indicates you were traveling at less than ten miles per hour at the moment of impact," Snow said. "Do you always drive that slowly?"

"I don't have any idea how fast I was going. I didn't look at the speedometer."

"What were you looking at when you looked away from the road?" Alice said.

She shrugged. "I don't know. I just happened to look out my side window."

"You don't remember what you saw?"

"Not really, no. I guess I was just looking at the scenery."

"Is there a lot of good scenery to look at on Sahara Avenue over by Burnham?" Snow inquired.

She smiled. "I don't know."

"You don't remember what you saw when you looked out your side window?"

She narrowed her eyes and shook her head.

"A car dealership," Snow said. "That's what you would have seen if you looked out your side window just before you rammed into that truck at the corner of Sahara and Burnham. It seems to me you would have remembered that."

"I guess I'm a little bit absentminded at times," she confessed.

"Where were you headed at the time of the accident?" Alice asked.

Joyce thought about that. "The Strip," she said. "To do a little gambling."

"Where on the Strip?"

She thought some more. "The Sahara."

"You go there often?" Snow asked.

"Oh, sure," she said. "I love it there. It has a lot of history."

"History is the right word. Have you been there recently?"

"Sure."

"Well, you must have broken in," Snow said, "because they closed the place down almost a year ago."

Joyce Phillips raised her eyebrows, smiling. "Oh, that's right. I'm thinking of the Stratosphere. I always get that one mixed up with the Sahara. That one's not closed, is it?"

"No, it isn't."

"Joyce," Alice said, "how long had you been looking for a used car to buy?"

She turned to Alice. "Off and on for a while."

"Why did you suddenly call about that cheap old clunker so late in the evening?"

"I just happened to run across it in the listing, and it sounded like what I was looking for."

"And what were you looking for?"

"Something cheap."

"Why did you feel the need to rush over to the seller's home and look at it so late at night?"

"It wasn't late by my standards."

"I guess not," Alice conceded. "And you just happened to wreck it the morning after you bought it."

"Yeah," Joyce Phillips said. "Good thing I didn't make it to the casino, with that kind of luck." She grinned.

CHAPTER 31

They stood at the front door of Dean Kale's home, Snow holding a twelve-pack of Heineken in each hand, Alice holding her purse.

The door opened to reveal Kale, wearing a black T-shirt and baggy tan shorts. Though he was clean-shaven and less rumpled than the previous day, he appeared more haggard than ever. His eyes were so bloodshot, it made Snow wince to look at them.

"You two don't ever give up," Kale muttered.

"We can't stay long," Snow said, raising the cardboard containers at his sides. "But I brought some luggage—along with an apology. We would have called first, but I'm sure you would have told us to get lost. So we thought a surprise visit would be better—unless you're busy."

Kale lowered his gaze to the beer and shook his head grimly. He sighed. "No, I wasn't doing anything. Just staring at the living room wall, trying to figure out my limited options. All right. Come on in."

Alice and Snow stepped inside. Kale took the two containers of beer from Snow. "I'll put these in the refrigerator," he said. "Make yourselves comfortable."

He headed toward the kitchen with the beer. Over his shoulder he asked, "Anybody want a glass?"

"None for me, thanks," Snow said. "I was never able to wean myself off the bottle."

"I'm fine with the bottle," Alice chimed in. "Don't trouble yourself."

They went into the living room and sank down onto the sofa, glancing around the room.

Leaning up against a corner near the front door Snow spotted a Winchester lever-action rifle. He noticed Alice also staring at it.

Kale walked into the room a moment later, holding three open bottles of beer. He handed two of them off and sat down with the third one, across from Alice and Snow.

"I suppose I should apologize also," he said, wedging the beer bottle between his legs. "It doesn't pay to shoot the messenger, but I've been having a tough time of it with everything. I'm sure you understand."

"Certainly," Snow said, resting his beer bottle on his thigh. "Speaking of shooting the messenger, I noticed you have an addition to your domestic arsenal over by the front door. Are you expecting an Indian attack?"

Kale glanced at the rifle. "You never know. You always get struck down by what you weren't expecting. The older I get, the more I expect—and not good things either." He took a slug of his beer and shoved it back down between his legs. "Actually, I was out shopping, since there's not much going on today at many of the tracks. I ran across that rifle in a gun store. It reminds me of all of the old cowboy movies I used to watch, so I brought it home and put it over there where I can look at it now and then. It's like a piece of western art, but it also provides a feeling of security."

Snow took a sip of beer and nodded. "Nice-looking rifle. But wasn't it mostly the women in those old westerns who used those rifles? The men were partial to handguns. What happened to your 9mm?"

"I don't know," Kale said. "I can't seem to find it."

"You could have bought another one."

"I didn't feel like waiting three days for the background check to clear. Besides, the rifle is more accurate at longer distances."

"Like if someone is coming at you with a 9mm handgun," Snow suggested. "Speaking of which, you never registered your father's 9mm, I take it."

Kale shook his head. "I know I should have. I didn't want to bother."

"If you had, you wouldn't have to wait the three days for a new purchase," Alice said. "When you register a handgun in Clark County for the first time, you get a blue card. For any handguns you purchase after that, you just present that card and you don't have to wait."

"I'll keep that in mind," Kale said.

"What happened to your snub-nose .38?" Snow blurted. "Did you lose that too?"

"If you're referring to my father's .38," Kale said, "I told you before: I tossed that in a ditch."

"That's right." Snow grinned. "I forgot." He took another sip of beer. "You know, a funny thing happened this morning on Sahara Avenue. Gina Ryan's brother Lance was rear-ended by an off-duty hooker, and a snub-nose .38 with wooden grips—just like your father's—fell out of his bumper onto the pavement. It's also a Model 36, just like your father's gun. Isn't that a strange coincidence?"

Kale's mouth had fallen open. "What?"

"Yeah," Snow said. "Hard to believe, isn't it? Makes me wonder if somebody found your dad's .38 in that ditch outside Victorville, brought it to Las Vegas, and used it to shoot your buddy Billy Ryan."

Kale swallowed and wet his lips, staring at Snow. "You're full of all kinds of good news," he said. "Every time you come here, you've got something crazy to report."

"I just wonder," Snow pondered aloud, "was the serial number on your father's .38 ground off when he owned it?"

"I don't know. I didn't notice any grind marks. Where would they be?"

"On the bottom of the butt."

"I didn't look at the butt."

Snow nodded. Referring to Claudia, he said, "I guess you're not a butt man. You're more of a boob man. Right?"

"What happened to the gun?" Kale said, ignoring Snow's insinuation.

"The crime lab has it. They're running a ballistics check to see if it matches up with the bullets used to kill Billy Ryan."

"But that won't do them much good without any fingerprints or a serial number. Right?"

"There's always DNA," Alice put in. Without drinking any of it, she set her beer on the coffee table. "And the serial number can easily be restored using magnets and various chemicals."

Kale's eyes popped wide. "Fuck," he said.

"So, the bad news is this," Snow said. "If that's your father's .38, and it has your DNA on it—you're in big trouble. You can wipe all the prints off a gun. But unless you tossed it in the wash with your other dirty laundry, that stuff can hide in cracks and other hard-to-reach surfaces, just waiting for those lab techs. But they really don't need that. The serial number will be enough, along with everything else, to establish probable cause."

Kale stared down at his beer, his eyebrows drawn together. "What was that gun doing in Lance Brown's bumper?"

"That's what we're trying to find out," Snow said. "Of course, it's possible Lance put it there and he's lying about it. It's actually a pretty clever place to hide a gun as long as it's strapped in securely. But it wasn't." Snow stared hard into Kale's face. "You didn't put it there, did you, Dean?"

Kale looked up from his beer to Snow. "You say it was inside his bumper?"

Snow nodded. "His rear bumper."

"What was holding it there?"

"A single strip of duct tape," Snow said. "Just enough to let go with a good jolt from a rear-end collision."

Kale looked back down at his beer. He shook his head and blew out a breath.

"Man, that is really, *really* fucking stupid."

His head came up then. He turned it toward the rifle in the corner near the front door and stared at it.

"Dean," Snow said. "It may not sound like it, but we're here to help you. If there's anything we can do for you … if there's anything you want to tell us … just let us know. Okay?"

Kale said nothing, just continued to stare at the rifle.

CHAPTER 32

It was a few minutes past ten p.m., Monday night. Coffee at Denny's on Boulder Highway.

Snow was returning from the men's room to find Cassie Lane sitting across the table from Alice. There were dark circles under her eyes, and her hair was disheveled as though she'd been riding in a convertible with the top down and hadn't bothered to brush it.

Snow pulled his chair out from the table and sat down. He took a sip of coffee.

Cassie turned her head to him and forced a tense smile.

"How are you coping, Cassie?" Snow asked.

"I'm okay."

The waitress came with an extra cup of coffee and set it in front of Cassie. "Anything else?" she asked.

"You want some pie?" Snow asked.

Cassie shook her head. "No, thanks. I'm not hungry. Coffee is fine."

Snow glanced at Alice with raised eyebrows. She shook her head.

"I guess we're good," Snow said to the waitress, and she walked back behind the counter.

"Cassie," Alice said, "have you been getting enough sleep?"

Cassie shrugged. "I don't know. When I'm conscious of it, I go to bed at eleven, but I usually can't fall asleep until one or two in the morning. And then I wake up around six or seven and can't get back to sleep. But I can't always be sure of what time I went to sleep, because Claudia is out and she makes that decision. And— this must sound funny, but I'm just grateful when I wake up in my own bed."

"Since you're not working right now, what about taking a nap during the day?"

"I've tried that," Cassie said. "I can't get to sleep."

"Whose bed have you slept in lately," Snow asked, "if not yours?"

Cassie hesitated. She stared into her coffee cup. "This is embarrassing."

"You don't have to share that information," Snow said. "But it might be helpful if you did."

To her coffee cup, her voice barely audible, she said, "Sunday morning I woke up next to Gina Ryan. We were in her bed and neither of us had any clothes on, so I can only guess how I got there or what happened. I only remember driving away from your house, and then I blacked out."

"Was that the first indication that something was going on between Gina and Claudia?" Alice asked.

Cassie looked up at Alice and shook her head. "I have some vague recollections, bits and pieces of her interactions with Gina that made me realize what was going on. I've known for quite some time that Claudia is interested in women as well as men. I told Dr. Rodgers about that and she seemed very interested in it, and we talked about it quite a bit …"

Thinking about this, Snow took another sip of coffee. It seemed odd that Dr. Rodgers would dwell so much on this one aspect of Claudia's personality. He tried to remember any phrases or body language that might have revealed Dr. Rodgers's leanings toward lesbianism—not that this information would help with the investigation in any way. Snow was always curious about the unusual behavior of desirable professional women.

"Anyway," Cassie continued, "the reason I called you and wanted to meet with you again was to tell you that I'm starting to remember more."

"Well that's good news," Alice said. She drank some of her coffee and set the cup back on the table. "Are these recollections from the distant past or something more recent?"

"Both," Cassie replied. "I'm beginning to get flash-backs to when I was seven or eight, I think. They're quite disturbing—and depressing. I've had them before, but always pushed them quickly out of my mind. I'm trying to force myself to be more audacious in dealing with everything, but that's easier said than done. I'm just not a very strong person emotionally."

"It sounds like you're making tremendous progress," Alice said. "You mentioned earlier that you remember seeing Dean Kale with an ankle holster and a snub-nose revolver. You said you thought he was getting undressed at the time?"

"Yes, but it's really vague. These memories that materialize in my head are like fragments of a dream."

"Do you remember anything else that might have to do with Billy Ryan's death?"

"Yes, and that's the main reason I called you. I have an image of that same revolver appearing suddenly in front of me, pointed away from me, and firing twice, and kicking back with each discharge."

"Who was holding it?" Snow asked.

"I don't know," Cassie said. "That's not clear. I don't remember a hand holding the gun—just the gun itself. I don't even remember seeing what was being shot at. I can't visualize that. But it was fairly dark."

"What color was the gun? Was it silver?"

"No," Cassie said. "It was dark blue, almost black."

"Is it possible Dean Kale was holding the gun?"

"I don't know who was holding it. I don't even know who else was present at the time, or even if there *was* anyone else there."

"Is there anything else you remember?" Alice asked.

"Yes. I get this feeling of being in a car that's accelerating with the engine revving. I can feel my back pressed into the seat from it. And I see a man's face. It's a round face, fairly young, with black hair and a mustache. And he's wearing a red ball cap with black letters across the front of it. Four letters; I think it says 'UNLV.' And his eyes are big and wide, like he's terrified of something."

"Was it anyone familiar to you?" Snow asked.

"No," Cassie said. "It's a face I never saw before—possibly Hispanic, but I'm not sure of that."

"Where was he?"

"I don't know. I only remember seeing his face and how terrified he seemed to be … but, no … terrified isn't the right word. Shocked … he looked like he couldn't believe what he was seeing."

"Would you recognize him if you saw him again?" Alice asked.

"I think so."

"Do you think he might have witnessed the shooting?"

"I don't know."

"Maybe we can get a sketch artist to draw up a facial composite," Snow suggested.

"What'll we do with that?" Alice asked.

Snow shrugged. "Go around knocking on doors again. Show it to people. Ask if the guy looks familiar."

"I don't know," Cassie said. "I don't remember his face clearly enough to get the details accurate. I just remember him having a round face with the black hair, mustache, and red ball cap. That's all I can tell you."

"What did his nose look like?" Alice asked. "Big or small, rounded or pointed?"

"Average size," she replied. "I guess it was rounded."

"Lips? Full or thin?"

"I don't know. Average I suppose. I think his mustache was bushy enough to cover most of his mouth."

Alice finished scribbling in her notebook. "Well, that's a start at least," she said. "Is there anything else you remember that might help?"

Cassie didn't respond. She was staring into her coffee cup with a detached look, her head wavering slightly.

Alice reached out and put her hand on Cassie's forearm. "Are you alright, Cassie?"

She blinked slowly then lowered her head until her forehead was resting on her outstretched fingertips. She moaned softly.

"Cassie?" Snow said. He stood up and hurried around the table, sitting down next to Cassie. He cocked an eyebrow at Alice. "What do I do?"

"Catch her if she falls forward," Alice said.

Snow put his hand on her upper arm.

Cassie's eyes were shut tightly now. She sat still for over a minute.

Finally her head moved slowly up off her fingertips. She leaned back in her chair, grinning across the table at Alice.

"Are you feeling okay, Cassie?" Alice said.

"I'm fine," she said, quietly.

Abruptly her right fist swung upward from out of her lap and slammed into the corner of her right eye.

And then the left.

And again with both fists.

Her smile faded. She gasped and winced in pain.

Snow quickly leaned into her, wrapping his arms around her, holding her arms pinned against her sides. She squirmed violently, turned her head, and bit Snow's nose.

Snow yelped and jabbed his elbow into her midsection. Her mouth opened for an instant. He jerked his head back, sprang up out of his chair, gripped her wrists, and wrenched them behind her.

Grabbing a set of handcuffs from her purse, Alice hustled around the end of the table and snapped them on Cassie's wrists behind her back.

"Let me go!" Cassie gasped.

"We're not going to just sit by and watch you beat the shit out of yourself," Snow muttered.

He opened his wallet and removed a ten and dropped it on the table. Alice picked up Cassie's purse from the chair next to the one she'd been sitting in.

Amid inquisitive stares from two waitresses, a cook, and a score of patrons, Alice and Snow guided their client out through the front door of the restaurant and into the parking lot.

Crossing to Snow's Sonata, they helped her into the backseat. Alice walked around to the other side of the car and slid in beside her. Snow got behind the wheel and turned halfway around in his seat.

"Have you been drinking at all tonight, Claudia?" Snow asked.

"No! And if I want to beat myself up, that's my business."

"What's the sense in that?" Snow said.

"That's just a message from me to her," Claudia panted, "to let her know she better keep her mouth shut. The next time she looks at her face in the mirror, she'll know she fucked up again."

In the faint glow from the overhead lights Snow could see the sides of her face were reddening. Swelling had already begun.

"It's your face too," Alice said. "You're hurting yourself."

"No pain, no gain," Claudia hissed. "I warned her. The bitch wouldn't follow my advice. I guess she thought I was bluffing. If you want to help Cassie, just terminate this investigation right now, and refund her whatever she has coming. Or keep it. I don't give a shit."

"What difference does it make to you?" Snow asked.

"That's none of your business!" Claudia snapped. "I didn't hire you—Cassie did. Look, Cassie's gone. I already came in of my free will and gave you a statement. I have nothing more to say to you. Now, let me go!"

"We will," Alice said. "As soon as you calm down to the point where you won't be a danger to yourself, I'll take the handcuffs off."

"I don't need to calm down," Claudia said. "I'm not angry. I just did what I had to do. It's over. Now let me go."

"I think we better call Dr. Rodgers," Snow suggested. "Let's get her involved in this."

"I agree," Alice concurred.

"Don't call that bitch!" Claudia screeched. "You do and I'll dive over that seat and bite your fucking nose clean off from your face—handcuffs and all!"

"This situation is out of control." Snow shook his head and leaned to the side, digging into his front pocket for his phone.

"Alright, alright, alright," Claudia chanted. "I'll cooperate. What do you want me to do?"

Snow turned his eyes to Alice. "What do you think, Alice?"

"I don't know," Alice said. "If we call her doctor, she'll probably just talk to her on the phone to calm her down, but I don't think that will work."

"It won't," Claudia insisted. "I'm already calm. I promise I won't hit myself again."

"Dr. Rodgers might want to have her committed," Snow said. "That might be best course of action at this point. She seems to be getting worse."

"It's not best," Claudia murmured, leaning toward Snow. "Look, I've never been institutionalized. Why start now?"

"Do you mind if I look through your purse?" Alice asked.

"Sure, there's nothing in there," Claudia insisted. "Unless you're interested in a stick of gum—help yourself."

Alice unsnapped Cassie's purse and dug through it. Satisfied there were no weapons, she clasped it shut and set it on the seat next to Claudia. She got her key out of her own purse and unlocked the handcuffs, then dropped them into her purse.

"You can go," Alice said.

Claudia brought her hands back out from behind her, leaned into Alice, and gave her a kiss on the cheek. "Thank you."

"You're welcome."

Claudia opened the backdoor and swung her legs out. She shut the door and began to walk back to her car.

"Be good to yourself," Snow called after her. "And stay in touch."

Claudia turned and winked at him. "We'll be in touch. Don't worry about that."

She turned back around and kept walking.

CHAPTER 33

Jim Snow's sister Karen had a friend who worked with a woman whose daughter was a talented art student at University of Nevada–Las Vegas. The James & James Detective Agency outsourced all of their sketch composite needs to her for a paltry fee.

The following morning they stopped by her home in Summerlin and provided the young lady with the description Cassie had given them of the man with the red ball cap.

With photocopies of the drawing in hand, Alice and Snow went door to door, canvassing the neighborhood of Billy and Gina Ryan, asking if the man in the sketch looked familiar. A few of the residents recognized the ball cap, having seen it around town on the heads of Running Rebel fans.

Snow was between houses when his cell phone chirped.

The caller identified herself as Metro Homicide Detective Marcia Stevens.

"Well, I haven't talked to you in quite a while," Snow said, by way of greeting.

"I can't imagine why not," Detective Stevens said. "We got along so well while we were partners."

"We did have our disagreements," Snow allowed, "but I only remember the good times, which is probably why I draw a blank whenever your name comes up in conversations." He laughed. "How are Larry and the kids?"

"The kids are doing great as always, but I divorced Larry two years ago."

"That's too bad," Snow said. "Something counseling couldn't fix?"

"Larry's the one who got fixed," Detective Stevens said. "He underwent sex reassignment surgery before the divorce was even final."

"Oh," Snow said. "That's hard to believe. That's quite a departure from his football days at USC."

"Fifteen years of marriage to the guy. I could write a book," Detective Stevens said. "So, how are you doing? Did you ever get married again?"

"Why?" Snow asked. "You want to go out with me?"

She laughed. "Not after what you did to my cousin on your first date with her."

"I didn't do anything that wouldn't meet the dating standards of the National Organization of Women."

"If I remember correctly, she said you started undressing her in her living room halfway through her first glass of wine."

"I thought I saw a wasp crawl inside her blouse."

"Yes, she thought that was hilarious."

"Unfortunately, I didn't find the wasp or anything else worth looking at inside her blouse. And I got a kick out of the rat's nest on her head. Why would a natural blonde dye her hair red?"

"She didn't dye her hair. It was naturally strawberry blonde."

"Her hair was red," Snow insisted. "You could tell by her temper."

"I'm so grateful I don't have to work with you anymore," Detective Stevens said. "You are such an asshole."

"Nice of you to call and remind me," Snow said. "Was that the main objective of your call or was there something more important?"

"Actually there is … I have a note addressed to you. It's from Dean Kale."

Eyes narrowed, Snow stared down at the sidewalk. "What are you doing with a note from Dean Kale?"

"It was discovered on his kitchen counter in an area that wasn't completely littered with dirty dishes."

"So you were over at his house doing his dishes? Does the section chief know you're moonlighting?"

"Ha-ha, ha-ha …"

"What does the note say?"

"It's like a short poem. It reads: 'Jim Snow, thanks for the beer. I'm out of here.'"

"Do you have any idea where he went?"

"The living room," Detective Stevens replied. "He was found by the first responder in an easy chair with a single bullet wound to the head."

CHAPTER 34

In her early forties, Detective Marcia Stevens appeared younger and more attractive than Snow remembered her. Fitting curvaceously into her gray skirt and white blouse, she looked like she'd been working out, he speculated. Clearly, she was trolling for a new husband.

While she had still been married, her posterior, hips, and thighs had been much wider. Snow had never seen her wear anything but pants in those days, and they were always made of stretchy material to allow expansion while she was sitting and bending over. Her face had always looked swollen and drooping, as though it were filled with jelly. Now her facial skin was tight and sleek, revealing high cheekbones and even features.

Snow shook her warm, delicate hand and embraced her, noticing a temporary stirring of attraction he had never felt toward her. She seemed like a different woman, and Snow wondered why some poor bastard hadn't latched onto her and her excess baggage by now.

Alice, standing beside Snow in the lobby of James & James Detective Agency, gave Detective Stevens a quick hug nearly at arm's length, then stepped back, looking at her.

215

"You look fantastic," Alice said. "Single life must agree with you."

"You too, girl," the detective said. "I don't see a ring on your finger yet. Are you seeing anyone steady?"

Alice smiled and nodded her head toward Snow.

"Oh, how cute," Marcia said. "Good luck with him. I think you'll need it. Along with a stun gun."

Alice forced a laugh, and Snow's grin turned into a grimace, the brief attraction he'd felt for his former partner curdling into disgust.

Detective Stevens turned her eyes to the cardboard cutout standing behind the counter. With a smug grin on her face, she said, "I see your sense of humor hasn't changed, Detective Snow."

"What's funny about it?" Snow asked. "Betty Boop's a classy dame. I'm proud to have her on our team."

"Well, I have to admit, that is classier than an inflatable doll with a fat cigar sticking out of its mouth. Do you still have that?"

Snow shook his head. "Somebody lit the cigar at the last bachelor party she attended. It melted part of her face."

Snow escorted the two women into Alice's office, where Marcia seated herself in one of the client chairs. Alice rounded her desk and took her chair. Snow dropped himself into his swivel chair to the right of Alice and leaned forward, with his fists folded together under his chin and his elbows resting on his knees.

"So, what's the story with Dean Kale?" Snow asked. "Who shot him?"

Detective Stevens leaned back in her chair, crossing her legs, allowing her skirt to ride up a couple inches over her firm thighs. "He shot himself," she said.

"What? Are you sure about that?"

"No question about it, even if he hadn't told the 911 dispatcher he was going to do it. The handwriting on the note matches. The lack of a struggle, the position of the body, gunpowder residue—it all points to a self-inflicted wound. He used a 30-30 Winchester rifle he'd bought earlier that day. He propped it up under his chin and blew the top of his head off. There were over a dozen empty beer bottles strewn all over the living room floor, indicating he was probably in a suicidal state of mind before he started drinking. And then, shortly after two a.m. this morning, just before he shot himself, he called 911 and revealed his intention to the dispatcher."

"He didn't seem like the type to do himself in. In fact, Alice and I were there when he started drinking. I brought him the beer."

"Whatever you said to him must have pushed him over the edge," Marcia said. "You have a talent for that, Mr. Snow, and not just in the interrogation room. Did he seem depressed before you started in on him?"

"Sure, he was depressed," Snow said. "His best friend was murdered two weeks ago, and he'd been losing his ass at the sports book, probably wondering if he'd be able to generate any sort of income for himself in the future. But a lot of people endure worse than that and manage to muddle through."

"How did he sound on the phone when he talked to the dispatch operator?" Alice asked.

"He sounded very calm and very drunk. He told the dispatcher that he would leave his front door unlocked for the police, so they wouldn't have to break it down. Did you know he was under investigation for the murder of his father for the second time?"

"I wasn't aware his father was murdered more than once," Snow declared with a straight face.

"Ha-ha, ha-ha, …"

"You probably know we visited with the detective in San Bernardino who's reopening the investigation."

"Yes, he told me," Marcia said. "It sounds like you suspected Dean Kale of the Billy Ryan murder long before that planted revolver fell out of the bumper of Lance Brown's pickup."

Snow nodded. "I don't always like to brag, Detective Stevens, but we were way ahead of you on this one."

She ignored the comment. "Who are you working for on this case?"

"It's not usually our policy to reveal that—as long as we're not covering up a felony. What difference does it make? It's someone who's extremely interested in finding out who killed Billy Ryan. That's all I can say."

"I'm assuming it was Gina Ryan."

Snow pressed his lips together. "You're a brilliant detective, Marcia. I'll give you that."

Detective Stevens beamed. "Would you mind sharing whatever you have?"

"If you'll lay *yours* on me," Snow countered, arching his eyebrows suggestively.

Alice shook her head and tittered.

"I'm glad *she* thinks you're funny," Marcia said. "Alright. I don't see any harm in it. Besides, I'm ready to wrap this one up. It would be good to add anything you can tell me to the file. What do you have?"

"I'll defer to my associate," Snow said. "Alice keeps better notes than I do."

Alice opened her notebook and went over the high points, explaining what they had seen on the video footage at Beaver's Oasis, the argument that had taken place in the car, and how Cassie had exited the vehicle on Greenawalt Road, indicating that Billy Ryan and Dean Kale had probably driven on to Billy Ryan's residence in a state of anger.

She went over the statements taken from casino employees stating that Billy Ryan had been winning, Dean Kale losing. And Billy had rubbed it in Dean's face, causing Dean Kale's increasingly agitated state.

They were both intoxicated, which obviously escalated their emotions and diminished their judgment.

Cassie had told them about Dean Kale wearing an ankle holster with a snub-nosed revolver.

Dean Kale had lied about everything, changing his story from one interview to the next, and seemed to them capable of murder.

Marcia nodded after Alice had finished. "That's entirely consistent with what we uncovered," she said. "We were able to expedite the ballistics report and learned that the revolver taped to the bumper of Lance Brown's truck matches the bullets used to kill Billy Ryan. They recovered the serial number and found that the gun was registered to Samuel Kale, and the serial number had just recently been ground off, probably right after Billy Ryan was shot with the gun."

"That's pretty conclusive," Alice agreed. "What about fingerprints or DNA?"

"The only prints on the gun were from Lance Brown, from when he'd picked the gun up from the street. They found DNA samples on the gun from three different people. Brown was one, obviously. The other two haven't been matched up yet. We had a DNA sample from Dean Kale's remains submitted, but the third person is a question mark. But not a big one, since we have enough circumstantial evidence to conclude that Dean Kale shot Billy Ryan with his father's gun. And now he's avoided arrest by killing himself."

Snow nodded. "That's a tough way out. We felt sure he was capable of murder. But I never thought his instinct for survival was so weak."

"Enough alcohol can change anything," Marcia said. "It breaks down inhibitions, releases the inner demons to run rampant."

"Yes, indeed," Snow said. "Alice and I should have you over for margaritas one night, Detective Stevens. It should be a wild time."

After walking the detective to the door, Alice and Snow returned to Alice's office. Snow fell into his chair. Alice sat down in the same chair Marcia Stevens had just vacated.

Snow blew out a breath. "Well, it looks like that's it. I guess we can call our client and give her the mixed news."

Alice leaned her elbow on the armrest of the chair and put her fingertips over her lips. "There's one loose end that's bothering me."

"The third DNA sample on the revolver."

"Yes."

"That's not worth losing sleep over."

"I know," Alice agreed. "But it makes me wonder who it belongs to."

"I'm guessing Claudia. But he might have just let her handle the gun—to satisfy her own curiosity, since she'd undoubtedly already seen it. Or it might be someone he showed it to in the past."

"Or maybe he taught her how to shoot it. And what about the 9mm Dean said was missing?"

"I don't think it was missing," Snow said. "I think he threw the 9mm in the ditch outside Victorville and kept the .38." He put his hands behind his head and looked at the phone on Alice's desk. "You want to call her—or should I?"

Alice got up and went behind her desk. She sat down, picked up the handset, and punched in the number for Cassie's cell phone, then switched it to speaker.

A recorded voice announced that the number had been disconnected. There was no referral to a new number.

Alice hung up and tried again. Same result.

She punched in Cassie's home phone number.

A similar recorded voice came on, making the same sort of announcement.

She set the handset back on the cradle and leaned back in her chair, staring at Snow.

"Now what?" Snow asked.

"If she wants to talk to us, she'll call us. But I'm worried that she might not be able to because Claudia won't let her. I was afraid this might happen."

"She's paid up. It's out of our hands. That's the end of it."

Alice shook her head. "It bothers me. This feels like Cassie's been kidnapped and she may not be safe."

"She's never been safe with Claudia around," Snow said. "We can't track her. Not until she settles in somewhere... but I think she'll call eventually. She always has."

"Possibly," Alice said. "Or maybe her name will show up in the news after Claudia does something else Cassie will live to regret."

CHAPTER 35

Alice and Snow spent the remainder of the day beginning work on a couple of new assignments that had come in over the last few days. Shortly after 6:00 p.m., a call came in from Lance Brown, requesting a meeting as soon as possible. Lance Brown told Snow he and his brother had disturbing news and were considering hiring the duo to investigate their sister Gina.

Snow told their prospective clients to stop by Gina's home to discuss it. The men said they could be there in twenty minutes.

Lance greeted them at the front door and invited them to the dining room table, where Damon Brown sat down with a forlorn look on his ashen face.

"What's this about?" Snow asked after everyone had been seated.

"Gina," Lance said. "She's gone. No warning. Just up and left while Damon and I were at work."

"Where did she go?" Snow asked, bewildered.

"We don't know," Lance said. "When I got home from work I found this note on the table."

He stood up and fished it out of his back pocket. It was two pages long. He unfolded it and slid it across the table in front of Snow. Written neatly in longhand, it read:

Dear Lance and Damon,

It is with mixed emotions that I write this because we've been so close for the last few years. Too close I guess. I'm afraid you both have come to depend on me more than you should. You've both gotten weak and lazy. And I feel trapped here living with you. When you first moved in, it was nice having family around, but gradually that got old. Putting up with your crude humor, sloppy living standards, and belching and passing gas whenever the urge strikes you has taken a toll on my patience.

I think it's best for all three of us if I just leave. I won't tell you where I'm going because I don't want the burden of you both showing up out of the blue to visit, which would probably turn into an extended stay once again. Don't try to call me, because I've had my cell phone disconnected. When I get settled, I may call to see how you're getting along, but I doubt it. The thought of having to talk to either of you again makes me want to puke. I know that's harsh, but it's the truth. Possibly, time will heal the rift that has developed between us. But it could be a very long time because the constant bickering that developed over the last few days has changed the way I feel about both of you worthless losers.

Living with you has even made me begin to feel like a loser myself in spite of the years of success I enjoyed with my career as a model. I'm hoping, in a new location I may possibly be able to pursue that level of success once again.

There is no sense trying to trace my location because I've sold my car this morning to a used car dealer, taken all of my money out of my accounts, and closed those.

Both of you may continue to live in this house that Billy and I so graciously provided for you—as long as you pay the *mortgage, taxes, and insurance. The statement comes in the mail once a month from the lender addressed to Billy. They don't know he's dead, and I doubt that they give a shit as long as someone keeps making the payments. Of course those are pretty substantial since Billy bought this house near the peak of the housing boom. It's now worth a third of the price the dumb shit paid for it, so it doesn't bother me to walk away from it since Billy is dead and not making the payments anymore.*

Obviously, it would be cheaper for you two to find a house to rent. I'm sure you could find plenty of them for $600 a month or less.

I hope you won't hate me for abandoning you, but I think at this point you both could use some tough love— and a swift kick in the behind.

Love and kisses,
Gina

Snow slid the letter over to Alice.

When she had finished reading it, she turned her eyes to Snow. They exchanged a look.

Snow leaned back and looked at Lance. "This is a shame. What would you like us to do about it?"

"Damon and I talked it over," Lance said. "We're convinced Gina had Billy killed so she could run off with his money. We think she had that gun taped to the bumper of my truck. She probably did it herself, trying to pin the murder on me. Now that she's run off—that proves it."

"Unfortunately, it doesn't prove anything. Gina has been cooperative and helpful during our investigation. Apparently, neither of you got the word about Dean Kale."

"What about Dean?" Damon asked.

225

"We spoke to the homicide detectives this morning," Alice said. "The preliminary ballistics report came back and indicated the gun in Lance's bumper originally belonged to Dean's father. So, of course, the gun can be assumed to have been in Dean's possession since some time after Dean's father's murder."

Lance's eyes widened. "Dean's father was murdered?"

"A long time ago, when Dean was a teenager," Snow said.

"You're saying *Dean* planted that gun in my bumper?"

Snow nodded. "It looks that way. The police are convinced of it. They're concluding their investigation of Billy's murder."

"So Dean's been arrested?" Damon's eyes were wide, his mouth hanging open. Snow wondered how long it had been since he'd had his teeth cleaned.

"I'm afraid that's not possible," Snow said.

"*Why the hell not?*" Lance bellowed.

"He's dead," Snow said. "He shot himself last night."

The brothers looked at each other with big eyes.

"What a coward," Lance said.

"He seemed like such a nice guy," Damon said. "Always had kind words for us and Gina. After Billy split up with Gina, I was hoping Dean and Gina would hook up."

"Why did he shoot Billy?" Lance asked. "I don't understand that."

Snow shrugged. "A sudden fit of rage. Things weren't going well for Dean. He'd been losing a lot of money. Billy had been winning. Sometimes that's all it takes. I can relate. I think we all can."

"But then why did Gina leave?" Damon asked.

Snow nodded at the letter in front of Alice. "Maybe you should read that again. It's pretty specific."

"Maybe you could give us Cassie Lane's phone number," Lance suggested. "She might know where Gina went."

"That won't do you any good," Snow said. "Her phone numbers have been disconnected."

Lance looked at his brother. "That explains it. They ran off together."

"Oh, my God," Damon said. "This'll kill Mom and Dad."

"I'm not planning on telling them," Lance said. "They won't believe it."

"I can't believe it myself," Damon said. "If I hadn't heard it with my own ears. I could hardly stand listening to the perverted shit that was going on in that bedroom upstairs."

"I know what you mean," Lance agreed.

"What would you like us to do?" Alice asked.

The brothers looked at each other, then at Alice.

"How much would it cost us to locate our sister?" Lance asked.

"Why don't you just leave her alone?"

"We might want to send her a card now and then," Lance explained. "So we can reach out and touch her."

"She'll probably get all the touching she wants from that sleazy slot mechanic," Damon muttered. He looked at his watch, then his brother. "Well, that's water under the bridge. No sense dwelling on it any longer. What are we going to do about dinner?"

"We'll have to start cooking for ourselves," Lance said. "I'll run to the store and pick something up. What do you want?"

"What do you know how to cook?"

Lance shrugged. "Any idiot can cook a chicken. You just let it sit in the oven and crank up the heat until it turns brown. Or we could have Hamburger Helper. That's always good. And then there's Tuna Helper for a healthy heart."

Lance sighed and shook his head. "I miss her already," he murmured.

CHAPTER 36

Snow and Alice were parked on Wampler Street, fifty yards from the intersection of Greenawalt Road. At 3:15 a.m. there was little traffic and hardly any pedestrians. They'd been there for an hour, and no one matching the sketch of the man with the black hair and the mustache had walked past the stoplights.

"How long do you want to sit here?" Alice asked with a tone of impatience in her voice.

"You didn't have to come."

"And leave a nut like you out here alone to your devices?"

"Till four thirty?" Snow said. "What do you think?"

"I think we're wasting our time. We've already exceeded our billable hours for this case. Our client has apparently skipped, and with no way to contact her, obviously she is no longer interested in what we have to report."

"That's true," Snow agreed. "But I'm curious."

"If I investigated everything I've been curious about in my life," Alice argued, "I wouldn't have time for anything else."

"A couple hours sitting here won't hurt anything. Think of it as quality time together."

"We spend almost twenty-four hours a day together. That's plenty. This is cutting into my sleep."

"It's not like you to complain, Alice," Snow said. "What's wrong?"

"My worst fear is being realized. We've spent so much time together, I'm acting like you."

"You're complaining that I complain too much? Is that it?"

"This is a depressing pattern I've found in all my previous relationships. You spend the first three to six months sharing your thoughts and experiences, and after you run out of material, it's all downhill from there."

"Now I'm getting depressed."

"See what I mean? I read that married couples have similar blood pressure levels. That's just one more example of what I'm talking about."

"I don't think that was the case with either of my first two wives," Snow said. "They both lowered their blood pressure by raising mine."

"That's hard to believe. I read that married men live longer."

"That's because their wives won't let them drink."

"And that's a bad thing?"

"I'd much rather live seventy-four years as a happy beer drinker," Snow insisted, "than seventy-nine as a miserable teetotaler."

"Wait until you get to be seventy-three and see how you feel about it. And it's not necessary to be abstinent," Alice countered. "One or two drinks per night are good for you."

"That's a waste of good alcohol," Snow argued. "It won't give anyone a buzz. The reason booze seems to taste so good is from the mind anticipating the onset of a temporary level of euphoria you'll enjoy after six of them."

"Really," Alice said. "How do you feel when you begin running in the morning?"

"Like a zombie."

"So your mind isn't anticipating the onset of a temporary level of euphoria from a runner's high. It's just wishing you were back in bed sleeping."

Snow thought about this. "That's a good point," he said. "I never thought of that."

Alice smiled.

Snow noticed the form of a man in a straw cowboy hat come into view. He was walking briskly on the far sidewalk along Greenawalt Road. He was of medium height and build, and appeared to have dark hair and a mustache.

Snow raised the binoculars from the center console. The man appeared to be Latino, wearing a red T-shirt, jeans, and sneakers. With the exception of his headwear, he matched the sketch perfectly.

"That's him," Snow said, his pulse quickening. He handed the binoculars to Alice.

"Looks like it," Alice said, peering through the lenses, working the focus with her fingers. "You go ahead. I'll stay with the car."

"You sure?"

"Yes. Two people coming at him might scare him."

"Okay."

He pulled the keys out of the ignition, climbed out from behind the wheel, putting the keys in his pocket. Shutting the car door, he turned toward the intersection.

"Jim," Alice said.

Snow lowered his head and peaked through the open window at her.

"I might need the keys."

"Oh, yeah." He fished them out of his pocket and handed them through the window. "I'll just be a minute."

With that he jogged off down the sidewalk. At the intersection he looked both ways, then jogged across the street against a red light. He ran toward the man.

Fifteen feet away the man turned and glanced at Snow over his shoulder. He turned back around and began to sprint.

Glad to be wearing his oxfords with the rubber soles instead of his loafers, Snow raced after him, closing the gap quickly.

He hopped off the sidewalk and ran along the street next to the gutter. Clearly out of shape, the man was slowing, his breathing heavy.

Moving up alongside him Snow slowed to match the man's pace. He looked over at him grinning. "How's it going?"

No response. The man kept his head turned to the front, huffing and puffing.

"Nice night for a run," Snow said. "Are you training for a specific race or maybe just a fun run of some sort?"

Out of breath, the man stopped.

Snow stopped too.

The man dug his right hand into his front jeans pocket and brought out a large knife. He flipped it open and turned facing Snow, brandishing it in front of him. *"Back off!"* he bellowed.

"Whoa!" Snow jerked backward and raised his open hands next to his head. "Hey now, I'm just an investigator," he protested. "I'm just trying to find out about an accident on this street. This has nothing to do with you."

"Get the fuck away from me!" the man snarled.

Snow backed up a few more paces. The man took the same number of steps toward him.

"Take it easy," Snow said. "I'm not armed. I just need to ask a couple questions…"

The whine of an engine approaching on the street behind him broke the stillness. Snow stole a glance over his shoulder and saw his Sonata skidding to a stop a short distance back, with Alice at the wheel.

He turned his head back around and saw the man glaring at the car with apprehension. The car door slammed shut, the engine still idling.

Then came Alice's voice, loud and shrill: *"Lay that knife down or I'll shoot! Right now!"*

"It's alright, Alice!" Snow yelled. "I've got this under control."

"Do you even have a weapon?" he heard her yell back.

"I don't need one," Snow insisted. "If this fellow intended to stick me, he would have done it by now."

"He's pointing a knife at you!"

"That's just a form of greeting in certain cultures," Snow proclaimed, hoping his fear wasn't showing in his voice.

He could hear Alice's footsteps advancing now. "Put the knife on the sidewalk. I won't tell you again," she commanded.

The man complied, then put his hands out at his sides, fear taking control of his face.

"Jim, where's your gun?" he heard Alice say.

"Forgot it," Snow said. "Just as well. I couldn't run after this guy with a holster strapped to my leg."

Snow turned and looked at Alice. She had her 9mm in front of her with both hands aimed at the man's chest.

"Alice put your gun away before somebody drives by and sees it and calls the police."

She pulled back the flap of her blazer and holstered the weapon.

Snow turned back to the subject in front of him. "You can put your hands down. Like I told you, I'm just an investigator, and so is she. We're not cops. We just need to ask you about an accident. It happened at this intersection last Thursday."

The man lowered his hands to his sides. "I don't know nothin' 'bout no accident. I wasn't even here. I was home in bed. That was my day off."

Snow lowered his gaze to the man's T-shirt. In large, white letters it read "Arturo's Taco Shop."

"Why did you run?" Snow asked.

"You scared the shit out of me—you look like cops."

Snow wondered if he had an outstanding warrant. "Like I just said, we're not cops, and we're not interested in you. That's the truth." Snow pointed at the man's T-shirt. "You work there?"

The man shrugged.

Snow stepped up on the sidewalk in front of him. He leaned over and picked up the knife, closed it, and handed it to him. "Put that back in your pocket. You won't need it."

The man took it and slipped it into his pocket.

"What's your name?" Snow asked.

The man shrugged again.

Snow thought for a moment. "Is there another guy who works at Arturo's who looks like you?"

"My brother," the man said.

"Does he live somewhere around here?"

"In the same house," he said. "My whole family lives there."

"They own the restaurant?"

The man shook his head.

"Your brother work there on Thursdays?"

He shrugged, then nodded.

"Does he work the same shift as you?"

"Yes."

"So—do you guys take the bus home?"

The man nodded.

"Did your brother mention seeing an accident here last Thursday?"

"Yes."

"What did he tell you about it?"

The man shrugged.

"Would you mind giving me your brother's cell phone number so I can talk to him about the accident?"

"He doesn't have one," the man said.

Snow dug out his wallet, slipped two twenties and a business card out of it, and handed them to the man. "Ask him to call me. Tell him it's urgent. There's twenty bucks for him and twenty for you. Okay?"

The man looked at the card and the money and nodded.

Snow offered a handshake. Ignoring it, the man shoved Snow's business card and the money into his pocket, turned, and continued walking.

"Thanks!" Snow shouted after him. "Nice chatting with you." He turned to Alice.

She was frowning at him.

"You know, Jim," she said. "We were lucky this time. We should have approached him together and maintained a safe distance. You can't just run up to strange people like that. You could have been hurt or killed. It's like you don't think your actions out clearly. You're sometimes a danger to yourself and me. I really need to think seriously about our future in working together."

"What about the other side of our future?"

"At this point I'm not too sure about that either. I realize now it's a good thing we didn't move in together."

"Ah, come on, Alice," Snow said. "You're just having a bad day. Don't be bitter. Reconsider."

She shook her head, turned, and walked back to the car.

CHAPTER 37

To Jim Snow's surprise he received a call on his cell phone the following morning from a man named Carlos Hernandez, who agreed to meet Alice and Snow in the parking lot outside of Arturo's Taco Shop in east Las Vegas.

A little after 1:00 p.m., they spotted him getting off a bus on the next block. He resembled his brother, only a few years older, wearing an identical red T-shirt with the taco shop advertisement splashed across the front and a red UNLV ball cap.

Alice and Snow got out of the car as he drew near. Snow gave him a nod and a wave, and Carlos nodded back.

They shook hands all around at Snow's Sonata, then leaned against the front fender.

"I was afraid your brother wouldn't give you my card," Snow said. "When I approached him last night, he ran from me."

Carlos Hernandez stood with his legs crossed at the ankles and his arms folded, staring off in the distance at Frenchman Mountain. "My brother has a problem with authority," he said. "He's paranoid of the cops. And he has good reason. He spent time in prison for an armed robbery he didn't commit. They had no evidence, no gun, only the testimony of the clerk in the store

236

and some bad video footage from a camera over the cash register, which only showed the robber's cap. You couldn't see his face because his cap was pulled down over it. My brother looks like a lot of people, and I guess I do too, so I'm lucky it wasn't me that woman picked out of a lineup."

"How did they find your brother?" Alice asked.

"He walked into that same convenience store to buy some cigarettes. It's that one right over there." He turned and pointed across the street at Abel Market, half a block to the west in another strip mall. "That silly woman who works there freaked out and called the cops. She watched him walk across the street. The cops came over here and arrested him. I guess I'm lucky I don't smoke or it could have been me."

"That's a shame," Snow said, "but it happens a lot. People think they have a better memory than they really do … and speaking of memory, your brother said you witnessed a hit-and-run accident last Thursday on Greenawalt Road and Wampler. Is that true?"

Carlos nodded. "I saw the whole thing. That poor girl got knocked down and dragged out to the middle of the intersection. She got hit hard; must have split her head open when it hit the road."

"Why didn't you call 911?"

"What am I going to use to call with?" Carlos asked. "I don't have a cell phone. And I could tell that girl was dead. She wasn't moving at all, and that car just took off. And I don't want to deal with the cops. They might decide to arrest me for something. I figured somebody else would be along pretty soon, let them deal with it."

"How did it happen?"

"The car came from the west on Greenawalt. It passed me just before the intersection, and I could hear people arguing in the car. Yelling and screaming at each other."

"What were they arguing about?"

Carlos looked at Snow. "Hot dogs," he said. "They were hollering at each other about hot dogs; 'Fucking hot dogs' this and 'Fucking hot dogs' that. The car was swerving all over the road, so I could tell the driver must have been drunk or high on something.

"The car went down another hundred yards or so, then slammed on the breaks and made a wide U-turn, driving up on the sidewalk on the other side of the road in the process. Then came speeding back the direction it had just come from. All kinds of yelling in the car. By then that girl was in the crosswalk right in the middle of their lane. She had earphones on and couldn't hear the car coming I guess. It plowed right into her. It was awful.

"So, after it hit her, the driver slammed on the brakes in the middle of the intersection, with the girl halfway under the car. All three of them jumped out, screaming at each other. They ran up to the front of the car and looked at the girl's body.

"They didn't care about the hot dogs anymore. Now they were yelling at each other about what to do. One of the men wanted to call 911. The other man and the woman wanted to get the hell out of there because they could see she was dead."

"Who was driving the car?" Alice asked.

"The woman. And she looked drunk. They all did. They were all smashed, and now that poor girl in the crosswalk was smashed too."

Snow looked at Alice with a raised eyebrow. She met his gaze and shook her head.

Reaching into his back pocket, Snow pulled out three folded sheets of paper. He unfolded them, revealing photos of Cassie Lane, Billy Ryan, and Dean Kale. He handed them to Carlos. "You recognize any of these people, Carlos?"

"Yes," he said. "All three of them, I think. They were all in the car." He pointed at the photo of Cassie Lane. "She was driving."

"So, what happened then?" Snow asked.

"These two," he pointed at the pictures of Cassie and Kale, "they got back in the car. The other one stood there looking down at the girl's head. They were both yelling at him to get in the car. And he finally did.

"The woman backed up off from the dead girl's body and put it in drive and floored it. She made another U-turn heading back the original direction—"

"East," Snow clarified.

"Yes, they were going east. Then she sped off down the street."

"Did any of the three people seem to notice you?"

"If they did, they didn't let it slow them down."

"And what did you do after they drove away?"

"I kept walking," Carlos said. "Nothing could be done for anybody, so I did the smart thing and got the hell out of there."

CHAPTER 38

Returning to the office from lunch the next day, Snow unlocked the door and found the day's mail scattered on the floor. He leaned over and gathered it up.

Among the bills and credit card offers, he found a plain envelope with no return address but with his name on it.

He got out his penknife and slit it open. It was a six-page letter, handwritten in an uneven scrawl. Taped to the top of the first page was a tiny flash drive. The letter read:

Mr. Jim Snow,

I debated for a long time over quite a few of my last beers whether or not to write this letter. But ultimately, I realized I want someone to know the truth about everything. Not that it matters much, I guess, because I'll be dead by the time you get this.

I'll have to walk this to the nearest drop box. I can't risk getting picked up for drunk driving tonight. That would really throw a monkey wrench into my already screwed-up life.

I know this will surprise you after all the fine detective work you did, but I want you to know I didn't shoot Billy. I can't say the same for my dad, unfortunately. That son of a bitch left me no alternative. He had me backed into a corner with only one way out—and that was over his dead body.

With my born-again best friend shooting his mouth off, I can see it's only a matter of time before I will need to confess to that crime. I always thought I got off too easy; funny how your luck can turn on a dime. I'm sure I don't have to tell you about that—you being an experienced gambler yourself.

Now that Cassie has fucked me over by planting that gun in Lance's truck, I'm completely screwed. You convinced me of that this evening when you told me about the certainty of the gun being traced to me. Keeping that gun was a big mistake. Although, like I say, I'm screwed anyway since the police probably won't need it to arrest me for my father's murder. The testimony of an ordained minister along with my stack of lies will seal my fate.

So it really doesn't matter if the DA convicts me for Billy's murder. The best I could hope for with my father's killing would be life in prison. What harm can one more charge against me do?

But sitting here comfortably, getting plastered for the last time, I feel the need to let the truth out, the whole truth, and nothing but the truth. Ha-ha, ... this may sound strange, but I'm actually feeling more jovial now that I've decided which course of action to take. Even if the plan is to blow my brains out with my beautiful new rifle. In case you're wondering, I didn't buy that rifle to kill myself with.

I bought it to protect myself against Cassie. I'm sure she took my 9mm handgun and is probably intending to shoot me with it if the mood strikes her. And she gets struck by a lot of moods—some of them really weird. However, I will admit she was good in bed, and that counts for something. Amazing how hard it is to turn away a good piece of ass. I never have. But those are small mistakes when compared to the big ones I've made.

As for Billy—that guy caused his own death indirectly. If he'd kept his mouth shut, he'd probably still be alive. He should have just shut up about the hot dogs. He was the only who wanted to stop for them—but he always thought those hot dogs at Beaver's were good enough to die for. Well, he did that.

We were still arguing about stopping at Beaver's when we pulled onto Greenawalt Road. We were screaming at each other. It was crazy. I could have told Cassie to pull into Beaver's, but I was so pissed at Billy for kicking my ass at the crap table and rubbing my face in it—the last thing I wanted was for him to get the satisfaction of a bunch of kosher hot dogs smothered in mustard and relish. I'd rather have a good hamburger—but that's Billy. That guy loved his kosher hot dogs.

After Cassie started Billy's car up and left the parking lot at Boulder Nugget, I realized how drunk she was. Billy and I were pretty well toasted, but Cassie seemed to be getting woozier by the minute. Those shots will do that to you.

Anyway, we rolled through the intersection of Wampler Street without incident. And then I made the mistake of telling Cassie to let Billy have his hot dogs. I told her to turn the car around and head back to Beaver's. If the bastard wanted his hot dogs so damn bad, let him have them.

She turned the car around almost ramming it into a sound wall in the process and stomped on the gas. She had her head turned, yelling at Billy in the back seat. I was looking out my window, thinking I should just shut up at that point. And that's when we slammed into that girl.

We all got out and looked at her. Boy, was she ever dead! Billy wanted to call 911 and wait for the paramedics. I told both of them to just get back in the car and get the hell out of there. That girl was dead and we were in big trouble—especially Cassie—because I knew she was over the legal limit for alcohol.

We all jumped back in the car and took off, this time arguing about going back to the scene of the accident. Billy wouldn't shut up about it.

I usually carry my dad's old snub nose .38 in an ankle holster. I know that sounds stupid, but it wasn't used in any crime, and I didn't grind the serial number off. Cassie must have done that later. And I never took the gun in the casinos with me. I always left it in the trunk, and strapped it on after we got out of the car, to keep from getting robbed.

Cassie knew about that gun. I made the mistake of taking her to the firing range a number of times to practice with it. Big mistake. She got to be really good with it.

When we pulled up to drop Billy off at his house, he got out and looked at the damage to the front of the car. He still wanted to call 911. I don't think he was thinking straight. He was really plastered and could hardly stand up.

I told him to just shut the fuck up and go in and go to bed—that I'd put the car in my garage when I got home, and we'd decide what to do with it the morning.

He finally turned his back and started walking to the front door. That was when Cassie reached down and pulled the .38 from my ankle holster. I know I could have stopped her, but I guess a part of me really didn't want to. Because I just sat there and watched her jump out of the car and put two slugs into Billy's back.

That bitch is cold. Without a word she just jumped back in behind the wheel, put the gun in her lap, and took off out of there.

I didn't want to touch that gun again. I just let her keep it. Then I got the bright idea to take out my phone and started it recording audio, so I'd have that as proof that I didn't shoot Billy.

We abandoned the car where the police found it, and we walked home. I went to my place, Cassie I guess to hers.

I saved the recording on the flash drive that's taped to this letter. It doesn't really matter now, but you can listen to it.

I'll let you decide what to do with this letter and the audio file. I really don't give a shit at this point because I'm only a few beers away from meeting the grim reaper.

Good luck to you, Jim Snow. And thanks again for the beer.
Regards,
Dean Kale

Snow peeled the tape, along with the flash drive, from the letter before handing all six pages to Alice. She stood there in the lobby, reading it, while Snow went back to his office and slid the flash drive into a USB port in his computer.

He brought up the drive containing the audio file and sat looking at it.

A few minutes later Alice walked quietly into his office and sat on the edge of Snow's desk.

"You want to hear this?" Snow asked.

Alice nodded.

Snow opened the audio file and started it playing. He turned up the sound.

There was a lot of hysterical yelling back and forth between Claudia and Dean Kale, with Kale asking her over and over why she shot Billy, and Claudia insisting she had no choice, because, at some point, Billy Ryan would go to the police about the hit-and-run. That was the sort of person Billy was.

The audio evidence confirmed what Dean had written in the letter.

Snow closed the program and the directory. He pulled the flash drive out of his computer and set it on his desk.

He leaned back in his swivel chair and looked up at Alice. She was looking at the letter she held in her hands.

"What do you want to do?" Snow asked.

Alice met Snow's gaze. "We're required by law to turn this letter and the flash drive over to Marcia Stevens."

Snow nodded. "You know, if we give her this evidence after she's already closed the case, it will only piss her off."

"I know," Alice agreed. "But everything makes that woman angry."

245

"Right," Snow said. "I'm not looking forward to that."

"We could wait a couple days at the most. We need to try to locate Cassie and talk to her. She's still our client. She hasn't officially fired us again."

"What if we can't find her?" Snow said.

Alice sighed. "Then we'd better just take a drive down to Homicide."

Snow nodded, frowning.

CHAPTER 39

The next day another plain envelope arrived, with no return address, bearing a postmark from Denver, Colorado. This one was addressed to the James & James Detective Agency:

Dear Jim and Alice,

I'm so sorry for leaving Las Vegas without saying good-bye, and making you wonder what happened to me.

I can't tell you where we are, but only that I'm doing well. I haven't remembered anything more about my past or what happened to Billy. Claudia found out about Dean's suicide, which is so sad, but it looks like he was the one who shot Billy. That's what the police say anyway. So, it looks like: case closed.

Claudia and I are learning to get along very well. I'm trying to cooperate with her wishes, and she has stopped beating me. Actually, it was only that one time. She swears she won't ever hit me again as long as I keep my mouth shut, and I promised I would.

We communicate back and forth in a diary every day. That way I'm never in the dark, and I'm grateful for that.

It just amazes me how adventurous Claudia is. I find her actions scary sometimes, but what can I do? We're two completely different personalities. Claudia is Claudia, and in me, she has a captive audience. I can either try to enjoy what life presents to me or feel miserable, and I'm tired of feeling bad.

I've decided not to pursue therapy any longer. We've spent years on that, and it never got us anywhere, so Claudia and I will just continue on living together and try to make the best of it. She treats me more like a little sister now instead of an enemy, so the future is looking brighter for us.

Gina is also living with us and she's been very kind, if a little condescending, to me. Gina and Claudia seem to get along extremely well. Gina used to be a model when she was younger, and she's trying to talk Claudia into giving that a try. Gina says almost anyone can succeed as a model if they want it bad enough. I'm beginning to notice Gina is a lot like Claudia. They will probably end up starting an agency together.

One thing I've noticed that's different in just the last few days is that there are longer gaps between conscious memories for me. I seem to be losing interest in coming out to participate in life, and I wonder if someday I will just cease to exist.

That wouldn't be so bad. As a whole, life hasn't been that great for me, and I don't mind leaving it all to Claudia.

I appreciate everything the two of you have done for me. And please, please remember what I told you not long after I met you about me resigning myself to what-ever happens next in life. I'm just thankful for the small pleasures I've been granted along the way. Thank you so much for putting up with me—and Claudia.

Warm wishes,

Cassie

After they'd each read the letter a second time, Snow put it back in the envelope and set it on Alice's desk.

He flopped down in one of the client chairs. "I'm having trouble believing Cassie wrote that letter," he said.

Alice nodded. "It does look suspicious. My first thought was that Claudia is trying to cut us adrift. That she wrote the letter."

"But if Claudia wrote it, why hasn't Cassie contacted us?"

"Because, if she tried to, Claudia would beat her. Claudia is aware of everything Cassie says and does. Dr. Rodgers told us that."

"What do we do now?" Snow asked.

"We need to talk to Cassie," Alice said. "But I haven't found an address or phone number. They must still be in hiding. I checked with the post office, and Cassie has a hold on her mail delivery. So does Gina. Eventually, I expect they'll submit a change of address request now that Claudia knows the case has been closed. And she'll assume we won't be interested in locating Cassie, because we're not being paid."

"We can't sit on this evidence until the two of them decide to run out and buy a house. Let's just get in the car and dump this problem on Marcia Stevens."

Alice was gazing at Snow as he said this, but she seemed to have a distant look in her eyes. She turned her attention back to the letter. Picking up the envelope, she removed the letter and read it again.

"This part where she mentions telling us to remember what she told us about resigning herself to whatever happens next..."

"What about it?" Snow asked.

"Cassie didn't just tell us she was resigned to whatever happened to her in general. Remember? She specifically told us she was resigned to what would happen to her if we come up with evidence tying her and Claudia to the crime. She wanted us to let her know first. Then our final task would be to accompany her to the police, where we'll explain to them everything we know. She said, if it comes to that, then they can lock her up. You don't remember that?"

"Now that you mention it, I do recall her saying something to that effect."

"I think this letter is a veiled message to us to find her."

"Okay," Snow said. "I guess I agree. And now we know she's in Denver."

"Right. And I doubt that they rented an apartment or moved into a motel, because the police could have easily tracked them. It's most likely that Gina and Claudia are staying with family or friends—of Cassie."

"Why not family or friends of Gina?" Snow said.

"I doubt it. Claudia likes to be in control. She wouldn't feel comfortable hiding out with someone she doesn't know."

"I'll go along with that, but there's no longer a need for Claudia to be in hiding."

"She hasn't given the post office a change of address," Alice argued. "That indicates to me they haven't found a place of their own yet, though they're probably looking. We need to talk to Cassie's parents and find out if Cassie has any relatives living in Denver. And get some names. Friends from high school she may have stayed in touch with. I think we should split up. You talk to the father; I'll talk to Cassie's mother."

"Cassie's father? Why would that creep tell me anything?"

"Just keep your emotions in check," Alice said. "Try to make him feel like you're there for the welfare of the entire family."

"What family?" Snow muttered. "The Manson family?"

"Just try to be professional. Stay calm. Don't insult him."

"Alright, alright...I'll just calmly knock his fucking teeth down his throat."

"Jim," Alice said, "I know you don't mean it, but it really bothers me when you say things like that."

CHAPTER 40

Gordon Lane was a criminal defense attorney working as a partner with two other lawyers in a prominent firm in Henderson. He was a round-shouldered man in his late fifties, with a full head of gray hair, deep-set eyes, and a pallid and deeply creased face.

Snow followed him into his office and stood across the desk from him, with his hands on his hips, feeling tense enough to explode out of his own skin.

Lane watched him without expression. But there was a hint of fear in his eyes.

"Have a seat," Lane said.

They both sat down, Lane in the leather swivel chair behind his executive-style desk, Snow in one of the padded chairs across from him.

Lane leaned forward, his hands together on his desk. "You didn't tell me much on the phone. What's this about?"

Snow sat stiffly in his seat, his arms folded. "Cassie hired us to investigate the murder of a friend of hers—are you aware of her disorder?"

"Her mental disorder?" Lane asked.

"Yes."

"Her therapist called me about it quite some time ago and explained it to me. I'm not sure I agree with her diagnosis."

"Why?"

"You have to know Cassie the way her mother and I do. Cassie isn't always truthful. She likes to play games. You can't trust anything she says. Her mother and I learned that the hard way over the years."

Snow stared at him for a long moment. Lane let him do it, blinking impassively at him. Waiting him out. Yes, it was possible Cassie had invented the stories her therapist had accepted at face value. She was a disturbed woman. Disturbed people often made up stories, even if they didn't know they were doing it.

All these things were true, but it was like Snow had to shout them to himself against a steady gale. He knew what and whom he believed.

"When was the last time you talked to your daughter?" Snow asked, feeling his throat constricting.

"I don't see where that's any of your business," Lane replied.

Snow took a breath and let it out. "Mr. Lane, the reason I'm here is that your daughter has disappeared, and we need to locate her."

"She owes you money?"

"No. She paid us, but we haven't concluded the investigation she hired us to conduct."

Lane gave his head a little shake, like he was having a hard time making sense of Snow's errand. "If she disappeared without notifying you, that means she's not interested in you continuing with it."

"It's not as simple as that," Snow said.

"Because of her mental state."

"Yes."

"I haven't spoken to Cassie in years. What makes you think I could tell you where she is?"

"We've tracked Cassie to Denver. I'm hoping you could tell me whether you have any relatives living there who Cassie might want to stay with."

"We don't have any relatives living anywhere in Colorado."

"What about friends from high school? Someone she might have stayed in touch with over the years."

Lane shook his head. "I don't remember any of their names."

"You sure about that? It seems to me you might remember at least one or two of them." Feeling the bile in his stomach beginning to rise, Snow had been fighting a losing battle with himself. And now he stopped fighting it. "Or maybe you only limited the manifestations of your sick behavior to your own two kids."

"What the hell are you talking about?" Lane snapped.

"I don't know for sure," Snow said. "Why don't you tell me?"

Lane's eyes widened. "What is this investigation really about?"

"It's not about you," Snow muttered. "Although the whole mess started with you—or maybe before you."

Lane pointed a finger at Snow. "You've stepped well over the line, now, Mr. Snow. I think you'd better leave."

Snow pushed himself up angrily out of his chair. "It was a waste of time coming here in the first place."

Lane stood up. "Then why did you?"

"I guess I just wanted to see what a slimy, rotten slug like you looks like close up." Snow took a step toward the desk, his fists clenched at his sides.

Lane took a step back, glaring at Snow, and pointed at the door. "Get out of my office—right now!"

"I'm leaving." But he took another step and leaned forward, his upper thighs pressing against the edge of Lane's desk.

"You're not moving in the right direction," Lane complained. "If I have to call the police to have you removed, you'll be going to jail."

"I've got a feeling you'll be heading there before me," Snow lied—knowing full well how unlikely that was. "And I want you to know that I know—you're a sick fuck, Gordy. There's no hope for you. And there shouldn't be."

With that, Snow turned on his heel and strode out of the office, wondering how he would explain the exchange that just took place here to Alice.

——

Snow was northbound on Boulder Highway, heading back to the office.

His phone chirped and he pulled the Sonata over to the shoulder.

He picked the phone up off the passenger seat and put it to his ear.

"Alice."

"Jim!" She sounded excited. "I've got it. Natalie Leonard. She and Cassie were best friends since they were kids. She's never been married and she lives in Denver. She's got a Facebook account with photos of her and Cassie taken at the Luxor last year."

"How did you manage to get that? Maggie Lane's husband wouldn't tell me anything."

"I don't think she's as bad as we thought. I didn't press the issue, but the impression I got was that it was Gordon who dished out all the abuse. I think Maggie Lane took her share of it too. I think she's been in denial all these years. She told me she's planning to leave him. She was very helpful."

"That's great," Snow said. "Where are you?"

"I'm sitting in my car in a parking lot in a strip mall. I'm making airline reservations for us right now. So you need to get home and pack a bag. Call me when you're ready to come pick me up."

CHAPTER 41

By the time their rental car pulled up in front of the three-bedroom home in Denver, the sun was setting behind the mountains.

They hadn't called Natalie Leonard, hoping to catch her at home.

She answered the doorbell, and after Snow introduced Alice and himself, she graciously invited them in. She was a petite woman, the same age as Cassie, with short black hair and a nervous smile.

She told them Cassie and Gina had been staying with her for a few days while they looked for an apartment. She was aware of Cassie's condition and had cultivated friendships with both Cassie and Claudia since her disorder had been diagnosed a year earlier. She said Gina and Claudia had been arguing since their arrival, and suddenly Gina got her bags together the night before and drove off, headed for Chicago. Cassie had just found an apartment earlier that morning and was still out shopping for furniture while Natalie had been at work.

They went into the living room, and Alice explained to Natalie everything that had happened with Cassie and Claudia and the murder of Billy Ryan. She concluded by telling her they had received new information incriminating Claudia.

Natalie seemed shocked. "That explains it. Claudia's been acting really weird," she said. "I mean, as I mentioned, I've known about Cassie's disorder and about Claudia since Cassie was first diagnosed with DID. Cassie has always been wonderful, and Claudia was always friendly toward me. In fact..." She paused. "It's a little embarrassing."

Alice and Snow exchanged a glance.

"We don't need to know," Alice said. "We have all the information we need. We just need to talk to Cassie so we can close out our investigation."

"I don't want you to get the wrong idea," Natalie said. "I know that Gina and Claudia are or were... involved. But Claudia and I never were. I mean, she made advances toward me at one time, but I rejected them because I knew Cassie wouldn't be comfortable with it. We've always just been friends."

"You mentioned that Claudia has been acting stranger than normal?" Snow said.

Natalie nodded. "Yes. She seemed really anxious and paranoid when they first got here, and she was always looking out the front window at the street, so I knew something wasn't right. And now that you're here, after what you've told me, I understand."

"Is she still acting that way?"

"No, she's calmed down in the last couple days. And even more so now that Gina is gone."

"I'm glad to hear that," Alice said.

Their conversation veered off from there into mixed topics of small talk for the next half hour as the three of them waited with apprehension for Cassie or Claudia to arrive.

And the living room became still when they heard the sound of the front door opening and closing.

The three of them got up and waited for the footsteps to draw near.

Finally Cassie came into view. She glanced at Snow and stared hard at Alice. Snow could tell by the hostile look on her face that this wasn't Cassie.

"What the fuck do you two assholes want?" Claudia demanded, glaring at Snow with her fists on her hips.

Alice stood erect with her legs slightly apart, her purse hanging by its strap from her shoulder. Her handgun was inside the purse along with a pair of handcuffs and a can of mace. "We need to talk to Cassie," she said.

"Why?"

"We need to get her permission to close out the investigation."

"Why? You won't be getting any more money from us."

"We just need to talk to her."

Claudia crossed her arms. "No!"

Alice reached into her purse and brought out a folded piece of paper. She stepped toward Claudia and handed it to her. "You should read this."

Claudia's eyes widened. She took the copy of Dean Kale's letter, unfolded it, and began to read.

"That's just a copy," Snow said. "If we aren't able to talk to Cassie, we'll take the original to the police."

Claudia continued to read. When she was finished, she folded it and put it in the back pocket of her jeans. "So, if I let you talk to her—then what? You'll leave?"

Snow shrugged. "Probably," he lied.

Claudia glanced at Natalie, then stared down at the floor, shaking her head. Gradually, the headshaking stopped, and she whimpered softly for a moment. Then she looked up at Snow and then Alice with a confused look on her face like a child waking up from a nightmare.

Her expression spread into a weak smile. Suddenly she appeared to be weary.

"Cassie?" Alice said.

Cassie nodded.

"We got your letter this morning."

"I'm glad … but I have to tell you that most of it was a lie. And before I say anything more I want you to do me a favor."

"What's that?" Snow asked.

"I want you to handcuff me, because I never know for sure when I'll lose what little strength I have left—and Claudia will come out—and I think that will be about *it* for me. So please …"

Alice got her handcuffs out of her purse, stepped behind Cassie, and snapped them on. Then she walked over and stood beside Snow.

"I think I can stay out for as long as I need to," Cassie said, "and do what I know needs to be done, as long as I continue to concentrate. And I know this will be the last time for me. I just don't have the will to continue with any of this, knowing what I now remember."

"What do you remember?" Alice asked.

"Everything, I think. Well … not every detail of my life and Claudia's life. But I remember the important things. I remember what my father did to me, and I remember what happened to Billy and that girl in the crosswalk."

"We know about it too," Snow said. "We got a letter from Dean Kale yesterday. He mailed it before he committed suicide. The letter details what happened. A copy of it is in your back pocket."

She nodded and her eyelids seemed to droop like someone falling asleep.

"*Cassie!*" Alice snapped.

"I'm okay," she said. "I'm still here. I just feel so tired."

"We understand," Alice said. "You've been through a lot."

She nodded again. "Claudia shot Billy and she ran over that girl on the street. She wasn't paying attention."

"The girl in the crosswalk or Claudia wasn't paying attention?" Snow asked.

"Neither." She pressed the tips of a thumb and forefinger to her eyes and took a deep breath, then took the hand away and looked at them. "I know you must be wondering how I can suddenly remember so much when, at the same time, I'm losing control of my mind."

No one replied to this. Snow glanced over at Natalie to see how she was taking these revelations. Her face was ashen, and her eyes were wide and glassy. Snow had seen victims in the morgue who looked better.

"Natalie, maybe you should sit down," Snow told her.

She immediately fell into the flowered rocking chair behind her and gripped the arms of it as though it were about to take off.

"I've been fighting with myself for days to concentrate and try to bring back what I could of the past," Cassie said, "because I know now for sure I don't want to go on anymore. I guess it's like a dying person having their life pass before them. I think that's what happened to me.

"The nice thing about having DID is that I don't have to commit suicide in order to leave this earth. All I have to do is give in and allow myself to sink down inside the depths of my own mind—and never come back. And that's what I intend to do."

"I wasn't aware you could control that," Alice said.

"Yes. It's the only real control I have. Claudia has always been much stronger than me. I've been deluding myself into believing I could win the battle against her. It isn't fair, I know, because she's so evil. Billy and that girl aren't the only two people she's killed. There've been others, and I want to tell the police about them just as soon as you can get me to the station. Will you do that for me?"

"Of course," Snow said.

"Good," Cassie said. "I don't like to use strong language, but for once in my life I know Claudia better than I ever wanted to and I feel like that *bitch* needs to get what's coming to her!"

"You know she can hear everything you're saying right now," Snow said.

"I'm sure she can," Cassie said. "That's good. Because I want her to know there are two souls inside this body, and I know mine will go on to a better place—while hers can rot in hell!"

Snow winced at this declaration. He knew Claudia must be writhing around inside there, listening to this, wherever she was, down in the smoldering inner reaches of Cassie's brain.

"And while I'm at it," she continued, "I also want to file a criminal complaint against my father for what he did to me. Can we do that here in Denver?"

"Yes," Alice said. "You can make a video-recorded statement and sign it in front of witnesses, and that will go with you back to Las Vegas. And you say there were other victims in the past?"

"Yes."

"I'd probably better call the FBI field office," Snow said.

"There is a lot of cash in my purse," Cassie said. "Take whatever I owe you. I don't care what happens to the rest of it. Claudia won't need it where she's going."

"Don't worry about the money," Snow said. "You're pretty much paid up."

"What about Gina?" Alice asked. "Did she have anything at all to do with Billy's murder?"

"No," Cassie replied. "She didn't even know it was Claudia who killed him. She and Claudia just had a little fling, I guess. Those are two wild women."

"I can imagine," Snow said, then winced as he realized what he'd just said.

Alice just shook her head.

Cassie turned to Natalie. "I'm sorry Claudia dragged you into this mess, Natalie. I hope you can forgive me."

Her face frozen in grief and her eyes welling up with tears, Natalie shook her head and gave a wave of her hand before covering her mouth with it as though she might be sick.

"Well, we'd better go," Cassie said. "I have a lot to say and do while I still have the opportunity this evening. I can't really stay out late. I feel so very sick and tired. And the next time I go to sleep—I find comfort in knowing that I will never wake up again."

Snow stared at her in disbelief. "I think you're worn out and distressed, Cassie. You get a good night's sleep, and you'll feel stronger in the morning."

Cassie calmly shook her head. "I've been thinking about this for months. There is no sense continuing this struggle. It's obvious I'm losing the battle. But even if I won out against Claudia eventually—I could never live with what she has done."

"But that was Claudia," Alice said.

"I know," Cassie said. "But she's always been a part of *me*. So we both have to pay the consequences. But I've paid enough— I'm leaving."

Snow sighed. "What a mess."

CHAPTER 42

Three months had passed.

Alice and Snow were sitting in Alice's office, having coffee and discussing their caseload, when there was a knock at the front door.

Snow got up to answer it. When he opened the door, he found a familiar face smiling at him.

"Cassie?" Snow asked.

She stuck out her hand. "I'm Caroline."

Staring at her in disbelief, Snow shook her hand.

"Are you and Alice busy?" Caroline said. "I just stopped by to say hi."

"I'm surprised to see you," Snow said. "We heard you were…"

"In the nut house?" Caroline said. "They let me out." She giggled.

Snow stepped aside and let her in. They walked past the cardboard cutout of Betty Boop, down the short corridor, and into Alice's office.

Alice stood up and stared at Caroline.

Snow introduced them, and then Caroline plopped into one of the client chairs, smiling up at the flabbergasted Alice.

Snow took his usual seat in his swivel chair at the side of Alice's desk, and Alice eased herself back down into her own chair.

"What happened to Cassie and Claudia?" Alice blurted.

Caroline crossed her legs and let out a heavy sigh. "Well, you know what happened to Cassie. She got fed up and cut out. Claudia stuck around a little longer. She actually had hopes of walking away from all these problems she created for the two of them. But with Cassie gone, I think she lost her nerve. Two days after they sent us to Rawson-Neal for evaluation, Claudia departed.

"That left a perfectly good body sitting there drooling all over itself. So I had to come out and take over. It's like being on the battlefield and two are down, and you're the only one left, so you're in charge—even though you haven't seen any action."

Alice and Snow exchange a perplexed glance.

"Wait a minute," Snow said. "How long have you been inside…?"

"Since the beginning," Caroline said. "I saw it all. My entire life."

"And you never came out?"

"Not once," Caroline said.

"Why not?"

She leaned forward. "Would *you*? With all the shit that was going on? I didn't want any part of it. It was bad enough I was stuck inside there watching it all, like a lifelong horror flick. I only came out in the hospital because I had no choice. They would have started shock treatments."

"So they released you," Alice said, still staring at her.

"Yes! Just yesterday. Well, it's been three long months inside that place. But I explained everything to them and stuck with it for the entire time I was there. Dr. Rodgers has been wonderful.

She helped a lot too. Of course, I have to keep seeing her once a week. But it will be wonderful because I just love that woman."

"I'm glad it turned out so well for you," Alice said.

"Yes. Thank you, Alice. But what could they do? You can't prosecute somebody whose mind is like the inside of an empty bus terminal. Right? I'm the only one left, and I wasn't even active when all of those crimes took place."

"But how can anyone be sure Claudia or even Cassie won't come back—out?" Snow said.

"Well, nothing's ever certain except for death. And a lot of people have sworn they've seen Elvis." She laughed.

"What about the case against your father?" Alice asked.

"Oh, that was Cassie's thing. I don't want to pursue that. My father is suffering in his own living hell. Believe me, I don't think he has had a moment's pleasure his entire life. His attorney came to see me in the hospital—imagine a lawyer having a lawyer—and we managed to strike a deal that will be quite lucrative for me. And I can always use the money. I'd love to go to Paris, but they won't let me leave the area. So I'll have to settle for the Paris Casino on the Strip." She giggled.

Snow had begun to feel uncomfortable. "What are your plans, Caroline?"

"Nothing different," she said. "I like my job, so I'll keep that. Maybe I'll find a nice guy to settle down with … I don't know if I'm ready to think about children yet."

"Better not to rush into that," Snow agreed.

"Well," she said, standing up, "I just wanted to zip in and thank you both for what you did for us. I really appreciate it. Maybe we could get together for drinks sometime."

Alice and Snow stood up too.

"That sounds like fun," Alice said.

"Yeah," Snow said. "Don't be a stranger."

Caroline stepped toward Snow and gave him a hug. And then Alice.

"Oh, honey, you smell good," Caroline said.

"That's soap," Alice said.

"I know. I'm just fucking with you." She laughed. "You don't have to see me out. I can find my way. I know you need to get back to work."

She wiggled her fingers at them.

Alice waved back and Snow nodded.

Half a minute later they heard the front door open and close. They sat back down.

Snow turned to Alice. "Who the hell was that?"

"I'm sure that was Claudia," Alice replied.

"I don't think so," Snow said. "Claudia has never done anything that didn't have a selfish motive behind it. Why would she stop by here to visit us?"

"To gloat," Alice said.

"The money she's extracting from her father?"

Alice nodded.

"That makes sense." He fixed his gaze on his coffee cup and shook his head. "That is one scary woman. You never know what she'll do next." He turned his head back to Alice. "So...you interested in breakfast?"

Alice laughed. "So, we go right from the Black Widow to breakfast, huh?"

Snow shrugged. "I'm hungry. What sounds good?"

"The Boulder Nugget buffet?"

"I'll leave it up to you," Snow said with raised eyebrows.

Alice sighed. "Alright. I'm not in the mood for any pouting from you today."

"I don't pout, Alice. And you're the one who made the suggestion. I think you secretly like the place, but you feel guilty about your waistline, so you put it on me."

Alice laughed again, and then the two of them walked down the short corridor into the lobby.

Snow looked to his right and stopped. "Do you see what I see?" he asked.

"And you thought that wasn't Claudia," Alice said.

"But why did she steal my Betty Boop cutout?" Snow asked. "She hated it."

"I'm sure, if you call her, she'll bring it back. That's why she took it. She wants us to call her. I think she likes us."

"I'm not calling her," Snow said. "I'll order another one. She can keep it. I don't ever want to see that crazy woman again."

"I wonder how many more there are just like her out there driving the streets of Las Vegas—looking for love."

"And hot dogs," Snow said. "Don't forget the hot dogs."

END

ABOUT THE AUTHOR

Rex Kusler was born in Missouri and raised in a small Iowa town. After calling Silicon Valley home for thirty years, Kusler relocated to Las Vegas to indulge his love of the desert and his fascination with gambling and probability. A mechanical designer by profession, Kusler began his writing career in the early 1980s, selling short stories to regional magazines before trying his hand at novels. He is the author of *Angela, Family,* and the Las Vegas Mystery series.